Lost Survivor

Thomas R. Jones

Published by:
Pitch-Black LLC in association with J Publications

Senior Editor: Bridget Ingebrigtsen
Cover Design: Greg Walbert
Line-Editor & Layout: David Pitchford
Proof-Readers:
Siobhan Pitchford, Jerod Ingebrigtsen, and Job Conger

J Publications
PO Box 7458
Springfield, IL 62791
Phone: 217-793-8632
Email: lostsurvivor@jpublications.com
www.jpublications.com
www.lostsurvivor.com

Pitch-Black LLC
3232 South First Street
Springfield, IL 62703
Phone: 1-800-963-1070
Fax: 217-529-9246
Email: pitch@pitchblackbooks.com
www.pitchblackbooks.com

ISBN 0-9758840-6-9 (Pitch-Black LLC)
ISBN 0-9773874-0-2 (J Publications)

LOST

SURVIVOR

The Novel of a Black Soldier's Journey to Vietnam and Back.

Historical Fiction

From Man Into Soldier—And Soldier Back to Man

THOMAS R. JONES

ACKNOWLEDGEMENTS

I was blessed to have many people provide inspiration, patience, ideas, criticism, insight, and other assistance, both personal and professional, in bringing *Lost Survivor* out of my mind and into the pages of this book. In particular:

My wife, Carol, for her love and patience during the twists and turns of the creative process for twenty years.

Jim Wassell, the first reader of the manuscript, for his encouragement and support for twenty years.

Bridget Ingebrigtsen, President of The Word Authority and my writer's consultant, who helped me give birth to this book with her insightful guidance and editorial expertise, all while having her own baby in the process.

Greg Walbert, President of Greg Walbert Design, who turned ideas into beautiful visual representations.

David Pitchford, Project Leader of Pitch-Black LLC, who co-published the book. His knowledge and experience smoothed rough spots I didn't know existed. And Daniel E. Blackston, Senior Editor and partner of Pitch-Black LLC.

Our Webmaster, Mike Standley.

My consulting readers: Kathryn Jones Mayberry, Vivian Maxine Johnson, Thomas Stringer, Bernie Armbruster, Scott Fessler, Darla Austin and her sister Sue, Joe Stanley, Brett Cox, Monica Melton, Carla George, Rob Nelson—a Nam brother, Cecil Turner, Amanda Dow, Vince Williams, Kym Hubbard, and Linda and Carl Kelderman, Lynn Ralph, Louis Broccardo, Melissa Orrill, Melinda Mavis, and Job Conger.

To the men and women who served their country in Vietnam, those who served before us, and those who have served and continue to serve after us.

Tom Jones, October 2005

FOREWORD

This book represents a fictional account of an American soldier. The story told herein is based on actual events in the author's life. JD, the protagonist, could be any soldier in any war; the details change, but the heart of the matter is survival. He happened to be a black American soldier. The war happened to be in Vietnam. Yet this story likely holds as much or more truth than the historical events themselves, and it is hoped that the narration makes their sense and nonsense much more readily apparent than any factual telling could. Those truths are inextricably bound in our history; truths of racism and brotherhood, truths of values and actions, truths about right and wrong and when they matter.

The field of battle is clearly a place for soldiers. Philosophers and deep thinkers must become what they are not in order to survive in crisis. Their challenge is to find their identity when crisis has passed and revise it given the reality of their experiences. A man who believes that killing is wrong damns himself the moment he pulls the trigger that causes his enemy's death. Can a man survive once he's damned himself? Is it really survival? *Lost Survivor* is wonderful fodder for conversation. I offer my deep gratitude to the men and women of our armed services, past and present, for the safety I enjoy while pondering such deep philosophical issues.

CAVEAT: the views of the narrator are not statements of opinion by the author, editors, or publishers. The narrator is as fictional as the account. While based on factual materials, all persons and events described in this book are fictional. Any resemblance to persons living or deceased is coincidence.

David Pitchford, October 2005

*Show me a hero
and I will write you a tragedy.*

F. SCOTT FITZGERALD

CHAPTER 1

In Nam, minuscule distances separated pain, death, and God.

Explosions fractured the night, jarring JD from a deep sleep. He sat up on his cot in the darkness, straining to determine if the explosion sounds were incoming or outgoing shells. Since explosions didn't call out their affiliation, it took an extra heartbeat to sort out incoming enemy fire from outgoing friendly fire.

The shrill scream of a shell overhead erased any doubt—enemy fire. He flipped off the cot like a startled cat. The explosion boomed through the air.

He stood up and in one continuous motion grabbed his flak jacket and helmet off the floor, the combat web belt from above his cot. His right arm snaked under his pillow to grab his lucky .32-caliber automatic pistol and a curved-blade knife.

"Fucking gooks," he muttered. "Three weeks to go and you got to fuck with me." He jammed the weapons into their holsters on his combat belt and bolted out the door into the night air. He jumped the two steps outside the door and ran toward the bunker a few feet to the left.

An incoming shell—eerily shrieking "you"—burst nearby. He dove to the ground and rolled into a fetal position.

A hailstorm of incoming shells gushed from the sky. The updraft of an exploding blast sucked him up with dirt and rocks, then flung him hard to the ground on his back. He lay dazed, in a state of shock, unable to move his body. Fuzzy blue and white spots danced in front of his face every time he blinked.

The horrifying scream of another incoming shell jerked his mind out of the murky veil. Lying on his back facing the unprotected sky, he watched the stars twinkle. The bunker's dark shadow entrance was now to his right. He flipped onto his stomach and crawled on his hands and knees across knife-sharp rocks that caused piercing pain to run down his legs. He cursed at the pain but kept crawling.

He dove into the dark tunnel. Two shells exploded so close he could hear the sickening whiz of steel into the bunker's sandbags, wood, and metal behind him. On his stomach, dragging his combat belt behind him, he crawled into the dark hole. When he tumbled onto the dirt floor of the heavily mildewed and musty bunker, he gasped for air. The fear of death drenched his body with sweat and tormented his stomach with spasms.

His six-foot, four-inch body didn't take up much space when he stood up in the eight-foot-deep and eight-foot-wide bunker. The murky, damp ceiling was layered with planks of wood, strips of runway matting, sandbags, loose dirt, and more sandbags. The bunker was solidly built, but it wouldn't survive a direct hit.

No outside light penetrated the twists and turns of the bunker's tunnel entrance, designed to prevent grenades being tossed into it. He blinked his eyes a couple of times to make sure they were open. He felt small. The darkness engulfed him. Whenever a shell exploded nearby, he instinctively bent his head and hunched his shoulders in an attempt to become a smaller target. The high-pitched scream of a siren—warning that *death's-a-coming*—provided background accompaniment for the clatter of exploding enemy shells.

Two shells shattered the ground so close that the bunker's walls shivered, rumbled, and caused loose sand to fall down from old, torn and tattered sandbags in the ceiling. A small stream of sand cascaded down his back, between neck and collar. It collected at his belt line, then trickled into his pants where it mingled with his sweaty grime.

The sand grains between his legs felt like they were multiplying. He had stopped wearing underwear in Nam because it rubbed the crotch raw and caused jungle rot, a rash that never seemed to heal. He stamped his feet to force the sand down his pant legs.

He heard squeaks and scurrying noises on the floor to his right. He jumped left a couple of steps and stared into the darkness.

Rats! They knew incoming artillery fire killed, and they, like men, fled to the bunkers during these attacks. Surviving thunderbolts from the sky made strange bedfellows of men and rats. Both were willing to do anything to survive with or in spite of each other. Rats, however, had an edge over men—they instinctively knew how to survive in the dark.

JD had to share a bunker with rats before, but never alone. When other men were around, they would make light of a rats' presence by telling jokes and stories. But nothing was funny about being the only non-rat in a dark bunker. They would become bold and attack if they were cornered or if they thought men were invading their homes. Rats ate anything they could get their teeth into, including human flesh.

When he was eleven years old, JD had had an experience with rats that still haunted him. The city had been working on the sewer system near his street and the workmen scared big sewer rats out of the bowels of the earth. One night, two rats crept into JD's bedroom and attacked him. He still carried the scars and pain from that terror-filled night of teeth and claws ripping into his flesh.

A furry, thick body ran across JD's right foot. "Filthy fucking rats!" he yelled into the darkness as he tried to kick it out. The scurrying and squeaking stopped.

Trembling, he thrust his sweaty left palm into his pocket and pulled out his Zippo lighter. His hands shook so much he almost dropped it. He flicked it three times before a small yellow and blue explosion of light shot into the darkness. Through a hazy halo, he saw three rats the size of raccoons.

Dull, red-tinted, ember-glazed eyes glared up at him. Their whiskered, cone-shaped noses sniffed at the air as they bared sharp yellow teeth. The rats leaned forward, their bodies rigid, their hairless tails erect. Then the furry shadows ran into the dark behind him. JD frantically twisted his body around to keep the rats in the light and in front of him, reaching with his right hand for the pistol—

A hammer slammed into JD's consciousness. Vietnam, the bunker, the hazy light, and the rats disappeared into a swirl of darkness.

Sensations returned in irritating little spurts through a foggy veil, erupting in his arms, chest, back, and legs. He fought to suck air through his dry mouth, but instead swallowed sand and started coughing. Rough, grainy sand covered his body, and sandbags from the ceiling pressed down on his chest.

The bunker was hit! He didn't hear the explosion—the shell that drops on top of you is never heard.

He raised his arm painfully, and woodenly pushed through the sandbags on top of him, feeling open space. *At least the bunker didn't collapse*, he thought.

JD pushed sandbags off his body, slowly rolled over onto his stomach, and crawled up the tunnel. Outside the bunker, he rolled over onto his back, and stared up at a clear, black night sky peppered with stars. It was quiet. The shelling stopped. He turned and looked at the bunker, but saw no trace of the terror from the sky except a sag in the middle where the shell exploded.

The shell had hit the bunker roof at an angle. A few degrees down would have been a direct hit and would have buried him alive. In Nam, minuscule distances separated pain, death, and God. Intense memories filled his mind about collapsed bunkers and the men he had dug out before. He remembered how suffocation etched agonized death masks on their faces.

The base's 105-mm howitzers, located behind recon's area, spit fire into the night sky. Shock waves bucked him like a wild horse through the ground. The howitzers could dump forty-eight rounds of thirty-three pound shells into a target in one minute. They were not firing at specific targets—they simply fired in the direction of the incoming, presumably enemy, artillery.

The base was within artillery range from the Demilitarized Zone (DMZ) and at any time, day or night, the enemy shelled the base, either a couple of rounds to screw up your sleep, or at other times hundreds of rounds to punish you. All the firepower on the base couldn't stop enemy shelling.

JD's leg muscles shimmered like gelatin. The massive knots in his stomach forced him to take fast gulps of air. His head buzzed as if it was filled with angry bees. He wobbled back to the hooch. Short siren blasts in the background bellowed out the all-clear signal.

Inside the hooch, he grabbed a canteen and poured water over his face to flush the sandy grit out of his eyes and mouth. The cool wetness running down his chest caused a clammy, chilling wave to scurry through his body, which made his knees buckle. He grabbed the door to keep from falling.

In the dark, the far wall of the hooch was a mockery of the pitch-black night sky. The angle at which the shell hit the bunker caused flying strips of steel to skip off its top and spray through the wall. Moonlight peeked in through little holes in the wall. A dirty green canvas provided a dark backdrop for the little tunnels of light. Each death-hole sparkled like a twinkling star.

Hot metal blasted across his cot had left deep, jagged tracks in its wake. Had he been lying on the cot when that shell exploded, those rips would have been bloody valleys through his flesh.

He fumbled, finally finding the light on the desk. He sat down on the edge of the cot and dropped his combat belt on the floor. He sat motionless for five minutes before he slowly moved and grabbed for the box of joints on the shelf above his cot. He lit one, sucked the smoke deep into his lungs, and let it escape slowly from his mouth. He didn't know how or why he had survived. He didn't care. Only one thing mattered—he was still alive.

CHAPTER 2

The words of God were twisted to justify killing and destruction.

Vietnam was an ancient, mysterious world of villages that survived a powerful China next door for centuries. It had been occupied by the French for years and survived a Japanese invasion. The Vietnamese called their nation "Da Nuoc," which means "earth and water" when translated into English.

In Vietnam, a dead man had the same impact on the earth as the plop of water-buffalo shit—both became organic compost. The land was soaked for centuries with blood. Life in the villages continued on.

To be black and in combat in Vietnam in 1967 meant you had to either be crazy or be dead. Death honed the living, through brutal experience, into a servant of its continuous call. A person's mind, body, and soul were driven to the edge of absurdity by its puzzling hell.

It wasn't the permanent hell and eternal damnation he had been taught about on Sundays in his mother's Baptist church in Springfield, Illinois. That hell, John Douglas understood, was the devil's house—a timeless place located far below heaven for sinners who weren't forgiven.

In Vietnam, it was thirteen months, day in and day out, with no Sunday breaks. If you were fortunate, it meant pain, disorder, and cruelty with continuous fires composed of explosions and napalm. The fight for survival went on twenty-four hours a day—from the sky, from the ground, and from every angle in between.

The words of God were twisted to justify killing and destruction. Incoming became a momentous image of God, forcing men to bow and prostrate themselves before its terrible presence. Every day was the same; the Sabbath was as unholy as any other day to live through.

Words were adapted to fit the brutal, staccato pace: Vietnam became "Nam"; Reconnaissance became "recon"; and the Viet Cong became "VC," "gooks," or "Charlie." Ground troops were "grunts," and "non-grunts" were "wimps," "Rear-Echelon Mother Fuckers" (REMFs), "glory hounds," or "PX plowboys." New arrivals were called "Fucking New Guys" (FNGs) or "new meat." Getting killed designated one as "dead meat."

Three days after John Douglas arrived in Vietnam, his Nam metamorphosis began. His name was shortened to JD by a supply sergeant. Before Nam, he had smooth, medium-brown skin. Within two months, the Nam sun had deepened his skin color and changed the texture to a taut, rough, dark brown like a Midwest walnut shell. His city-soft body had been sculpted into 195 pounds of tempered muscle confined to a slender, agile frame.

His light-brown eyes hadn't changed color, but within his stare they seemed darker. Below his hard stare was a broad nose with wide, flared nostrils. According to his mother, he carried a true "Douglas nose," a trait that all the men folk had on his father's side of the family.

Deep lines etched into his face and a thin smile between thick lips gave his face a tight, constricted appearance. His high cheekbones, long facial lines, and small, round chin made his face look egg-shaped. He kept his hair cut boot-camp short. In Nam, too many creepy-crawly things looked for a home in long hair.

JD was twenty-five-years-old when he came to Nam. He was an old man compared to the nineteen- and twenty-year-old kids who composed the bulk of the recon company. Although he was older, his age didn't matter to hot metal zinging through the air. Being scared every minute of your life makes you old. But everyone killed in war dies too young.

He was an enlisted man, with combat medical training, called a Navy corpsman. As the highest-ranking medical person, a First

Class Petty Officer who was the main "Doc" to the Third Marine Division Deep Reconnaissance, he was in charge of four other corpsmen. The nearest "real" doctor with medical school training was at the medical battalion next to the airstrip on the other side of the base. The medical battalion building had nurses, technicians, a sterile environment, surgery suites, medical supplies, air conditioning, and concrete floors.

JD lived and worked in a hooch; a hooch is a shack with a wooden floor two feet off the ground, wooden walls, and screen wire running up to a rusty, leaky tin roof. All Nam hooches were a drab mixture of military-green paints, tinted with a reddish hue from the blowing dirt on the outside. A heavy, dark-green curtain, rolled up in the daytime for airflow, hung on the walls to keep light from showing outside at night. Most hooches were peppered with holes from past enemy shelling. The major difference between hooches was the number of men in them. Recon team members usually stayed together in a hooch. He was a member of a team, but as the senior corpsman, he slept in the back of the medical hooch. When out of the bush, he was on call twenty-four hours a day.

The medical hooch was divided into two big rooms. The front room was further divided into two sections by a thin piece of chest-high plywood. One side housed a cart, bandages, and equipment for sewing up flesh. The other side contained a beat-up desk and a couple of file cabinets. Across the back wall in both sections were shelves lined with various sized bottles of pills.

A green military blanket hung in the doorway, separating the front and back rooms. On the opposite wall past the blanket was the door that led outside. On one side of the back room was a safe where brandy and narcotics were kept. Next to the safe and facing the wall was an aged metal desk with a desk lamp. Between the desk and the back wall, boxes of medical supplies were stacked like uneven rows of children's building blocks.

On the other side of the room was JD's cot that he had not had a good night's sleep on for a year. Since he was so tall, he always had to sleep with his knees bent so his feet wouldn't hang over the edge of the cot.

He slept with two bedmates—a .32-caliber automatic pistol and a thick curved-blade knife under his pillow. He didn't leave the hooch without them.

His bush backpack underneath the cot was next to a battered brown suitcase tied with a dirty white rope. This obscure carry-all held all of JD's personal valuables: a pair of blue jeans, a blue suit he had picked up on R&R in Hong Kong, letters from home, and pictures of his wife, son, sister, and mother.

His M-16 rifle hung on two nails above his cot. Since the black, plastic-covered barrel and shoulder stock gave it the appearance of a toy gun, many men in Nam called their M-16 the Mattel™ gun. The M-16 was notorious for its sensitivity to dirt. JD didn't take any chances his rifle would misfire. He kept it meticulously cleaned and oiled with black tape over the end of the barrel to keep out grit.

Next to the M-16 hung his combat belt, which held his personal weapons of war: six lightweight, oval fragmentation grenades; two cylindrical smoke grenades used to mark landing zones for choppers; a white phosphorus grenade; and a tear gas grenade. The belt also held 400 bullets in twenty-round M-16 magazines, and holsters for the pistol and knife.

The other nail held his small, green Unit One bag filled with various-sized bandages, a surgery kit, morphine, and a few pills for headaches and malaria prevention. He only carried it on the base. In the bush, it was an identifier that could get him killed. Behind the bag was another belted holster with a Marine Colt .45 Ham had given him to protect the hooch; he kept it clean and ready for nights like this, but never carried the heavier sidearm in the field. A standard issue combat knife accompanied the Colt on the olive-drab belt, along with extra clips of ammunition for the pistol.

Above the nails, a shelf held his weapons against the war in his mind: a stereo, tape player, tapes, and books. Behind the tape player he kept his stash—a box of rolled joints.

JD heard a faint scraping sound on the outside steps to the back door. He turned out the desk light, yanked the Colt .45 from its holster, and aimed the barrel at the door. Gooks probed recon's side of the base a couple of times a week after incoming, and at least one always seemed to get through. Eight gooks had been killed within recon's area during the past five months. Five of them were killed around his medical hooch, including two he shot coming into the hooch. He was convinced that gooks thought the Red Cross symbol painted on the medical hooch was a bull's eye.

The door slowly opened and the partial shadow of a head and shoulders were outlined against the night sky. He hoped it wasn't a gook sapper who would throw a grenade into the hooch and run. JD tightened his grip on the pistol's handle, the sights over the barrel pointed directly at the shadow in the door. If it was a sapper, he was going to make the little fucker pay.

"You alright, Doc?" the shadowy figure asked in a baritone voice, "Ain't gonna shoot me with my own weapon, are ya?"

JD took a deep breath and eased his finger off the pistol's trigger. "Yeah. Come on in, Ham." Only one voice in recon had that distinct baritone sound—Sergeant Hamsel, the leader of the Valley Dogs recon team.

JD turned on the desk light, illuminating a big, black man with hair so short it was little more than a dark tracing on his head. His real name was Tulley Ike Hamsel, but to the men who served with him in Nam, he was "Ham," a massive man, standing six-feet, seven-inches and weighing over 270 pounds.

A thick, puffy crescent-shaped scar ran down the left side of Ham's face from his ear to the corner of his mouth. When he was angry and clenched his teeth, the thick glaring scar wiggled like a worm, twisting and turning as though it had a life of its own. The scar lifted the left edge of his mouth upward, which distorted his face into a grotesque snarl.

The big man looked at JD's sweaty, sand-streaked body. "You alright?" he asked again.

"How can I be *all right* with little, slant-eyed yellow bastards trying to kill me? The fuckers got damn close tonight. A round glanced off the bunker and sprayed the hooch. Three weeks . . . three weeks to go in this shit-hole, and I get a fucking round dropped on my head." A sharp chill jammed into JD's stomach, forcing him to take a deep breath. His voice rose to a higher pitch. "Shit. My insides are still shaking."

"Take it easy, Doc." Ham glanced at the holes in the wall and the gashes in the cot. "It's over," he said.

Ham's tone was too detached for JD. "No shit!" he snapped. "If I had been lying in that cot, it would've been over for me."

Ham hooked his thumb toward JD's desk. "Break out some of that good stuff from your private stock," Ham said. "I don't want none of that wet-season dog piss you give out."

During the wet season, men coming off patrol were issued a half-pint of whiskey to warm their insides. Some of the men, for various reasons, didn't drink, so JD always had extra half-pint bottles stashed in the medical hooch's safe. Ham called it dog piss. For JD, though, it was close to home; the Services got it from a brewery in Peoria, Illinois—a place Johnny Douglas had spent some time back in the *real world.*

He walked across the room to the old metal desk and pulled a bottle of Johnnie Walker from one of the drawers. He turned to Ham. His voice had a sarcastic overtone. "You want a glass?" JD asked.

"Nope, straight from the bottle is always fine with me," Ham said, taking the usual five steps from the door in two. He sat down on the edge of JD's cot. "Yeah, it looks like someone wanted your narrow little ass," he said. "If I didn't know better, I'd think someone feels your ass is worth something."

JD guzzled a long drink from the bottle. The first drink of scotch usually left a burning sensation, but his senses were dulled from the joint he'd smoked earlier. It allowed the liquor to slide down too fast and too smooth. He passed the bottle to Ham, who took a short drink and passed it back to JD.

JD quickly sucked down another drink. "Man, I'll be crazy as a fucking Looney bird, shacking up underground with rats for three weeks," he said. JD's body shuddered when the thought of rats passed through his mind, and he slugged another drink.

"Take it easy, Doc," Ham said.

JD's fear caused him to blurt out, "Take it easy? Fuck taking it easy. That fuckin' round landed on top of my head. How in the fuck am I supposed to be easy 'bout that?" He guzzled another drink from the bottle. "Everything's uptight—even my asshole."

"Well, I'll be damned. You finally got a short-timer's attitude," Ham said. "You're scared of getting your ass blown away because you're going home. Don't let the thought of going home fuck your head up." Ham waved his hand in the air as though he was shooing a fly away. "Hell, you know you have just as much chance of dying your last day as you do your first day in Nam. What difference does it make?" he asked.

"I know, I know, but God dammit, that round landed on top of my fucking head. All my days would've been yesterdays," JD said.

"Come on, Doc, get it together." The scar on Ham's face was

jumping, a visible sign he was agitated. "You're getting caught up in the gooks' head games. You know better. The first shell can land on top of your head at any time. What's important is hearing the last shell and knowing you don't have any holes in your ass." Ham laughed. "Fuck it. Take another drink. It's over."

JD took a long drink, and looked around the room. "Damn it, I'll be digging shrapnel out of my shit for a week."

"Well, at least you're not digging hot metal out of your ass," Ham said.

JD paced back and forth. "I'm ready to go back to the bush, where at least I can shoot back at the little yellow mother-fuckers. I can't handle this bullshit of playing hide and seek with the gooks' incoming in a dark hole with rats."

Ham spoke through a chiseled snarl. "Nigger, please. Who you tryin' to shit?" His voice got louder. "You can't walk home from the bush. Just keep your fucking head screwed on right and you'll make it."

Ham knew about staying alive. The hideous scars that dotted his face and body were a testament to his ability to survive. Ham had lived through more long-range reconnaissance patrols than JD would ever go on. He'd taught JD how to stay alive in the jungle on the jungle's terms. However, the cost of survival had made Ham ugly and mean when he needed to be and nonchalant the rest of the time. He was content just being alive in Nam. Nothing else mattered to him.

JD changed the subject rather than argue a losing point. "How bad did they fuck us up this time?" he asked.

"Ten or twenty rounds hit recon's area," Ham said. "Mess hall took a direct hit. No one was hurt, but breakfast's gonna be a few days late."

There were only two good things about mess hall food: it was hot, and the food had names like back home. Fried chicken. French fries. Ice cream. Pie. It wasn't much, but it beat the hell out of eating cold C-rations, or bush food. "They hit the mess hall? Days? My ass! We'll be eating bush food for weeks."

"I'll know later today how much damage." Ham stretched and yawned. "I'm slowing down. I'm gonna crash. See ya later." He stood up and walked to the door, then turned around. "Doc, keep your fucking head screwed on so you don't lose it." He walked out the door.

JD fell back onto the cot. After a few minutes he blurted out, "It's too fucking quiet." He sat up, grabbed the headset off the shelf, and flipped on the tape player. Soon the smooth voice of Otis Redding crooned, "Sitting on the dock of the bay." He hummed along with the words: "Sitting on the dock of the bay, wasting time . . . looks like nothing going to change . . . 2,000 miles I'd roam, just to make this dock my home." He lay back on the cot and clutched his cramping stomach. Pulsating throbs of fear coursed through him.

CHAPTER 3

*As the MPs escorted Julius out, JD wondered why
the crazy ones always made it home.*

Sunlight had just cracked the darkness of the night when he was awakened to sew up a Marine who was injured in a fight. Besides two broken ribs and bruises all over his body, the Marine had a deep cut on his forehead and three stab wounds in his belly. JD sewed up the wounds, immobilized his ribs, and sent him to the medical battalion. The trickiest part had been to find and clamp the lacerated vein from which the man would have quietly bled out in a matter of hours—so often it was the wounds that didn't show that killed you outside the bush. The Marine was lucky to be alive.

Men became cruel animals in combat, explosive and dangerous as an attacking tiger, and as fearsome to their own kind as to the enemy. There were men like Dancing Dan, who pranced through the company's area to a beat only he could hear, with live grenades in both hands, pins pulled and primed to explode. He approached all FNGs and asked them to dance. If they refused, he'd throw grenades down at their feet. He never killed anyone, but JD had to remove shrapnel from a few Marines' behinds after they encountered Dancing Dan.

Then there was Booby Trap Bobby, the best man in the company for setting or disarming booby traps. He'd set booby

THOMAS R. JONES † 15

traps in the latrine. When someone sat down to take a dump, his weight would trigger the booby trap. When a victim heard the ping of the grenade pin, he would invariably run out the door with his pants down around his ankles. Booby Trap would wait outside the door with a camera and take pictures. He had a legendary overstuffed photo album of FNG bare asses.

Men who had been around awhile knew not to sit down in the latrine when Booby Trap was in from the bush. Not because they didn't want to be in Booby Trap's bare-ass album, but because they didn't want to get killed in the shitter.

Then, there were men who would hear or see something in their minds and, without warning, would attack because of a careless word or misunderstood movement. These men were crazy—dangerous to be around. And not in the sense of glory hounds who bragged constantly of being "mad, bad, and dangerous-to-know." Simply madmen, a hazard to all.

After sending the wounded Marine over to the medical battalion, JD finally got a chance to take a shower. He carried his combat belt, the one with the .45 and Marine issue combat knife, over his bare shoulder and wrapped a towel around his waist. Ham had taught him to always have a weapon nearby, even when naked. The shower was a homemade contraption, with unheated water from a storage tank that flowed into a fifty-five-gallon drum with holes punched in the bottom. Taking a shower in the morning was like standing naked under a waterfall of icicles.

He was called back to the medical hooch midway through his shower. A recon team had come in from the bush. He cussed as he stepped out of the shower, bitching about how nothing, not even a cold shower, could be finished in Nam.

He had to work through and over rubble from the previous night's incoming, treating the men for jungle rot, bandaging small cuts, and removing leeches.

A few minutes after the team left the hooch, the military police (MPs) brought in Julius, a brother who had just received a "Dear John" letter from his girl. His girl had a new man back home and wrote to say goodbye. Julius tripped out on whiskey and rage, jammed a magazine into his M-16, and started shooting at everything that moved. Even in the medical hooch, Julius grabbed one of the MP's pistols and shot off two rounds before they could wrestle it away from him.

Four big MPs had to hold the raging man down. "Fuck this shit. Fuckin' Jody! Fuck this shit," he cried over and over between clenched teeth. His face was a mask of painful desperation woven into helplessness. JD knew, even as he injected him with the temporary comfort of a standard-issue sedative, that sooner or later Julius would be diagnosed as crazy and sent home. As the MPs escorted Julius out, JD wondered why the crazy ones always made it home.

It was late in the afternoon before the traffic of hurt and suffering Marines stopped streaming through the medical hooch door. The smell of sweat and body odor lingered in the hot, muggy air. He opened both doors to get air flowing through the hooch and collapsed on his cot.

CHAPTER 4

Every day of survival took something away from his yesterdays.

JD drifted off into memories of his home—Springfield, Illinois, the state capital, located about 200 miles south-southwest of Chicago. Springfield was famous because Abraham Lincoln had lived there. Lincoln freed blacks and gave them the chance to stand as equals in places such as Vietnam.

Springfield was a middle-American town with oak- and elm-lined streets. Changes of seasons meant a mixture of green and brown grass during the summer, multi-colored leaves in fall, and cold, white winters. In spring, warm rain fell down on rich, black dirt, which farmers loved for raising corn, beans, winter wheat, and that greatest of all seasonal foods, watermelon. Nam seemed to have only two seasons—wet and chilly, or hot and dry. Nam never changed color; it stayed green all year.

Springfield was his home in the faraway "real world." Every day of survival took something away from his yesterdays. Childhood memories of play and fun were the first to go. He could remember events, but couldn't remember the kids who were there.

Back in that world, there had been times when his mother and father could make him feel safe with a few comforting words. Strangers were a neighbor's out-of-town visitors. Danger was falling off a bike or the random bruises incurred by the boys-being-boys things he and his childhood friends engaged in. The worst thing in his life back then was his parents' anger and a butt-whipping. Tomorrow always came.

JD folded his hands under his head and lay on his back in the hooch, wondering where those kids were now back in the 'real world.' What were their names. . . .

"Johnny, c'mon man, we gots to get home!" he said. This was . . . what was that girl's name? She, and her brother now screaming at him, lived over off Fourteenth somewhere. The two boys had been playing dare games at the construction on Eleventh Street— what was it they were building? JD fought to focus on the memory as it sped past.

It was after dark. He'd better get home before his pops or there'd be a belt-whoopin' for staying out so late. It was hard to run because of the swelling of a bruised knee he'd gotten from jumping off the steel girder after—that fine girl's brother—had dared him. He'd hit his elbow on a cinderblock as well, but the evening chill took the sting from that. He pushed himself past the pain; he felt miserable making his mother worry.

Springfield was a new place at night. Johnny had never seen such colorful people. A white man in a fine looking car was talking to a lady down on the corner; she was pretty, but Momma wouldn't like the clothes she wore or all the makeup. Johnny raced past, panting hard enough to see his breath. Five or six young black men were gathered on the corner a few blocks down, blocking his way. He'd have to turn at the corner onto Stuart Street to get home. A stab of insecurity caused Johnny to run faster toward and then through the gang of young men though he wanted to go around them.

"Future track star!" one of the punks shouted.

"That's the Douglas boy! Let 'im be. Old man Douglas ain't worth fuckin' with!" That was the first time he heard the 'f-word'. He ran faster, only a little way left to go. His side started to pinch as Johnny took deep breath after deep breath. The pain from his knee had gone. His head felt light—he felt like he might be able to fly if he could just run a little faster. He felt powerful and real, felt better than he could ever have imagined.

"Hey Johnny! What you doin' out so late?" That was Momma's best friend, why couldn't he remember her name? The fine feeling turned to anguished disappointment. He had to stop and catch his breath.

"Cat got your tongue, boy. . . . Oh, can't speak for breathin'. Well, best come in an' have a glass of lemonade. We'll walk home together and tell your Momma you was helpin' me out in the yard and we lost track of time."

Johnny followed the lady into a very familiar house—yes, this was . . . . his Momma's friend's house. She was a sweet lady who always looked out for everybody but herself. Short, plumpish, and dark as coffee, she was like an aunt. JD looked at her while she poured the lemonade into a plastic cup. She was Momma's friend, that's all he could remember. His forearm tickled suddenly as though being harassed by gnats; he swung his elbow to shoo them away, then looked down at the blood drop falling to the floor.

"Sorry 'bout your floor, ma'am." Johnny said.

"What about my floor, young man?" said the woman, now holding the plastic cup out for Johnny to take.

"Oh my Lord! Mercy Jesus. What'd you gone and do to yo'self Johnny Douglas? How'm I gonna 'xplain that to Misses Douglas? Guess you musta fell from the roof when you was a-helping a poor old woman."

JD woke with a start. He was vexed at the dream; his stomach knotted as though trying to squeeze the memory away. He rubbed his eyes and looked at the puffed scar on his left elbow, trying to recall the incidents that led to the scar—trying to remember who Johnny Douglas was.

He clearly remembered that he had thought the girl was something special, and that he had gone to the construction site with her and her brother just to spend time with her and try to impress her with his bravado. JD laughed at the irony, then struggled to find more of the memory.

The boy had cajoled Johnny into climbing onto a steel girder, and when that hadn't seemed to challenge him enough the boy told Johnny if he was a real man he'd jump straight down and not have to climb down. What made him do it, though, was the concern Johnny saw in the girl's eyes—so pretty, warm, like a long-distance hug from his Momma. Johnny jumped. He hit his knee on the ground and fell forward to strike his elbow on a stray cinder-block.

Right after, Johnny had stood up without wincing and telling the boy it was his turn. The boy declined. The girl—she was so special then, at the age of nine—told him he was silly, but had asked him to hold her hand while they picked their way through the rubble to a sidewalk.

What was Momma's friend's name? JD decided that it didn't matter. That was the *real world*, it was worthless here. This was Nam. There were gooks to kill and grunts to patch up—but mostly gooks to kill.

CHAPTER 5

"I've never been this scared in my whole life . . ."

Nam's green had washed away many multicolored memories of home and created new, more vivid ones, like the impressions of his first day in Vietnam. He'd flown on a Braniff plane to Vietnam from Okinawa. It was the first time he ever flew on an airplane. In fact, he was the only one among his friends or family to fly on an airplane. Black folks just didn't fly. They would drive a car, ride a bus, or take a train if the distance was too far to walk. The flight from Okinawa was long and mostly over water. During the flight, he was afraid of crashing into the ocean and drowning. He had never been in water where he couldn't see land.

There were 125 corpsmen, twenty-three Marines and twelve nurses on the plane. As he waited to board the plane, he met up with the ten corpsmen he attended Field Medical Services School with at Camp Lejeune, North Carolina. JD was popular because he was so smart. He'd helped a few of the corpsmen get through some of the tougher classes. After the recognition hellos, they started joking about why they were being sent to Nam. It was most likely Master Sergeant Lou's revenge a few of them said. Sergeant's job was to turn corpsmen into some watered-down version of a Marine. One of his pet peeves was corpsmen washing their cars on the grinder, the parade grounds. It was for military activities only, he would holler and write up corpsmen for disciplinary action. Somehow Lou's medical records had gotten sent to Washington DC. Not to a particular office, just to the city of Washington DC, which meant he had to re-take all his shots. The tough man had fainted. He suspected it was a plot against him, though he couldn't prove it. It seemed many of the corpsmen in the company at the time were going overseas, a lot of them to Vietnam.

Sitting next to JD on the flight was a corpsman named Mel. He was short and stocky with sad brown eyes that shifted from side to side. In Okinawa, some Marines on their way home from Nam had fed him a bunch of shit. They told him, "You'll get a weapon and flak jacket on the plane. As soon as the plane lands, run off the fucking plane like a bat out of hell, or your ass will be blown away your first day there." Mel believed what they said. The sweat of fear had caused his uniform to go limp and his whole body emitted a pungent odor.

Mel bugged JD most of the flight about when they would get weapons. JD told him those guys were just messing with his head. Mel didn't believe him.

"Why would they blow smoke up my ass?" he asked. "They've been there. They should know. It's war, man, a fucking war. Shit! I'm scared to death. I've never been this scared in my whole life." His voice became a whimper. "I don't want to go to no fucking war."

"Mel, you're in a plane," JD said. "It's too late. You're on your way."

He squirmed in the seat awhile before asking again. "Damn it, when are they going to give us our fucking gun?"

Fear had many different expressions on that flight. A couple of rows up, on the other side of the plane, a loud-mouth Marine was bragging about how Nam would give him a chance to kick some yellow ass. He was talking to himself more than he was talking to anyone around him. Everyone recognized the raw fear behind the boasting. He'd yak it up a bit and then quiet down, apparently feeling better for having stated how brave he was going to be.

JD remembered how sad he felt for Mel and the loud-mouthed Marine for being so scared. He also remembered the fear in his own stomach. He had never been that scared before either. Questions bombarded his mind: *How will I act in combat? Could I kill a man who's done nothing to me? What is it like to kill someone? What do I need to know to stay alive? Will I get killed?*

He felt queasy and light-headed from all the unanswered questions that floated around in his mind. He wondered how his fear had been expressed and, though he couldn't remember, he didn't doubt it was as visible as Mel's and the loudmouth's.

The pilot's voice boomed over the PA system. "Good afternoon, Marines and ladies. This is your pilot, Captain Stevens. The land mass on the right side of the plane is the Republic of Vietnam." Seated on the left side of the plane, JD had to lean over people and seats to catch his first sight of Vietnam. The view was a blurred contrast between blue water and hues of green.

The red "Fasten Seat Belt" sign flashed as the captain's next words drifted through his memory. "We are starting our descent to land at Da Nang, Republic of Vietnam. The temperature outside is 103 degrees—but the ground fire is light to moderate." The pilot laughed. "Good luck to all of you, and I hope you fly Braniff when you leave for home one year from now."

The captain's words echoed in his mind—one year from now. Vietnam would be his home for a year.

When the plane door opened, he got his first whiff of Vietnam. It stunk like shit. The smell blasted in. He almost dropped to his knees. The entire aircraft quickly filled with the odor of warm shit. His lungs fought for air in the stink. Everything instantly felt dirty and greasy. The air turned hazy, and a coat of grime seemed to form on his skin.

He stepped through the door into a sun so bright he had to squint. He was drenched with sweat as he took his first steps into Vietnam. His starched and pressed uniform clung to his body like wet tissue.

Besides the heat and odor, the rabid racket around him, especially explosions, banged in his ears. When he heard the dull thud of helicopter blades and the sharp crack of rifles firing, he wondered if Mel was right. Maybe they should've had flak jackets on and rifles ready before they left the plane.

His eyes had flashes, vague images of hangars, silver butler buildings, airplanes, and helicopters on the ground, as well as trucks, jeeps, and pallets of ammunition. People swam in and out of focus. Green seemed to be on everything except the ground, which was rusty red. Barb wire and sandbags stretched as far as he could see.

Silvery coffins were stacked on the tarmac near one of the runways. He had never seen so many coffins. He couldn't stop staring at the gleaming packages of death. Different faces and bodies became the same under those metal covers. He wondered if it was arranged for new men landing in Vietnam to see the coffins when they came in, as if displaying the only option of a quick return home.

The wind caused the stiff brown tags to flap against the coffins like the nervous tapping of fingernails on glass. The bright aluminum boxes were loaded into the USAF C-141 Starlifters just like any other crate of freight—tied down and securely latched for the long flight home.

Men milled around in groups like herds of anxious animals. It was easy to identify the ones who were leaving. They had leering looks and scars. They grunted more than they talked, and they smelled like shit. Those arriving smelled of sweat and urine.

He left Da Nang with twenty other Marines on a C-130 transport plane to Dong Ha via Phu Bai. In Phu Bai, he could see the wreckages of war. Pieces of helicopters and a burned tank lay next to the runway like landmarks of catastrophe.

When the plane took off from Phu Bai, the crew chief gave each of the men a flak jacket. JD had asked the chief if he was to take it with him when he got to Dong Ha. The chief laughed and pointed to small round holes in the side of the plane. He told him to sit on it in case they received sniper fire when taking off to keep a bullet from going up his ass.

He had his first personal experience of unseen danger. The war became real to him. He understood that people whom he had never met would try to kill him. At that moment, he realized he had a personal stake in the war—his ass could get shot or blown off.

What didn't make sense, though, was why he would have a flak jacket under his ass when there were five giant fuel bladders in the center of the plane. A direct hit to one of them, and the whole plane would blow up. It didn't make sense to him, but he didn't want to get shot in the ass either, so he sat on the flak jacket.

CHAPTER 6

*"You crazy Marines can have these jungle-bunny games
I don't want to play anymore."*

The sound of footsteps in the front room of the hooch snapped JD's link with a day that seemed so long ago. He looked up just as Ham's big black hands parted the curtain between the front and back of the hooch.

Ham came in laughing from deep within his belly. "Damn it, Doc, the left side of this hooch looks like someone sprayed it with a double-barreled shotgun. You piss the little yellow people off?"

JD didn't say anything and grunted. "Come on, Doc, loosen up," Ham said. "You're still uptight."

JD pointed toward the front room, and spewed out his bottled-up fear and frustration in a belligerent tone. "The front floor is full of broken bottles and pills, the bandages are filled with shrapnel, and the medical records are peppered with holes. Shrapnel is every-fucking-place," he said.

Ham laughed. "So what? There's no shrapnel in your ass. What are you complaining about?" he asked.

"There it is, eh, Ham, the bottom line," JD said.

"Hey, in Nam, being alive is all there is on the best of days," Ham said.

JD laughed. "I hear you, Ham."

Ham smiled thinly. "Captain Masters wants to see you," he said.

"What's up?" JD asked.

Ham's eyebrows lifted and wrinkles cut into his forehead. "You're the Doc, and you're leaving," he said. "He might want to know what to do when you leave in three weeks."

"You're shitting me," JD said. "The old man can't think that far ahead. He's still trying to figure out who's here from last week."

Ham walked over and sat on the safe. He lit a cigarette. The puffy scar on his cheek worked like some kind of small, agitated snake. "Doc, what're you going to do your first day home?" he asked.

The question jolted JD. He only thought of going home, not about what he would do once he got there. He answered with a flippant tone. "Kick Jody's ass, feel my wife's ass, and hold my son. That's the usual hero's return."

Jody, a universal nickname, was the dude back home fucking the wives and girlfriends of men in Nam. Nightmares about some Jody between his wife's legs almost drove JD crazy during his first month in Nam. The thoughts turned into a nagging rage that burned holes in his stomach. The emotions and passions of survival ruled in the end. Rage eventually smothered down into cold ashes.

"What duty station you request?" Ham asked.

"I didn't request a duty station," he said. "I've asked for a school—Radioisotope and Nuclear Medicine School."

"What the fuck is that?" Ham asked. "Sounds like outer-space shit."

"Hell, I don't know," JD said. "When they asked me what duty station or school I wanted after leaving Nam, I asked them what the most difficult corpsman school to get into was. They told me that school was hardest to get into." JD reached toward his stash box, but Ham put a big hand on his arm and shook his head.

"The school only accepts six students once a year from all US military departments worldwide," he went on, sitting down so he could face Ham and still have full sight of the hooch door. "I liked the sound of that, but what was more important to me, I've never seen or heard of those people being in Nam. That's what sold me on the idea of going there." He pointed at Ham. "You crazy Marines can have these jungle-bunny games. I don't want to play anymore. I didn't join the Navy to go hopping around in the jungle with little slant-eyed, yellow mother-fuckers trying to kill me. Fuck this."

"Fuck that. The Navy's too boring," Ham said. "You know you love the Marines. Where else could you find so many interesting people in one place?"

"That's easy—in the nearest asylum in any city," JD said.

Ham shifted the subject. "Marines make you feel lucky. You're a lucky mother. I heard you were a big winner in a poker game last week. How much you walk away from the table with?" he asked.

"Ten-thousand American greenbacks. Real money you can spend anywhere in the world," JD said.

Military scrip was issued to military personnel in Nam and could only be spent in certain places. JD regarded it as Monopoly money passing for the real thing. He preferred American money because it made him feel like he was holding a piece of home.

"I bought a car through the PX and sent the rest home so I wouldn't fuck it up," he said.

Ham rubbed his chin. "Not a bad stake. You've got a nice little nest egg and a new car. Of course, none of that counts while you're still in Nam. You have to leave this shit-hole in one piece—with your head together."

"Don't worry, I'm not going to freak out and go crazy in some bunker."

"You don't understand. It's not just going crazy here. You have to think about doing things at home. It's different, and you have to be ready for it. You can't go home cussing everyone out or just blowing someone away 'cause they piss you off. It's not that way back home. Being an animal is okay here. Shit, everyone is a damn animal here. At home, those are your folks, your people," he said.

JD stood up and walked toward Ham. "So, what's this shit you're giving me about doing things at home?" he asked. "We both know nothing counts 'til I leave this fuckin' place. Conversations about home are useless; just fuck up your mind."

"How in the fuck do you know?" Ham asked. "You've never been home from Nam before." Ham's voice got louder. "You know so fucking much. Why? It sho as hell ain't 'cause you've done it!"

Ham softened his voice. "Doc, you got three weeks before you go home, and I'm telling you, you can't live there like you have here."

JD walked over and opened the door. He hesitated, then turned back and faced Ham. "When I get off the plane in the *real world*, I'll think hard about what I'm going to do. Right now, I better get my ass moving. The captain is waiting."

"Doc, the habits of war die hard," Ham said. "You have to think about what you're going to do at home . . . can't take this crazy shit with you. You have to start thinking differently."

"Yeah. Sooner or later I will." JD left the hooch.

CHAPTER 7

No doubt, for crazy and dangerous missions,
the Valley Dogs were the team to send.

JD knocked on Captain Masters' door. He heard rustling papers and a desk drawer sliding closed. He knew it was the sound of Masters putting away the bottle of gin he stashed in his top desk drawer. Masters often pulled out a bottle to share with team leaders and JD after hot patrols.

"Come in," Masters said.

JD stepped inside the door. "You wanted to see me, sir?"

"Yes, come in and sit." Masters shifted in his chair. "Any casualties from last night's incoming?" he asked.

"No, sir," JD said.

"I heard the medical hooch got hit—how bad?" Masters asked.

"A few new holes in the wall, lots of broken bottles on the floor, but I'm still in business," JD said.

Masters shifted his body in the chair. "Good. Did Ham say anything to you before you came over?" he asked.

"Just said you wanted to see me," JD said.

Masters started to rise from the chair, but sat back down. His voice lowered. "I wish I didn't have to be the bearer of this news, so I'll give it to you straight. Tomorrow the Valley Dogs go out on a special mission." He hesitated a few moments. "You go out with the team. This will be your last patrol, Doc."

JD glared at Masters. "You've got to be shitting me, Captain. You can't be for real?"

"Orders are direct from General Scott," Masters said.

"This is a crock of shit and you know it. Why does the general want me to go on patrol with only three weeks left in this shit haven?" JD asked. He stood up abruptly, placed his hands on the desk, and leaned forward, staring into Masters' eyes. "This doesn't make any fucking sense. I'm a short-timer. Three weeks to go. You should be taking me out of the bush."

Masters stood up and walked around the desk. He faced JD. "Doc, I wouldn't send you if I had a choice, but the orders came directly from General Scott. What the fuck can I say or do? I know you just have three weeks left in this shit-hole. Unfortunately, the patrol is tomorrow."

JD didn't move, didn't say a word. He glared at Masters. His flared nostrils took in the scent of tobacco and gin on the man's breath. His insides were a tightly stretched rubber band ready to snap. JD wanted to attack Masters. One swift raise of his right fist and the man's throat would collapse. It was a crazy, murderous thought. But crazy, dangerous people go home quick and safe.

Masters had good reason to feel fear. Even though JD was a corpsman, he had killed more men than he would ever save or help. Like most of the men in recon, JD could kill suddenly, showing no outward emotion to warn in advance or register what they'd done.

Masters grabbed a pack of cigarettes off the desk. He raised the pack in front of JD's eyes. "Cigarette?" he asked.

"No," JD said. "Must be some really heavy shit. We just came off a hot patrol and the general wants us to go back out?" He put his hands into his pants pockets. "Yeah, it must be a hot shit-patrol or you would've sent another corpsman."

"Now Doc, you know the Valley Dogs. They either start shit or step in it."

"Yeah, I guess you got a point there." JD relaxed. Both men laughed. "Oh, what the fuck, it don't mean nothin'." JD hunched his shoulders. "What time we go out?" he asked.

"Early. Take a seat, Doc," Masters said.

He knew Masters would offer him a drink and start talking about the mission. Masters was being friendly because he didn't know if JD would be alive or just pieces of meat scraps in a body bag next time he saw him.

Masters pulled the bottle of gin from his drawer and offered him a drink. JD took a long swig from the bottle and passed it back.

Masters shifted uncomfortably in the short-back, swivel contraption with padded armrests worn down to the metal. The seat was hard and dirty with a jagged split running down the middle. In any other office, the chair would've been thrown away as junk a long time ago. However, it was the command chair for the Third Marine Deep Reconnaissance Element, a special company organized for deep and long-range reconnaissance into enemy territory. That chair molded men to its contour.

JD and Masters had arrived at the recon company about the same time a year ago. A quirk of fate had put Masters into the chair. He never had any desire to lead or be in command of men in combat.

Masters had been sitting on his ass in a soft chair behind a desk in an air-conditioned office pushing papers for the war effort. He was just another Marine staff officer attached to the Military Assistance Command Vietnam Studies and Observation Group, MACV-SOG. Usually referred as SOG, it was military mumbo jumbo for the joint service, unconventional, warfare task force that engaged in highly secret operations throughout southeast Asia.

The Marine Reconnaissance Company was the only Marine combat element of SOG. Recon teams of six to twelve men operated deep inside North Vietnamese Army (NVA) territory with no friendly troops around for miles. They were in Laos, Cambodia, and North Vietnam more than South Vietnam. Most of the information the military wizards processed, analyzed, and turned into intelligence and strategy came from these recon patrols. Their main mission was intelligence gathering; however, sometimes they kidnapped and/or disposed of Vietnamese suspected of being VC leaders.

On paper, the reconnaissance company was assigned to the Third Marine Division in I Corps. However, the company's Command and Control Central Headquarters was in SOG and separate from the Third Marine Division Headquarters in Da Nang. SOG determined when and where the teams would go, debriefed the teams, and determined who had access to their information.

JD's company operated out of Dong Ha in South Vietnam's

most northern province of Quang Tri, a few miles south of North Vietnam. Military expediency had imposed a new set of reference points over Vietnam's older, truer being. This imposition had begun simply with the division of one country into two. Then, military logic made it easy to partition South Vietnam further into four clearly defined tactical corps. The company operated in I Corps tactical zone, a 1300-square-mile area from just below Chu-Lai to the DMZ—which included Khe Sanh, Hue, Phu Bai, Da Nang, A Shau Valley, and Tam Ky.

Standard procedure for SOG was to dispatch staff officers periodically to the field to verify the type and quality of intelligence reports. Most staff officers regarded such fieldwork as a reward. Marine officers who served with recon had a statement put in their service records with the impressive verbiage: "Served in a combat zone with Long Range Marine Recon Company." That deceptively simple statement enhanced and improved a staff officer's chances for early promotion. Even though a staff officer's service record would say he served in a combat zone, he actually spent his time safely inside a command bunker.

Masters had received orders for a three-month monitoring tour with the recon company to evaluate its handling of classified information. However, twenty days after he arrived in Dong Ha, Captain Brock, commanding officer of the company, was killed during enemy incoming. Since Masters' twenty days counted as combat experience, he was the highest-ranking officer in the company and ordered to take command.

The previous commander was left-handed, six-feet, four-inches tall and weighed over 250 pounds. His weight molded the seat of the chair into the form of his ass.

Masters was right-handed, with 160 pounds on a six-foot, one-inch frame. When he sat in the chair, his small body was like a sports car in the deep ruts of an eighteen-wheel truck. He couldn't sit straight in the chair because he slid off the middle hump either to the right or to the left. The chair leaned more to the left when the weight of worry and concern pressed down on Masters. His body twisted into an awkward angle that forced him to lean on the desk for balance.

Everyone, including Masters, shared their pain, their suffering, their fears, and their thoughts with JD. He was their Doc—their medical man for body and mind. Masters told JD about his life before Nam and how it pained him to give orders that caused men to die. He hated writing letters to "Killed in Action" (KIA) families. He didn't know what to say about strangers to their families. His letters were merely informational bulletins to families whose loved ones had been killed in conflict.

JD didn't like SOG's Marine commander, General Scott, because he didn't mingle with field personnel, and his colonels carried his orders to his field commanders. When General Scott did visit the field personally, it was for one of three reasons: to have his picture taken with bush monkeys while he congratulated them and presented medals; to give an ass-chewing in the field while surrounded by his staff; or to order a shit-mission that would get someone killed.

General Scott didn't even smell like shit. Anyone in Nam for more than a week usually did, other than the occasional R&R. The general even wore aftershave lotion. In the bush, cologne attracts bugs and irritates the skin in the hot, humid weather. It was also dangerous. JD usually smelled like funk, sweat, and other body odor, but General Scott smelled clean. That smell didn't belong in Nam.

"So, is this another grand idea of the general to win the war in thirty days?" JD asked.

"I'm not sure it will win the war, but it might shorten it," Masters said. "Since January twenty-first, as you know, the Khe Sanh Marine base has been under siege. The North Vietnamese have thrown everything they have at the base—artillery, rockets, mortars, and ground attacks. They want the two Northern provinces—Quang Tri and Thua Thien. The provinces' proximity to North Vietnam means shorter lines of communication and supply routes into South Vietnam. If the NVA overruns Khe Sanh, North Vietnam would have an unobstructed invasion route into South Vietnam. They're trying to turn Khe Sanh into another French at Dien Bien Phu. The general was very clear that the United States Marine Corps will have no damn Dien Bien Phu."

On May 7, 1954, thousands of triumphant North Vietnamese had shattered the defenses of an isolated French garrison in the mountains called Dien Bien Phu. North Vietnamese General Vo Nguyen Giap, against every prediction and in spite of all the impossible analysis, delivered enormous quantities of shells and supplies to the distant battlefield. He pounded 13,000 French defenders into submission on the fifty-sixth day of a terrible siege. His peasants' army had out-generaled, out-supplied, and out-fought France's finest soldiers.

Now, twenty-three years later, General Vo Nguyen Giap, the architect of Dien Bien Phu, was commander-in-chief of the North Vietnamese Army facing the Americans. His army was one of the finest, best-equipped fighting forces in the world. He had over 400,000 men, a complete array of modern weapons, and an air defense system nearly as sophisticated as what Germany fielded during World War II.

"We have information that mixed forces of Viet Cong and NVA are gathering by the thousands in the mountains around the Khe Sanh area. Estimates range somewhere between twenty and 40,000 regular troops," Masters said. "Their units are widely dispersed in squads and platoons. Stopping their movement has been like trying to catch the shadow of a fly."

He shifted around in the chair. The talk of so many gooks so close made him jittery. "West of Khe Sanh, there's the NVA 304th division, and elements of the NVA's 320th division are holed up somewhere to the east. The NVA's 325C division is deployed to the northwest, and we know the 324B is somewhere northeast."

"If you know that much about the NVA movements, why not just bomb them?" JD asked.

Masters shifted in the chair. "As I said, they're moving in small groups. The real problem is their artillery—battering our bases along the DMZ. Marine Intelligence reports an unidentified NVA artillery division has moved up on the Laotian border to bombard Khe Sanh."

JD laughed to himself. It was common knowledge that Marine Intelligence usually meant they saw lots of hoof marks going in and none coming out.

"Their big artillery is dug so deep into the mountain sides, our B-52s can't reach them. The Chaine Annamitique mountain terrain, cloaked by triple canopies and thick monsoon mists, can hide whole divisions of NVA massed for an attack on Khe Sanh or some other place," Masters said.

JD was very aware of the Chaine Annamitique Mountains. The Valley Dogs had been operating in the area for the last eight months. The mountain range extend southeast from the DMZ for some 700 miles, almost the entire length of South Vietnam. It formed the country's western border, separates it from Laos and Cambodia. The jungle peaks range in height from about 5,000 feet to over 8,000 feet.

Masters leaned forward in the chair. "The radio spooks have detected heavy radio traffic in recent days in an area around Khe Sanh. SOG is convinced the North Vietnamese have moved one of their top command army headquarters into the area. If so, it's controlling all the forces around Khe Sanh, perhaps the entire northern region of South Vietnam."

Masters' voice turned dry and somber. "Lang Vei Special Forces Camp was overrun last night." JD leaned forward in his chair. He had friends in that unit. Masters continued, "Of the 500 Montagnard Civilian Irregular Defense Group, 200 are dead or missing, and seventy-five were wounded. Ten of the twenty-four Americans have been killed. Apparently, the NVA used thirteen PT-76 amphibious tanks in the assault."

The gooks had tanks? JD had heard there was a hell of a battle going on at the Lang Vei Camp, but this was the first time he heard the gooks had tanks in Nam.

"It takes a lot of men to support a command headquarters and tanks," JD said. "It should be easy to target them."

"If we knew where they were. They're spread out, hiding under dense jungle canopy. We can't see the little yellow bastards," Masters said. "General Scott wants to draw their forces out into an open fight—hopefully, away from Khe Sanh. Then, with our air force and firepower, we'll have a chance to devastate those thousands of troops in a single stroke."

Masters looked at JD intently. "We also have information that General Giap might be at that headquarters to personally command the attacks on Khe Sanh."

That explained why the general had come out into the field in person. Capturing General Giap, one of the world's most gifted military leaders, would be a big, bright feather in the general's hat. General Giap, as the Minister of Defense and the third-ranking member of the ruling council in North Vietnam, was the most influential voice in North Vietnam after President Ho Chi Minh and Prime Minister Pham Van Dong.

"General Scott needs hard information. That's why he asked for the Valley Dogs to go in and get it for him," Masters said.

JD gritted his teeth. "Sir, the Valley Dogs just came off patrol two days ago," he said. "The patrol was hot. We almost didn't make it out."

"The Valley Dogs is the best recon has to offer, and he needs eyeballs he can believe in on the ground," Masters said. "He didn't want to depend on those damn unreliable red agent reports from spies and prophesies of the Aerial Photo Examination Section. Neither is good enough in this case."

JD understood the need for an on-site team. But the Valley Dogs? The NVA had increased the reward bounty on the Valley Dogs' heads. Hanoi Hanna's radio program had blasted the whole country with her prattles about a special reward for any member of the team killed. The gooks wanted the Valley Dogs dead, and General Scott was sending the team into a hell nest of thousands of gook troops. It didn't feel right, didn't feel right at all.

"Sir, the recon company in Khe Sanh would be closer to the action and have a better feel for the terrain," JD said.

"The recon company in Khe Sanh has been there since the siege started and has taken heavy casualties during the past month," Masters said. "Right now, they're being used for emergency reserves to repel possible enemy breakthroughs."

"What do you expect the Valley Dogs to do if the men who patrol the area can't get out?" JD asked.

Masters looked into JD's eyes. "My orders are to have the Valley Dogs ready for insertion by chopper in the morning. Issue five days of rations and any extra ammo you want. The coordinates of the recon zone will be given to you in Khe Sanh," Masters said.

"Get the coordinates in Khe Sanh?" JD asked. "Captain, the mission is hairy enough without trying to stay alive in Khe Sanh."

"I know, Doc. But a lot is riding on this patrol."

Orders are orders, especially when uttered from the mouth of a general. Generals gave orders that killed thousands of men—what would five more mean? It damn sure wouldn't matter that one black corpsman had only three weeks left on his tour. His ass still belonged to the general.

Corpsmen were an integral element in the unique blend that composed a reconnaissance team; it was often the corpsman who acted as hinge pin in a team's survival once there were wounded. As senior corpsman of the company, JD wasn't required to be attached to a team and go on patrols. But, he had been a member of the Valley Dogs before he got the position, and, since the company was short on field corpsmen, he'd decided to stay with the team. Even if Masters hadn't ordered him to go, he would have wanted to. The Valley Dogs were so much a part of JD that he still wanted to be with them, even if it meant death.

The siege of Khe Sanh had started three weeks earlier. The NVA's TET Offensive kicked off two weeks after the siege began. Gooks penetrated with strength into Quang Tri City, Tam Ky, and Hue, and attacked US military installations at Phu Bai and Chu Lai. Every recon patrol for the last thirty days had experienced heavy enemy contact and had to be pulled out of the bush.

No doubt, for crazy and dangerous missions, the Valley Dogs were the team to send. The NVA respected and feared them. Anything that didn't come off the chopper with the Valley Dogs could be killed—grass, trees, any animal, and particularly enemy. Killing gooks meant a successful mission.

Ham insisted that every member of the Valley Dogs team understand and speak some Vietnamese words. He taught them how to think like the gooks, move like them, smell like them, and feel comfortable in the jungle with them. He knew it terrorized the gooks to have Americans move as easy as them in their own jungle.

Nam had a hell of a problem with venereal disease (VD); it seemed to be part of the gook war effort to give it to every soldier they could pimp their women to. Commonly called Vietnamese cockrot, some said the only cure was your pecker falling off, and then you would have no more VD problems. However, you'd have to squat to piss. The Valley Dogs had a motto: "VD: a special disease for gooks." The Valley Dogs' motto meant they turned NVA men into women, which infuriated the gooks. But, what really generated shame and loss of face for the gooks, was their inability to kill any of the Valley Dogs.

CHAPTER 8

Scared shitless, he still functioned.

JD left the CO's office. Masters' words floated through his mind: "Walk out of Khe Sanh." How would the Valley Dogs stay alive on the ground there? Khe Sanh had constant incoming, twenty-four hours a day every day.

The smell of shit pulled his thoughts away from the mission to Khe Sanh.

Military bases in Nam were like a large container of human waste: piss, shit, sweat, and funk. The hard-driving rains of the monsoon season had gone, but the sky still filled with flash downpours from dark clouds. The clouds didn't linger long in one place, but left misty rain tracks on the ground and produced a light fog over the base. The humidity restrained the stench close to the ground and gave a sticky feel to the air.

JD's stomach had the same tenseness he had in his gut when he took the first step out of a chopper into enemy territory. The gripping fear squeezed the pit of his belly like a tube of toothpaste, forcing bile into his throat when the choppers flew off. The realization hit him. There was no turning back. America left him. He was alone in enemy territory.

His whole world became absurd at that moment. Scared shitless, he still functioned. No matter how bizarre the surroundings, all that concerned him was the detail of the job at hand. He didn't know if he was efficient, numb, or just plain stupid.

The Temptations' "My Girl" blasted out of a hooch. JD stopped to listen to the melody. The music was a sharp contrast to the explosions, gunfire, and cries of pain. It provided temporary relief from the constant madness going on around him.

Radios, reel-to-reel tape decks, Akai tape stereos, and all types of component sets were cheap in Nam. Music came in many ways. The Armed Forces Radio and Television Service (AFRTS) programming included Wolfman Jack and American music that was performed by Filipino bands in Da Nang who couldn't speak English; they mimicked the songs perfectly, but JD had complimented one in Hong Kong to find out, to his own surprise, that the singer couldn't consciously speak a word of English. The song floating from the hooch kindled JD's memory of home on Stuart Street.

Stuart Street, the center of the roulette wheel his life had spun around, had been very small. It was a mile-long, unpaved street with tar, sand, and little white rocks ground to dust by cars. Wind created little dust-devil swirls up and down the street. The street ran from the black pool halls, taverns, churches, and businesses on Eleventh Street to Withrow School at Twenty-Fourth Street.

The city provided sidewalks to the businesses on Eleventh Street. Most houses on the east side didn't have sidewalks. JD's house did. One summer, his father and some friends had scrounged concrete from construction sites they worked on to build it. The house sat on a corner so the sidewalk was on two sides, which made it stand out as something special. His father wanted something to separate him from others on the street who parked cars in their front yards. "Country folks," his dad used to say, "are comfortable getting off their mules on their front porch and sitting on a couch."

Stuart Street was lined with old trees, their trunks thick and rough. The tree limbs stretched out over the middle of the street like a massive umbrella. The strong oaks, hard walnuts, wispy weeping willows, and tall pines provided cool shade through the summer and a beautiful multicolor canopy in fall.

Stuart Street was as diverse as the mixture of trees that lined it. Interspersed among the black folks were Germans, Slavs, Jews, Italians, Irish, and poor white folks with unknowable heritage. Their common bond was belief in God, family, hard work, and right and wrong.

The east-side neighborhood was populated with third- and fourth-generation homeowners. Most lived in small houses with the same floor plan—two bedrooms on one level with basements and attics. JD's father converted the attic into a bedroom for him when his mother thought he and his sister were too old to sleep together.

There were no strangers on Stuart Street. Everyone was a member of the Stuart Street extended family. Friends and relatives visiting from out of town were greeted by their first names by people they didn't know. There were stories of travelers going through Springfield on the bus or train and deciding to stay in town because of the people and their tempo. Springfield's rhythm was quiet, with a slow southern pace.

Though located in the center of the state, Springfield had a southern slant to its views and lifestyles. Railroad tracks that ran north and south on Tenth Street clearly defined the line between whites and blacks. Blacks lived on the east side of the railroad tracks. Two blocks on either side of Tenth Street, blacks and whites engaged in trade without having to venture too far across the line. It was a free trade zone, a melting pot filled with black taverns, whorehouses, Italian construction companies, and Jewish stores.

JD attended Withrow School, which housed the only black recreation center in town. Young blacks played ping-pong, basketball, baseball, and could swim in a swimming pool. Record hops were held every weekend, and a live band came every other Friday.

Springfield's white people allowed black folks to skate at Moonlight Garden Roller Rink once a month. Black kids usually loaded up in two or three cars and drove forty miles southeast, down Route 36 to Decatur, where blacks could skate once a week.

Springfield also had a big lake called Lake Springfield. There was a beach where blacks could swim called Lincoln Beach. Though Lincoln Beach was originally made for white people, they gave it to the blacks so blacks and whites wouldn't have to swim together. It was renamed Bridgeview Beach. The open green spaces and blue water gave distance to the daily grind of working and living. Black folks came from all over Illinois, Indiana, and Missouri to swim and socialize at Bridgeview Beach.

Lake Springfield provided some of the best memories of home. First and foremost, he met Jan, his wife, there. She came down from Peoria, seventy-eight miles northwest of Springfield, to spend the weekend with girlfriends. The first time he saw her was at the beach's water edge in a one-piece, yellow swimsuit. The way the blue water reflected the sun's rays on her body gave the impression she was surrounded by a golden glow.

Jan had long, silky black hair that draped down over her shoulders to the middle of her back. She had a smooth, cocoa-brown body. She was tall, at least six inches above her girlfriends, yet she moved gracefully. One look at Jan's soft, captivating brown eyes would make Johnny melt every time. The feeling of love slammed down on him like the whack of a hammer. He decided at that moment she had to be his girl no matter what the consequences.

The burning fires of love in his stomach had him driving the seventy-eight miles to and from Peoria at least twice a week to see her, sometimes on his own, other times carpooling with various interesting people. Her love had him pumped up. But Jan worried about him driving so far so often. She told him that she wanted to be close to her man, at least in the same town. Soon they got married, and Jan moved to Springfield to live with him. They found a cheap apartment and got used furniture from family and friends. It wasn't much, but it was their home and he felt like he was in heaven.

He worked two jobs. He was a full-time ambulance driver, and he cut grass and did odd jobs part-time on the west side of town, where the white folks lived.

He felt good just being next to Jan. He remembered how they used to lay next to each other, how he would stroke her long hair while they talked about what happened that day. During those special nights, they made a promise to each other that they would always share how they felt no matter how bad things got. When he first got to Nam, he wrote her every day, sharing his unfamiliar and unbelievable brutal experiences. Her letters were full of questions; when he answered, she sent more.

He stopped writing when his brutal experiences became familiar and no longer unbelievable. The cruel and crude became so common they weren't even worth writing about anymore. Besides, he knew she wouldn't understand. How could she?

CHAPTER 9

"We live as warriors. We die as warriors."

His mind tuned in to the mellow rhythm in his ears and stopped the flow of memories. His head bobbed to the beat as he walked to the hooch where the music was coming from. The sweet smell of marijuana greeted him when he opened the door. He stepped into a misty world of swirling smoke and saw four men sitting around a makeshift table playing poker. Three men stood while two others sat on the cots and watched the game.

Poker was the main money card game played in Nam. Blackjack was played for a change of pace. Then, there was bid whist. Good bid whist players often had street professorships conferred on them in whizology.

He knew all nine of the black men there. It wouldn't have made a difference if he hadn't, because a black was welcome wherever black folks gathered in Nam.

Uncle Sam was an equal-opportunity employer for black country boys who yearned for adventure and black inner city youths who were trying to escape the 'bad streets'. Black country bumpkins or city hustlers developed a common survival instinct that swept away differences. United by their blackness and their determination to stay alive, they were blood brothers. They called each other "Bloods," which bonded them beyond white friends or yellow enemies. Their rituals of hellos and goodbyes could take twenty minutes with the slaps of hands, elbows, knees, and butts. Whites thought it was some type of street dance, but it was in many ways a creation from home, and, more importantly, it was a black thing.

Recon teams were closer kin than Bloods. Very little blatant racial conflict surfaced in recon. Staying alive demanded too much energy. In noncombatant units, however, racial tensions did contribute an undercurrent to the continuous, jangled backbeat of Nam, adding further fear to the uncertainty.

Vietnamese didn't like or care for blacks and considered them a bad omen. In the early sixties, the NVA had put rewards on blacks' heads. The Vietcong initially tried to exploit the prejudice of their countrymen. They slandered black soldiers with the same stories propagandized previously in World War II—that black men had tails curled up in their pants and would rape their women, and that they practiced cannibalism and were demons raised from the dead. The NVA and the VC changed their propaganda approach in 1967. The VC ordered villagers to treat blacks as equals. Black soldiers were supposed to be embraced as fellow victims of US imperialism.

VC propaganda urging blacks to surrender hung on the walls of the hooch. One read: "Black people, your real enemies are those who call you Niggers. Vietnamese people and Afro-Americans rise together against our common enemies, the US aggressors and racist authorities: Johnson, Rusk, McNamara, and Westmoreland." These leaflets, and the fact blacks tended to congregate in groups, made more than a few white officers nervous.

Hanoi Hanna was North Vietnam's modern version of Japan's Tokyo Rose of WWII. She had a perfect American accent to her soft, seductive tone. She would rant about US atrocities in Nam, Wall Street's connection to the racist and imperialist American government, and capitalist exploitation of the working class. Her message had too many high-sounding words for grunts whose only concerns were their next meal, their next high, or the next bullet coming their way. Her words didn't mean much, but she played the most up-to-date, hottest music from the "World." The American station played songs that were six to eight weeks old in *the world*. Hanoi Hanna got songs from *the world* on the air within a couple of weeks.

Between the songs, her messages were meant to throw you off balance. She really messed with white officers' minds when Dr. Martin Luther King was killed. She said blacks were rioting back home. She enticed blacks to turn their backs on Nam, saying, "Soul brothers, go home. Whitey is raping your mothers, sisters, daughters, and burning down your homes. Leave before it's too late." Some of the white officers were so upset by her ranting that they stationed armed guards around their hooches for protection.

But, since blacks were used to and could easily identify head games, her comments sparked more conversations than defections. Nam, to most blacks, wasn't their home. Home was where Momma was. It had streetlights, concrete highways, cars, buses, houses, and black girls with sweet love for their men. Blacks knew just because a gook didn't call you a nigger during the day, it didn't stop him from trying to kill you with bullets and artillery at night. Too many Bloods had lost brothers in battles with the little yellow people.

Sometimes Hanoi Hanna would get personal information about a man and broadcast it on the air. Her program also let VC in the countryside know the reward on a particular man's head.

At one time, JD had three rewards on his head by the NVA. One was simply for being black, until the VC changed their tactics. Another one was for being a corpsman. The NVA figured if the corpsman was dinged early in a firefight, more Marines would be taken out of battle to care for the wounded. The third reward, the highest one, was for being a member of the Valley Dogs recon team.

"You hear the yellow bitch's program today?" a brother sitting on one of the cots asked JD.

"That bitch is always flappin' her lips. What was so special about today?" JD answered.

The man smiled, exposing a gold-covered tooth. "You. The ante went up on the Dogs' asses. Y'all number one on the hit parade. Y'all gonna make some little yella bastard a millionaire if y'all aren't careful," he said. "Y'all beginning to be worth more dead to gooks than alive to white folks."

Another man said softly, "Yeah, my man, walk lightly. Walk very lightly," and laughed.

"The old saying is still true. You got to bring ass to get ass," JD said.

"Ooh, listen to the super-coon talk shit. I like it," one of the card players said.

"Fuck the bitch and her bullshit. Who's sleeping with the joint?" JD asked. He didn't like the talk about him being dead.

One of the brothers standing gave him a joint. "Check out this smooth, bad shit. It's a monster, pure monster-shit," he said.

Marijuana was a major crop in some areas of Nam. Extremely potent marijuana was always available and easy to get. JD saw men have hallucinations from smoking the local weed. He hadn't smoke very much dope before Nam. He and a childhood friend, Jeff, started smoking dope two years before JD had come to Nam. Getting high felt good and was cool back in the "World." They were just a couple of kids finding a way to laugh, act silly, and feel nice. He could be that way without the dope, so getting high was nice, but not necessary.

However, after two hot patrols in Nam, that changed completely. Getting high was something he anticipated and needed between patrols. Everyone needed something that would numb the insanity. Some prayed to God, but most used alcohol or drugs. Dope didn't change the reality he lived in, but it did temporarily change his focus. Like everything he bothered with in Nam, weed was a tool for survival.

JD took a hefty drag on the joint. A light, tingling sensation flowed down into his legs. "Wow. Good shit. One hit and you're on your way." He sat down on a cot. "Where'd you cop this—and is there any more?" he asked.

A wide grin came on the man's face. "My homeboy, PK in Hue, copped it. Stop by my hooch later. I'll take care of you, Doc. You can't get shit like this back home. You'll have to take it with you," he said.

"For sure, for sure," JD said. The tingling oozed slowly upward in his body. He took another hit. His mind felt light, like a leaf floating in a gentle breeze onto a quiet summer pond. He peeked through half-closed eyelids at the men in the hooch. They were shadowy figures lurking at a distance.

A nagging question tugged at JD through the mist in his head. Ham knew what the captain wanted, yet he wouldn't tell him. Why not? There was nothing either one of them could do about it. That's the way it was. Like it or not, orders were orders.

One of the men put on a tape he'd received from home. A black disc jockey started rapping about Ultra Sheen for black hair while he played "Grazing in The Grass."

"All right," one of the men said as he started snapping his fingers. "Yeah, talk shit," another brother yelled.

Tapes were the link for blacks with their music and what was happening back home. The tapes were usually made from black radio stations that wove together music, commercials, and news that let the Brothers know their world at home still existed.

The news about Nam on the tapes was old and outdated, but at least you heard a black voice saying what was going on. No one really cared if the music was old. Some of the tapes had the sweet, erotic crooning of a black woman's voice. The deep-bass soul music drummed a moment of difference into the war.

The beginning chords of Marvin Gaye's "What's Going On?" flowed out into the hooch. JD's high, combined with the music, transported him to another level in his mind. It brought back memories of the party thrown for him at Budda's Tavern at the corner of Eleventh and Cook streets in Springfield before he left for Nam.

His family provided the food, and the owner provided drinks at half price. One of the hottest disc jockeys in town was hired to spin records. The place was packed wall to wall with family, friends, and freeloaders. Judy, his little sister, had gotten drunk, which upset his mother because she was underage and shouldn't even have been in the tavern.

They toasted and kidded him about coming back home a war hero. Several people, some he didn't know, asked him to send back war souvenirs. People cried and got drunk, or got drunk and cried. Some of the girls were sorry he was leaving because they were hot for him. They would touch his hand when they talked to him. He could've taken at least four of them to bed that night. But Jan kept close, touching him, and saying over and over she would wait for him.

His mother told him to be careful and watch out for wild animals. Watch out for wild animals? Old Tarzan movies were her jungle vision, a place where four-legged wild beasts roamed. But, it was different from the jungle he was living in. In Nam's jungles, the killing beast was the one that lurked within a man's mind and soul, and stalked the bush on two legs.

He could remember only one real conversation from the party. It was a conversation with Kareen, a friend from Peoria who painted pictures of black men busting through walls or hanging on crosses. Others were of sorrow-faced black women with tears or ones with perfect bodies that broadcast sexual desires.

Kareen wore a red and black hat with a cut-off brim and dashiki most of the time. He read books and magazines constantly about how white people were planning to get rid of niggers. Kareen's heart and soul belonged to the Black Power Movement. He was one of the few visible members of the Black Panther Party in downstate Illinois. Kareen had told JD that night, "You don't know what you're getting yourself into. This Vietnam crap is just another white man's mind trick to kill off you young, dumb niggers."

"White boys are fighting over there too, you know," Johnny said.

Kareen's voice got so loud he was almost yelling at Johnny. "*Poor* white boys are over there. I bet rich white cats don't have any sons in Vietnam. They're not stupid. They don't send their flesh to some dumb war with little yellow men that don't mean shit. Hey, look man, you don't owe these white mother-fuckers a fuckin' thing. Don't go."

"Don't go and do what? Sneak around here until the police drag me off to jail?" Johnny asked. "I ain't got no money, and I don't know how to run away to another country. What the fuck else can I do but go?"

"You don't have to go and get yourself killed for them. I have some friends that might be able to help," Kareen said.

"Your Black Revolution friends?" Johnny asked.

"Good friends who will know what to do and can help you," Kareen said.

"Don't go to war, join a revolution . . . you can get fucked up either way," Johnny said. "I'll go to Nam. It's only one year, and then it'll be over. Who knows when a revolution is over? I'll be all right. I can take care of myself."

His answer pissed off Kareen. "Johnny, you're just another dumb nigger trying to prove yourself," Kareen said. "Black folks are offering up their sons in this war to prove they're Americans. Nigger, have you forgotten 'American' means *white only*? What makes you think killin' yellow men is gonna change that?" Kareen asked.

As the poker game got louder, his thoughts came back to the hooch. The men in the room seemed like actors in a drama, with each gesture, frown, or smile expressing what cards a player held.

A swirling mist seeped up from the floor and engulfed the men up to their knees. The room became darker, yet light seemed to bounce off the men and the walls of the hooch. Outlines of men in the room took on a soft, hazy coating. JD closed his eyes and floated on the currents of the swirling mist.

The room turned into a jungle. Green vines wrapped around large trunk trees. Long, slender threads of sunlight broke through a high canopy. JD sat with nine African warriors around a clearing and prepared for a battle. Large palm leaves held mixtures of different colors they painted on their faces and bodies. They were naked except for loincloths. Spears lay on the ground next to each warrior.

The enemy had killed hundreds of their friends and they were the only ones left alive—just ten men. There was no talk of fleeing, just quiet conversation about the upcoming battle. They forged a bond of death among themselves, deciding to attack the larger enemy force. A warrior could not return home without the bodies of fallen friends. The ten of them couldn't carry the hundreds who had died that day. Their mission was to kill as many enemies as they could before they themselves were killed. Once they left this spot, there would be no tomorrows.

Booming drums echoed through the air. It was time. Their actions were slow and deliberate as they prepared each other for death. Each rubbed two fingers into the different colors and finger-painted symbols on their bodies. They faced each other, created a circle, and held hands. No words were spoken. They looked into each other's eyes, nodded their heads and smiled. One of the men grunted. They dropped their hands and picked up their spears.

As they walked abreast into the jungle toward the beating drums, JD floated two feet above and behind them. The jungle turned into flat, open ground as they approached a river. Across the river, thousands of the enemy stretched back to the horizon as far as they could see. There were so many enemy forces that when they stomped their feet, they kicked up dust enough to darken the sky.

The enemy horde charged like a giant tidal wave rushing toward a beach. The fast beating of drums could be heard in the background as thousands of voices cried up to the sky.

The ten warriors charged the thundering herd of men, chanting, "We live as warriors. We die as warriors." The human wave stopped as if it hit a tall brick wall. The drums stopped. Stillness draped the battlefield. The enemy horde quietly watched the warriors charge toward them. The warriors' chant boomed across the valley.

"We live as warriors. We die as warriors. We live as warriors. We die as warriors. . . ."

CHAPTER 10

Winning or losing money in a poker game really didn't matter because Nam was a no-win game for everyone.

JD blinked. "Doc, you want another hit?" He was back in Nam, in the hooch, with the card players.

"No thanks, I've got to get moving. Shit, that's heavy stuff," JD said. "I've got to find my legs."

"What did I tell you, Doc? That's some tough shit. Stop by my hooch before you leave for home, and I'll give you some for the 'World.' You'll need it," the brother said.

"It's definitely tough," JD said. "I've got to move. Check you brothers later." As he walked through the door, the Bloods in the game were getting loud. Someone won a big pot. Gambling in Nam was different than at home. Winning or losing money in a poker game really didn't matter because Nam was a no-win game for everyone. Using money or match sticks was just a way to keep score at the moment. Winners and losers shared the same chance of being dead the next moment.

JD walked down the dusty road to his hooch. The question flickered through his mind—what happened to the ten warriors that charged certain death? They died. End of story.

Ham's parting words engulfed JD's mind. He needed to start thinking about home.

What's the use, JD thought, *until I'm sure I'll be alive to go home?*

JD went to his cot and lay down to think about home. Instead of Springfield, Illinois, he found himself in memories of meeting Ham for the first time. He was filling in for the lead corpsman, who was on patrol, in the medical hooch shortly after Charlie had finished an hour of steady incoming. He had just mended up the last of the wounded Marines, and JD was smoking a joint to calm his nerves—back in those days it worked better. But then he'd heard someone outside the hooch. He swallowed the bile his stomach squeezed up into his throat and pulled his pistol from its holster. When Ham stepped in, JD was pointing the .32-caliber automatic at his chest and would have killed Ham if only he'd recalled to disengage the safety.

"What the fuck, nigger?" Ham said. "Gonna shoot a Blood, shoot him with a righteous weapon. That little thing just gonna piss me off—you'll need another corpsman to come down here and remove it from your little FNG ass."

They both laughed and the tension eased.

"Where the fuck you get a pea-shooter like that anyhow?" Ham asked. "Here, this is the real deal," he handed JD one of the belts off his waist (he always wore two when Charlie was likely snooping around—which meant just about any time they were out of the bush), "any little yellow mother-fuckers come through the door, use the thunder God gave the Corps—Colt-mother-fuckin-forty-five."

"Can't hit my own dick with a forty-five," JD explained. "Been shootin' tin cans with this *pea-shooter* since I was seven. I can put your eye out at thirty yards without thinking. Lucky to hit you from here with that hand-cannon."

"Don't matter," Ham said, "You got eight shots, and the first big boom gets Charlie to shit hisself—then you can use that nose to track him down with the next two or three. Besides, I'm sure you seen Marines put 'em down from twenty feet; you know it knocks 'em down and out with or without a kill-shot.

"Mind if I take a look-see?" he motioned and the pistol still pointed in his direction as the two took a seat. JD handed Ham the pistol, took the belt and holster from him and drew on the joint all but forgotten in his left hand. Then out of his natural sense of hospitality JD rose to find his secreted stash of Johnnie Walker scotch and handed the third-full bottle to Ham.

"I think it was a WWI sidearm for some unlucky bastard," JD told Ham. He squeezed the cherry off his joint and put it back into the stash box; he'd had enough for the moment. "Johnny Douglas, by the way." They exchanged a somewhat awkward greeting ritual—JD wasn't yet familiar with the intricacies of Blood relations in Nam, but the big fellow led him through it.

"Sweet little relic. Not sure I'd want it in the bush, though," Ham said dubiously, then pulled on the scotch bottle and offered it back to JD with a third less liquor in it. "You're alright, Doc. I seen you 'round. Your brother here is Ham. Expect folks 'round here to call you Doc for the most part and JD the rest of the time."

"Any time, Ham," JD said. He realized he'd been staring at the man's scar long enough to seem rude. "Sorry, man."

Ham laughed. "Easy, Blood," he soothed JD, "It's just a fuckin' thing. 'Round here, long as you got your ass and a heartbeat, all else is *just a thing.* You're a good brother, my friend. First corpsman ever bothered givin' old Ham here anything better than that dog-piss morale propaganda shit they give out. You're a straight guy. You need a thing—anything—you talk to me and I'll tell you who to talk to."

"Great to know you," JD felt he'd found a new brother.

"Any chance you know where I can find a good supply of ammo for that?" he pointed at the pistol Ham was still holding loosely in his right palm.

"Consider it taken care of," Ham replied. He checked the mechanics and maintenance of the weapon, then handed it back to JD. "Not impressed with the weapon, but I have to tell you, Doc, you care for it more like a Bulldog than a squid. Valley Dogs ever need a corpsman, I'm puttin' in a request," he put his hand on JD's shoulder, an iron hand that felt much too soft for the reputation it had for cruelty and killing efficiency. "Don't worry, Blood, Ham's got your back."

JD felt a mixed thrill of companionship and the certainty of death. He abruptly changed subjects while going back to his stash box for the rest of the half-roached joint. "You come here for a reason, or just to insult my Granddaddy's Colt thirty-two?"

"Hot fuck! A brother ready to take care of business," Ham laughed deep in his chest, then stiffly pulled his shirt down and turned his left shoulder toward JD. "Mind takin' that out? It's pissing me off somethin' fierce."

JD gaped at the hunk of metal sticking in Ham's shoulder. He couldn't imagine having remained so calm with that sticking in him. He moved a spot flood in place to inspect it more closely. Embedded within Ham's shoulder was a three-inch chunk of metal with blast blackened camo paint on one side—obviously not shrapnel, but a scrap of something blown apart during the storm of incoming. JD had seen men with lesser wounds scream or pass out.

"Jesus-God, Marine," he said, "doesn't that hurt?"

"Pain just weakness leavin' the body, Doc." Ham replied, "besides, it's just a pinch and a damned inconvenience. Bleedin' much? Can't tell blood from sweat runnin' down on a night like this."

"Seriously, Ham," JD said in his clinical voice, in charge now. "I need to know if you can feel it. I think it's stuck in your clavicle—your shoulder bone. . . ."

"What the Fuck. That ain't my shoulder blade. What kinda fucked up shit they teach you in that medical school?" Ham teased.

"Not the scapula, smartass," JD said sharply, half-jokingly, "your *bone*, not your shoulder *blade*." He cleaned around the wound, continuing to inspect it and go through the progressions he'd been taught in both civilian and corpsman training. He continued to mutter to Ham out of a habit he'd formed to comfort, or at least distract, the men he patched up. "Problem is it's close to some nerves and possibly your subclavian if it penetrated deeply enough—but it'd have to go most of the way through. How deep does it feel?"

"Well, can't. . . .God damn! Careful, Doc."

"You're not bleedin' enough. You always clot this quick? Thick-blooded *individual*. Here," he handed a bottle of the cheap whiskey to Ham, "Drain it like a man and set yourself for a shit-storm of hurt. I'm going to have to jerk this hunk of tin out and sew the wound shut. Should get you out of action for at least a week or two. I'll recommend you for in-country."

Ham swore under his breath something about dogpiss and disrespect to a true soldier of the United States of America, then raised the half-pint bottle toward the sky, "here's to my ass intact!" and poured the entirety of the amber liquid down his open throat. Nam taught you nothing if not how to drain a bottle of cut-rate liquor.

JD busied himself mending the big Marine's shoulder, having him lie face-down for a more workable angle. While probing, then cleaning, then sewing the wound closed, JD told Ham the story of how he'd come to point a .32-caliber pistol at him in a medical hooch in Nam.

Thomas Crawford Jackson was a soldier in WWI. He'd made it late on the scene in the trenches near Paris, having gone through the whole shuck-n-jive show it took a black man to get into action in France. Jackson wasn't there for any purpose other than to scavenge souvenirs and whatever he could find to carry home to give his family a leg up. He ran from every battle he was in—until that last day of hell in October 1918. Then he'd gotten caught in a little group of runaways led by some low-ranking WestPoint educated officer by the name of Johnson right in the middle of a firestorm.

Despite having been in a number of battles and surviving by shear cowardice, Jackson had never fired his weapon in combat. He loathed the heavy rifle with his entire being. But this fateful day he fired it like God was pulling the trigger for him. Somehow the group of nine had gotten themselves caught in the middle of a group of krauts that were either advancing or escaping, no one could tell for sure. It didn't matter. Both sides fought like cornered rats—the most fierce being a Mississippi nigger named Thomas Crawford Jackson.

Night fell and the four remaining soldiers grabbed up what rounds they could from among them, said a numb but sincere prayer over their fallen brothers-in-arms, promised the wounded to send back a corpsman, and ran together toward safety.

West Point Johnson, that's what JD's grandfather called the officer, led them out despite the bullet in his left shoulder. He got them to some creek embankment where the krauts shot him and the youngest of the four. TC Jackson led the other boy—a white son of a farmer from Indiana—away to find somewhere to hole up and figure out what to do. Before leaving their fallen, the two grabbed their ammo and TC grabbed the officer's belt, holster and sidearm—a Colt .32-caliber automatic.

"Sounds like goddam Hemingway to me," Ham laughed, "you sure your gramps wasn't shittin' ya about all that?"

"Could be," JD said reflectively. "He wasn't quite right in the head when he got back home to Mississippi. Momma's momma swears that's the way it happened, but some speculate there's less glory, more infamy there. Makes a good story to tell a brother when you're putting 28 stitches in his shoulder, anyhow."

"You just made that shit up, didn't you, Doc?"

"You ever read Hemingway?"

"Sure as fuck have. Man can write; seems to know something—sure as hell rather be in some pansy-ass European theatre than here in hell."

"Yeah," JD laughed, "and sure as you've read Hemingway, my family carries the story like I told it to you."

"Alright, Doc. It's just a fucking thing, Blood, just a fucking thing." He sat up, keyed that it was okay from the way JD touched his fingertips to Ham's shoulder.

"What you doin' there, Doc?" Ham asked, watching JD scramble a sheet of paper into the typewriter.

"Gotta stay out of the bush so that don't turn septic. Need a form for that."

"Bull-fuckin-shit!" Ham replied. "Valley Dogs go out twenty-nine hours from now, and they sure as death ain't goin' in the bush without my ass."

"You need to heal up. . . ."

"Look, Doc," Ham demonstrated unimpeded range of motion completely without signs of discomfort, "moves like a new one. Great job, Blood. You do great work. Now let me do my job."

"I ain't gotta write your letter home. Do what you gotta do, Ham." JD conceded.

"Not to worry, nigger. You're coming with me."

"What happened to 'if the Valley Dogs need a corpsman'?"

"Turns out we do, Doc," Ham grinned. "Ours got lost in Hong Kong day before yesterday. Fellow down at the corpsman hooch said you was likely the best choice on account of how good you play poker."

"Shit," JD exclaimed. "Guess that's the payoff for a lucky pot at last night's table."

"Heard you sported drinks all around. You're catching on, Doc, you're catching on. Thing's just a thing. Win it, lose it, it's all the same as long as you got your ass in one piece. Nam ain't nothin' but a lose-or-lose proposition."

Had that already been a year ago? It felt like another lifetime. *Shut up!* JD thought to himself, *just turn it off; Valley Dogs go out in the morning.* He fell asleep with the vision in his mind of Ham swigging Johnnie Walker from the bottle, and the sound of himself telling Ham the .32 was a piece of luck he'd brought from home. It had saved his life and health many times since.

CHAPTER 11

JD's mother raised him to fight only to protect himself—
now he was going out to find strangers to kill?

Ham waited in the medical hooch for JD to return. He was lying on the cot when JD came into the room. "You're still here? I thought you'd be getting the team ready for tomorrow's patrol," JD said.

Ham sat up and pointed to the empty scotch bottle on the floor. "Mister Johnnie Walker talked me into staying."

JD stood in the middle of the room. "You knew why the CO wanted to see me."

"I knew," Ham said. "The CO ordered me not to say anything to you."

JD walked over and sat on the cot next to Ham. "What fucking difference did it make if you told me?" he asked.

"When Masters told me you were going on this patrol, I told him it didn't make sense for you to go with only three weeks left in-country. I also told him I'd tell you to say no and go to the brig for three weeks. Pissed Masters off—he didn't want to fuck around with General Scott; ain't got balls nor brass to do it." Ham picked the bottle up from the floor and shook it to make sure it was empty. "He gave me a direct order not to say anything to you about the patrol until he talked to you." Ham lit a cigarette. "All I got to say Doc is, fuck 'em. You're too close, and you don't owe them a fucking thing."

"What fucking difference does it make what they owe me or what I owe them?" JD asked. "They say 'go' and I say 'when'?"

Ham's facial scars jumped and curled. "That's dumb Nam shit talking," he said.

"Hey, I don't want to die in this fucking place, but I don't think I can take being locked up behind bars in Long Binh jail. Uh, uh. No thanks. That's like being in a dark hole with rats." JD's body shuddered. "Fuck that shit."

Ham took a drag on his cigarette and blew the smoke toward JD's face. "You're a dumb shithead if you haven't figured out that jail is better than dead," Ham said.

JD shrugged his shoulders. "Nothing has made sense in this hell hole for the last twelve fucking months, so why should it start today?" he asked. "If it's my time to go, it's my time. What do you always say? Going out on patrol ain't no big deal. Getting back is the key. Hell, you've lived through Korea and two tours of Nam."

Ham ran his big black hands over his head. "I don't know how much of me being here is luck or how much is skill. Besides, Korea was different than Nam. Gooks may look the same to us, but underneath they're different."

"What's the difference between slant-eyed gooks in Korea or in Vietnam trying to kill you?" JD asked. "They're both after your ass. Dead is dead no matter where you're at or who kills you."

"There are differences between Nam and Korea," Ham said. "First of all, gooks look the same to you and me, not to themselves. In Korea, you knew who the bad guys were. In Nam, you can't tell the difference between the bad guys and the good guys. In Nam, everybody gets sucked into the fucking meat grinder, turning men into dead pieces of meat to be counted. The only thing that counts here is the number of men killed or mutilated. It doesn't matter who they are."

JD couldn't understand the differences Ham was talking about. He had no sense of how the South Koreans needed America. To JD, the South Vietnamese were parasites living off other countries. The war efforts built their national economy for a privileged few.

"Killing is the same in Korea or Nam," Ham said. "What you put your life on the line for is different. Korea had a lot of killing, but it seemed to serve some purpose. In Nam, the only purpose of killing is to live to kill again."

Korea was full of drab, treeless hills and vast, open spaces surrounded by brown mountain ranges. The weather was cool and wet, turning to cold and snowy during the winter season.

The weather in Nam was hot, wet, or both. A constant dampness lingered in the air because of the rain or from the gallons of sweat that ran off a man standing still. The southern part of Nam was more water than land. The northern part was mountainous and covered with jungle. The Nam landscape could be unfamiliar and foreign even when you returned to the same place a week later.

Ham told JD not to think about why the war was being fought. The reason is an illusion that can get you killed in a combat zone, he said. There is no illusion about killing and dying in combat. He taught JD that living on the edge is a series of adaptations to circumstances. Combat is beyond understanding. There is no right or wrong. You live through it and in it. Clarity demands you know you are there to kill and live and live to kill. Everything else is irrelevant.

The thumping of boots on the floor in the front room caught their attention. A high-pitched voice with Spanish overtones came from the front room. "Hey Doc, you back there?" Mex, pointman for the Valley Dogs, called out in the front room.

"Yeah, come on back," JD said.

The dark-green curtain parted and an olive-skinned Mexican slipped into the room. "Hey, Doc short-timer," Mex said as he thrust his hands out toward JD with palms up.

JD slapped Mex's hands. "You got it all, amigo," he said.

Jake, a tall, country-fed white boy, followed Mex into the room. He nodded his head toward Ham and JD, walked over, and leaned against the wall next to the back door.

"You're looking for us, Ham?" Mex asked.

Jake spoke before Ham answered. "What trouble are we in now?" he asked. "We've only been out of the bush two days."

Ham laughed. "It doesn't take long for you two to get in trouble. I know you've done something wrong, I just haven't heard what it is. However, this is your lucky day. I don't care to know. Pack for a five-day patrol. We're going out in the morning."

"What's so fucking lucky about going back to the bush after only two days of rest?" Jake asked.

"Whatever trouble you're in that I haven't heard about don't matter," Ham said.

Jake spoke with a very apparent southern twang. "I know it's gonna be some shit if they gonna throw our asses back into the bush so soon. I don't care, long as it ain't a fuckin' milk run. I don't think I can handle another milk run right now."

They laughed. Their last patrol was supposed to have been a "milk run," which meant no enemy contact was expected. The mission was supposed to be a reward because of the heavy enemy contact the team had encountered on every patrol for the past seven months. General Scott personally told them they had five days to stroll through the jungle and do some overnight camping. It was supposed to be five days of cooling out, getting high, and watching the sky without expecting enemy contact.

However, unbeknownst to SOG, one of the NVA's top fighting regiments set up a base camp in the area. The Valley Dogs were dropped into the middle of the camp area. They were so deep and hot in shit the choppers couldn't get down to the pickup zone. One chopper was blown out of the air when a rocket hit its gas tanks. Another chopper was shot so full of holes trying to pick them up, it left the area in flames.

The milk run was a nightmare. The mission turned into a death-defying act of desperate madness for the Valley Dogs. They walked through a shitload of gooks before finding a safe pick-up zone for the choppers. They all made it out alive, but a lot of gooks died trying to stop them.

"Don't worry, this won't be a milk run," Ham said. "I promise you it will be like walking on a frying pan from the moment we land in Khe Sanh."

"Khe Sanh? You got to be shittin' me," Jake said. "No one walks in or around Khe Sanh. Everyone crawls on their fucking bellies. Why the fuck are we going there?" he asked.

"I haven't told you the fun part yet," Ham said. "We're walking out of Khe Sanh into our recon zone."

"Walk out of Khe Sanh? We'll get killed before we get in the bush," Jake said. "Hey, if I'm gonna get taken out, I at least want to be in the bush, eyeball to eyeball with the little fucker that does it."

Jake was six-foot, four-inches, stout with thick shoulders and a small beer belly. His sharp blue eyes didn't portray any emotion or concern about danger. He was a corn-fed, red-haired, southern country boy who weighed in at 220 and was scared of very few things.

Back in *the world*, he was a high-school football star in his hometown of Pondville, Alabama, a little town in the middle of nowhere, located in the Talladega National Forest, twenty-five miles as the crow flies from Tuscaloosa, and ninety miles north of the state capital, Montgomery. There was little difference between a football game and war to Jake. The strategy was the same—get an edge over the other side.

Jake was ruthless. In his mind, every gook he killed was one less gook to worry about. When there was time, Jake would carve a "J" with two lines underneath it on dead gooks' foreheads—his personal message to other gooks.

He didn't get high, smoke dope, or drink hard liquor. Being alive in Nam was his high. Jake would have been judged insane back in his hometown, but in Nam he wasn't judged.

Jake was respected in the bush and feared outside it. His twisted sense of humor would surface at unexpected times. A month earlier, Jake, Mex, and JD went down to China Beach in Da Nang for in-country R&R. There, pallets of beer and Cokes were stacked out in the open and men lounged around on towels trying to get a suntan.

They ended up drunk in an Army club full of big, loud soldiers talking about a mortar attack that happened the day before. Hearing so much talk about one mortar attack bugged Jake. He started to taunt the soldiers with his deepest Southern drawl. "Well, I'll be damned, look a'here, real live he-roes. I bet ya mammies are proud of y'all."

The soldiers became quiet. Mex stepped a few feet away from Jake and joined in the taunting. "Hey gringos, you take any pictures of the war for your mommas? Show her how much of a man her little boy grew up to be?" he asked.

"Hey, this is unfair," JD said. "Three recon men against a room full of boys." He looked at Jake and Mex. "We should wait until they get help." He turned toward Mex. "No cutting. Remember, I'm on R&R, too," he said, recalling many times he'd gotten cramped fingers from sewing up cuts from rowdies out of the bush, usually guys who had cut or bruised each other till one or the other relented or got himself unconscious; often all parties involved would come to the medical hooch and pass drinks while 'Doc' performed damage control.

The soldiers swarmed around the three Marines. They weren't going to take any shit from a big-mouthed white boy, a Mexican, and a nigger on their turf.

A big, beer-bellied sergeant stepped forward. "Fucking bush monkeys. We're gonna kick your ass," he said.

Jake continued to taunt the men. "You don't know much about bush monkeys, but I'm gonna teach you," he said. "Let's play a bush monkey's game." He grinned as he pulled a grenade from his belt, yanked the pin out, and threw it up into the air. "Yeah, this bush monkey's game is called, 'We're all gonna die today'."

The men surrounding them froze. Their eyes followed the arc of the grenade up into the air and then down. When it hit the floor, men bolted like they just heard a shot from a starter's gun. They scrambled and clawed over each other, charging out doors and diving through windows. A few busted through the thin walls of the hooch.

JD and Mex dove behind the bar, hugging their heads. There was no explosion, just the sound of Jake's laughter. He'd removed the grenade's primer pin so it wouldn't explode. "Those fuckers will have more respect for bush monkeys next time," he said.

Jake only cared about men who went on patrol with him. Nothing else counted, except how many gooks he could kill.

"Looks like you picked a good patrol to miss, Doc," Jake said.

"Hey Doc, I'll bring you some ears. You'll have fresh meat to take home," Mex said. "Let the family know you're a big game hunter."

Mex had the innocent smile of a kid on his face, but he was an extremely dangerous killer. His finely boned frame stood six-feet tall, yet he weighed a lean 140 pounds. His smooth, beardless face made him look younger than his age of nineteen. He was born and raised in McCarmery, Texas, a small, hot, dusty Southwestern town full of poor people and large families. The town's biggest claim to fame was being next to Crockett County, home of the Texas Davy Crockett monument.

His family was so poor that all they had was family and God. He grew up believing no matter how far he was from his family, God was always close. He'd come to Nam eight months ago, a very religious kid searching for a family. Three months in-country, Mex thought he'd found a family. He became attached to a little South Vietnamese kid whose mother worked on the base. Ham made arrangements for the kid to meet the team at the chopper pad whenever they came in from patrol. Four months ago, the team came in and the kid was waiting for them as usual on the chopper pad.

However, this time there were two other kids and an old man with him. When the choppers landed, the kids ran toward the team. Ham knew something was wrong because the kids were too fat. In Nam, all kids were skinny. Ham yelled for the kids to stop. The old man with them pulled out an AK-47 and started shooting at the team. They returned his fire.

This was a VC assassination attempt on the Valley Dogs. Both the kids and the old man were wired with explosives. The team's bullets detonated the explosives. Their bodies turned into four explosions that left gaping holes in the chopper pad. The assassination attempt failed against the team; however, two choppers were destroyed and their four crewmembers were killed.

That day molded Mex into a nineteen-year-old professional killer full of cold, surly hate. Something always happened in Nam to produce hate in a man, forcing each back to his basic animal existence; these men were predators for the most part, survivors across the board.

After that day, Mex stayed high smoking pot and killing gooks. He displayed his combat manhood by wearing a necklace of gooks' ears that he personally collected.

Mex's offer of a gook's ear made JD's stomach churn. "Ugh. Forget it. The only meat I want to take home is my ass," JD said. Mex and Jake laughed.

"Doc can get his own meat. He's going on this patrol with us," Ham said.

The laughing stopped. "What the fuck's wrong with you?" Mex asked. "You're a fucking short-timer. Get the fuck out of here. Go home."

"That sure is stupid shit, Doc," Jake said.

"No choice. General Scott asked me personally," JD said. "Besides, what would you crazy fuckers do if you got hurt, and I wasn't there to hold your hand?" he asked.

Jake scowled. "It don't make any sense, but what the hell, Scott's a general. They never make sense to me. Fuck it. If you're going, you're going. It's dumb shit, but what's new?" He turned to Ham. "What time we shove off?" he asked.

"Choppers pick us up at daybreak. It's supposed to be a five-day patrol, but pack heavy on ammo and light on rations," he said. "In that area, we don't need to lug heavy packs with food. Besides, I doubt we'll be there long enough to do any cooking."

Mex gave out a dog yowl and shook his body. "Here we go! On the hunt again. The Dogs are on the prowl for meat. Let's go, Jake. See you later, Ham. Doc, you keep your head down on this one."

There were three other members of the Valley Dogs, but Mex, Jake, JD, and Ham formed the core of the team. Their blend of craziness, brutality, and bush knowledge gave them an edge for survival in combat. The other three were good in the bush—better because they were members of the Valley Dogs.

Mike carried the M-79, a grenade launcher that resembled a sawed-off shotgun and shot a 40-mm shell. Mike was a twenty-year-old white kid from somewhere close to Thurman, Colorado, a small town in the eastern part of the state. People would ask him about the Rocky Mountains, but he didn't know much about them. He grew up on a flat farm far east of the mountains. Nam had become Mike's ticket off the farm.

Swene carried an M-60 machine gun that spit out bullets at such a heavy volume of fire it was called the "Pig." He was a twenty-year-old white boy with thick shoulders, no neck and a back rippling with muscles. He was born and raised in Kelsy, Minnesota, a small town on County Route 52 to Tiola where the pavement ended.

Kelsy was dairy country. His family raised cows and made cheese. Swene never left Minnesota until he signed up with the Marines to see the world. Other than basic training camp, the world he was exposed to was Nam. A two-man crew usually handled the M-60, but Swene handled it like other men handled the lightweight M-16.

Vince, the radioman, a nineteen-year-old black kid from Detroit, was the only member of the team from a large city. He got caught stealing hubcaps. Even though it was the first time he was ever in trouble with the law, the judge gave him the choice of going to jail or joining the Army. Vince opted to join the Marines. Vince was the best radioman in the company because he kept his cool and was strong as an ox, an important trait when lugging a twenty-pound radio plus combat gear and a pack.

"Ham, have you told Mike, Swene, and Vince we're going out in the morning?" JD asked.

"I'm on my way to let them know now," Ham said. "Vince and I have to figure out new codes for the mission since the gooks got our codebooks from the team they overran last month."

"I got the feelin' I better pack extra medical supplies on this one," JD said.

Ham looked at JD and shook his head. "Doc, you know you're a crazy nigger for going on this mission." He walked over to the back door.

"I'm in Nam, and I'm alive. How can I *not* be crazy?" JD said.

JD sat on his cot after Ham left and smoked a joint. A tingling sensation flowed through his body. His mind slipped into memories of his first patrol in Nam.

The night before his first patrol, he ran to the shitter throughout most of the night because he was so nervous. His body dripped with sweat and shook with chills. The only patrols he had been on before were training missions. But this was real. There was no instructor there to correct his mistakes. There were no repeats. Every act was final. Mistakes could get him killed.

He wondered if he could kill a stranger, a person who'd done nothing to him. His mother raised him to fight only to protect himself—now he was going out to find strangers to kill? Unable to sleep, he tossed and turned and threw up until he got the dry heaves. Finally, in the early morning, exhaustion forced him to sleep.

The first patrol was a blur until he stepped off the chopper into twelve-foot elephant grass flattened into a circular pattern by the down blast of the chopper's blades. The chopper hovered about three feet off the ground. He was told to jump. When his feet hit the ground, the extra weight of his pack, combat belt and extra ammo for the M-79 sent a jarring pain through his whole body. He moved away from the chopper a few feet and took a defensive position like he was taught in jungle warfare school. He turned and watched the chopper fly up into the sky. His heart pounded in his ears like the beat of a bass drum. The team moved quickly out of the elephant grass into thick jungle. After a few yards, the team leader halted them.

Plants, trees, and vines around him blended into a green blur. He tried to focus and see shapes in the sea of green that encircled him. He tried to distinguish the sounds around him while his eyes searched for the source. The intense smell of decay assaulted his nose. His mind became consumed by the overwhelming sensations.

He believed the enemy knew they were there, alerted by the sound of the choppers. Dark spots in the green jungle wall became windows for the enemy's guns. He expected enemy bullets to slam into his body. Fear took control. His breathing became fast and shallow. Sweat flowed in streams down the length of his body.

The patrol leader, KC Joe they called him, slid next to him. "Doc, close your eyes and take deep breaths. You're hyperventilating. Relax."

JD closed his eyes and took some deep breaths. He heard scraping sounds. Something was moving close to him. He had to see if it was an animal or the enemy. He opened his eyes. The sight of green flooded his mind. He swung his rifle toward the sound of movement to his right. A man knelt there with a rifle. *He's going to shoot me*, JD thought. KC grabbed his rifle before he fired. He had almost opened fire on a member of the team. "Damn it, Doc, we don't need *you* to shoot us. There are enough gooks around to do that. Now sit still and take long, deep breaths. I know it's your first patrol and you're scared. We're all scared. But we don't need to be scared you'll shoot us."

On the ground only a few minutes and the first man he was going to shoot was a member of his own team. The thought made his body shake.

"Doc, just breathe, you'll be okay," the team leader said.

He shook his head up and down. His eyes were still closed. He became aware of other things beyond his fear—how his pack cut into his shoulders, air going in and out of his lungs, and the wetness that covered his body from sweating. He opened his eyes. The wall of green was still there, but he could see leaves. "I'm okay," he said.

"Good, we've been here too long. Choppers attract gooks." He snapped his fingers. The other team members looked at him. He pointed in a direction, and the point man started moving.

KC helped JD get up. The pack got heavier and his legs weaker when he sat down. They moved through the jungle for about two hours. He fought little green and yellow wait-a-minute vines that wrapped around him and his pack. The more he wrestled with them, the more they grabbed him. They were winning the fight. The team stopped several times to let him rest. One of the team members knelt next to him. "Doc, don't fight the vines. You can't win. Move them out of the way with your hands." The advice worked, but the little stickers on the vines scratched deep into his hands. JD had gone to jungle warfare school in the Panama jungle, but Nam's jungle, with its clinging vines and enemies, was so different he felt ill-prepared.

KC halted the patrol when they reached the top of a small hill. A ridge line across a deep valley surrounded the hill on three sides. Behind the team was dense bush that opened into a flat field of elephant grass. They planned to stay there until it was almost dark, then move across the valley into denser bush to spend the night.

The team was laying down on their packs when the first shots rang out. Bullets whizzed through the air, tearing up leaves and smacking into trees. KC warned them that the incoming fire came from the left ridgeline. The team focused their return fire in that direction—except for JD. He was too scared to look up. He hugged the ground. Gunfire erupted from the ridgeline to the front and to the right. There was movement in the elephant grass behind them. The gooks had the team surrounded.

KC called in artillery on the gooks in the elephant grass. First, white smoke spotter rounds popped in the open field. They were on target. He then called for a full barrage. The ground shook like a herd of elephants was stampeding past the hill. The flying, twisted steel of exploding shells sliced through the elephant grass, leaving large, round death zones. He couldn't see them, but he heard men screaming as the steel fragments found flesh.

Bullets zipped above his head. The gooks were shooting at him. Every bullet flying in the air seemed aimed at him. Strangers hidden in the green of the jungle on the ridgeline were trying to kill him.

Fear plunged deep into his stomach. His body froze. The bits of metal zinging through the air would smash into his body if he moved. He felt a warm wetness between his legs; he'd pissed himself. His mind filled with rapid glimpses of his wife, mother, and other people who loved him. He cried out "Momma" into the clamor of explosions and whizzing bullets. Tears filled his eyes. He was going to die.

"Doc, your momma ain't here," KC screamed in his ear. He hit him on the top of his head and pointed to a tree. "Get over to that tree and kill some fucking gooks."

He didn't want to kill anybody. He didn't want to be there. He wanted to go home. He crawled over to the tree, closed his eyes and fired in the general direction of the ridgeline. If he was going to kill someone, he didn't want to see it.

Movement in the bush to his left caught his eye. He thought it was another team member, but it was a small yellow man in a brown uniform crawling out of the bush on his hands and knees. JD pointed his rifle at the man, but didn't fire. He just watched him. *He's the enemy? He's just a man, like me, who probably doesn't want to be here*, he thought. The man saw him. Their eyes locked. He dropped to his stomach and swung his rifle toward him, and JD instinctively pulled the trigger. The bullet splattered the yellow man's face, went through his skull, and exploded out the back of his head.

JD had killed. His first time. That was it.

He looked at the yellow man's bloody face. The bullet tore the man's nose off and blew one eye out, leaving a bleeding dark hole. JD turned his head away and threw up. *I didn't* want *to kill that man*, he repeated over and over in his mind. He remembered what an old gunny sergeant once told him: "When you kill a man, there are two graves—one in the ground, the other one in your soul."

He started to cry. He wanted to apologize to someone.

Then, from a murky place within his mind, another thought floated up. It was okay to kill a man if he was the enemy. He could see the brown uniforms moving in the green of the jungle. They were swarming down the ridge opposite the hill. Now he could see the enemy clearly. He started shooting at the brown uniforms. He wanted to kill the enemy.

He lived through his first mad minute, the beginning of a firefight. Bullets fly thick in the air, and you don't know from where. It is total confusion. It is the most dangerous time in a firefight.

He lost his virginity—his first firefight. No matter how much training you have, who you think you are, or what you say you will do in a firefight, no one knows how they will react until it happens.

It's the coming-to-Jesus moment, when everything in you is stripped away—leaving just you and your fear. You might lose control of your bodily functions—cry, piss, or shit yourself. You might call out for your momma. You might freeze from your fear or stand up and try to run from it. It doesn't matter. What matters is what you do after that. Did you cover your team member's back? Did you fight? If you didn't, no one wanted to be in the bush with you.

He killed his first man with hesitation, but he never hesitated after that. They were *the enemy*. They were *gooks*. The more gooks he killed, the fewer there were who could try to kill him.

KC called jets in to drop bombs. He told the team to hug the ground. Johnny looked at the sky behind him. A faraway jet dropped two bombs from its wing. The jet pulled up, the bombs headed toward the hill where the team was. One exploded on the slope of the ridgeline. The other one clipped the hill and exploded. The team got caught up in the blast. Hot metal blew over Johnny's head, slicing through bush and cutting down trees. He was tossed into the air and slammed down hard to the ground. Dirt covered his body. Dazed and confused from the blast, he rubbed his eyes franticly to clear the dirt out of them. The gooks were still shooting at him.

"Doc! Tim and Ray are hit," the team leader yelled.

He could see the two men to his left crumbled on the ground. He crawled to them. Bomb fragments had shredded their bodies. Tim was dead. Ray was bleeding from so many wounds he wasn't sure where to start. Life was slipping from Ray's body. JD had seen dead people and people dying in hospitals, but he had never seen wounds like these or so much blood. What should he do? Blood was gurgling out of holes in Ray's chest. If it filled up his lungs, Ray would drown in his own blood.

The first wounded man he treated in combat put him on the verge of shock. His stomach knotted even tighter, forcing up bile and he vomited. He wiped his mouth with his sleeve, leaving the taste of Ray's blood in it. His hands shook too much to be effective. He couldn't watch the man die. He had to do something.

His training taught him to stop the bleeding and make sure the man was breathing. He ripped the plastic cover off some pressure bandages, covered the holes in Ray's chest, then put on the pressure bandages. The gurgling sounds stopped. He wiped the man's blood and his own bile from his mouth, held Ray's nose, and started mouth-to-mouth resuscitation. He spit out blood and bile coming up from Ray's throat and kept trying to push air into Ray's mouth. It was no use. Ray was dead.

He crawled over to KC. "Tim and Ray are dead."

"Get your head down. The jet is coming in for another bomb run," the team leader yelled.

He turned and searched the sky for the jet. This time the jet was coming in from the team's right side. He wondered how it was going to drop its bombs. The distance across the hill and the ridgeline was too narrow for a jet to fly between them. The valley was filling up with brown uniforms. There was no way the team could defend against so many. Just before the jet entered the valley, it turned sideways. As it streaked past, the cockpit was even with the hill. He could see the top of the pilot's fly helmet and the markings on the wings. It was strange seeing a jet fly at that angle so close. He watched it straighten up after it left the valley. The roaring sound of its engine followed a few seconds after the jet passed. Then the sounds of the napalm bombs and men screaming shattered the air.

Brown uniforms scurried back up the slope of the ridgeline, their attack thwarted. Choppers came in and took the team out. The patrol was over.

After debriefing, showering, and sleeping, Johnny went outside and lay on top of the bunker outside the team's hooch. He stared into the dark sky. The events of the day replayed in his mind—what happened, what could have happened, and what failed to happen.

KC Joe came out of the hooch and jumped on the bunker next to him. "You did good for your first patrol, Doc. You survived."

"I almost shot a member of the team. That can't be good," he said.

"Don't hang on to what almost happened or could've happened out there," KC said flatly. "What counts is what *did* happen. We've all had our first patrols, did dumb things, and sometimes our mistakes get our own killed. First or last patrol, you survive. That's what's important. You do what you have to do to get out of here alive." He jumped off the bunker. "You made it through your first hot patrol. You know you can live through a lot of shit. Knowin' that'll help you on every patrol to come." He walked off into the darkness.

Yes, he'd survived. But—why did he feel so terrible inside? In the midst of his fear, he'd almost shot his own team member.

He'd killed.

He'd felt the last breath of a dying man in his mouth, and his attempt to save the man failed.

He felt confused.

Johnny no more. He was a bush monkey now. He was JD.

That first patrol . . . it seemed so long ago. Now, he killed so often it didn't even matter to him.

CHAPTER 12

Where was God in Nam?

JD's last patrol in Nam was thrown together like a cowboy outing. Missions based on, "Get your gun and fly off into bad man's land," usually get people killed.

It wasn't the Valley Dogs' routine to just fly off into the bush with guns blazing. They memorized codebooks and studied map overlays with proposed and alternate routes of movement. Everyone had to know escape and evasion routes in case the team became separated. Weapons were test-fired and radios were checked. A helicopter would fly over the insertion zone at first light. On its return, the pilots would be called in for an S-2, a pre-insertion briefing in which the brass and other anonymous, elite bastards would discuss what intelligence was necessary for the team.

On this mission, the only thing JD knew was that the team would meet at 7:00 hours on the chopper pad to fly to Khe Sanh. Missions always had an uncertainty about them, but more so this time. The doubt in his mind was partly because his tour of duty was growing so short. His major concern was that the mission would be too fast and sloppy, and *that* increased the chances of mistakes and was a sure sign people were going to die.

There was nothing he could do about the patrol except make sure he was prepared. He went through his usual pre-mission ritual—loading his M-16 rifle magazines, eighteen rounds with the lead tips facing outward so that if a stray bullet hit the magazine pouches, they would explode away from his body, and a tracer round in the last five so he would know when to reload. He sprayed his boots and pant legs with DDT to ward off leeches and would spray them again in the morning.

He taped anything that rattled or made noise with black tape. He filled his canteens and picked out rations he would take. He moved things around in his pack until the weight rode easy on the straps and high on his back. Everything he needed was where he could instantly get it into his hands.

The hardest part of any mission was the waiting. His stomach ached so bad he made hourly trips to the latrine. The night was hot, yet he had chills. Sitting on his cot, he thought about his mother's church and said a quiet prayer. "Dear God, forgive me for the things I've done in this hellhole, and I pray you let me go home safely. I know I'm alive only through your will."

In his mother's church, God had been a simple, great white father with clear judgment of right and wrong within neatly written rules. Sin in church was evil, rooted inside you, a defect of spirit that kept you out of heaven. Sin was a sure ticket to burn in hell.

He was taught to pray for God's forgiveness of his sins and to be kept out of sin's way. His mother worked hard to keep him from dying in sin when he was young. He attended Bible study classes to understand *the good book*. He even attended summer Bible school and never missed a Sunday church service. It used to shame him to admit he did it to meet pretty girls, but shame was useless for survival. It had no room in his soul anymore.

The minister stood before the congregation every Sunday preaching the words of God so his flock could receive God's blessings. He told them about the blessing of giving and sharing. In search of blessings, the congregation gave—mostly to the minister. He was given a new car every two years, a house, trips, and whatever else he thought he needed to lead them to God. JD didn't understand why the minister's happiness was necessary to receive the goodness of God.

The minister always gave testimony to the goodness of God and His mercy. In his mother's church, people dressed in their finest clothes on Sunday morning in case God called them. The old and young sisters caught the spirit, danced, pranced, and screamed out in the name of the Lord. There was no doubt; God was there.

But where was God in Nam? Nam gave JD the license to kill based on how he felt. In his mother's church, he was taught that determining life and death was an act of God. In Nam, though, JD was able to determine death, which destroyed the simple notion of the God he'd learned about at home.

Praying was a request to God, but he wasn't sure if God heard everyone's prayers. He heard dying men hollering and begging, "Oh God, help me, please God," and that didn't help. JD didn't expect too much from praying. But, just in case God was listening, he would say a short prayer every so often.

Even in Nam, people needed to believe in something more than the continual battle to survive, something that transcended the day-to-day experience of dying. Ruthless men carried crosses or some symbol of faith on them. Mex wore a gleaming gold cross around his neck, but, to keep it from shining in the bush, he covered it with black tape. JD carried a wooden cross, given to him by his Aunt Kathryn, in his left breast pocket over his heart.

His first week with recon showed him the difference between death in Nam and death at home. As an ambulance driver in Springfield, he saw dead people after they were shot, stabbed, or hurt in car accidents. He'd seen death before, but always after the fact and hadn't known it so personally.

One day shortly after that first hot patrol, a group of recon men took him about fifty yards outside the base perimeter to a hill. The area was littered with piles of dead gooks. He'd never seen so many dead bodies at one time. The men pulled a body from one of the piles. When they moved the body, brain matter slid out of a hole on one side of the corpse's head.

The men told JD to kick the dead gook in the head. It didn't make any sense to him why he would kick a dead man in the head. He asked, "Why?" They laughed at him. "Why do you care?" one of the men asked. "You think you're going to hurt him? Kill him again?" They kept laughing. "Kick the fucking gook in the head, Doc. Kick! It ain't no big thing." They started yelling over and over at him. "Kick, Doc, kick! Kick! Kick!"

The yelling became a chant pounding in his temples, beating in time with his heart. He felt his foot move. He looked down into dull, vacant eyes staring up at him. His boot was inside the gook's head.

He yanked the boot out of the dead man's head. Partly dried, congealed blood and brain matter covered his boot. He fell to the ground and threw up. The chanting stopped. Someone grabbed his head and forced him to look at the dead gook he had kicked. "Look!" he demanded, then in an older-brotherly tone explained, "You kicked his fucking brains out. You're a bad mother-fucker now. You're a recon man. Nobody fucks with recon; they know we'll kick their fuckin' brains out."

JD became a bad mother-fucker, yet he was still a corpsman whose first duty was to help the wounded and save lives. He began to understand that, corpsman or not, he belonged to the same profession of killing and dying as everyone else in Nam. He fixed in his mind that his duty, his function on any recon team, was to patch guys up so they could continue their efficient killing of gooks. That moment of acceptance opened his mind to a murky infection. Madness was a root that grew within him once he accepted death as a necessity of survival.

Death claimed all possibilities and made all emotions secondary. Friend or enemy, in combat or not, dead meat was dead meat. A dead buddy was tough shit, but bringing your own ass out alive helped you get over it. Survival, no matter what the cost, was the bottom line.

Staying alive was reason enough to survive in Nam. JD had another force driving him—his son had been born just a few months ago. He carried a faded picture of his son taken in the hospital when he was born.

He looked at his watch. It was 5:45 P.M. He wondered what his mother and Jan were doing. Had his son learned to sit up on his own yet? Was the baby waking up his beautiful momma for an early morning feeding? The mental image of Jan's breasts made JD ache in too many places—he tried to focus on something factual. It was 4:45 A.M. in Springfield. They were probably still asleep.

CHAPTER 13

The jungle was a collection of strange noises,
confusing smells, and blurry green shapes.

The morning sunlight sharpened the edges of dark figures moving around the chopper's landing pad. Two Huey choppers flew overhead, skirting the treetops like dragonflies over water reeds. When they came down to land on the pad, the downdraft of whirling blades stirred up a swirl of debris. Dirt, pebbles, and twigs rippled over the ground in all directions.

A cloud of debris engulfed Mex, Mike, Vince, and Swene. Mex jumped up, cursing in Spanish interspersed with English cuss words. Swene waved the machine gun in the direction of the choppers. "I should swat these flies for the hell of it," he said.

The team's green, short-brimmed bush hats were filthy and helped provide camouflage in the jungle's elephant grass, bamboo, and vines. Recon only wore helmets and flak jackets on base for protection against the sharp metal spears of enemy incoming. They were too bulky and noisy in the bush. The team's unwashed, baggy uniforms were splattered with dried mud and grass stains and impregnated with a lingering stench. Their eyes, noses, and cheeks, which were splashed with patches of black and green, mimicked the pattern of the jungle.

Each man carried four canteens of water, a five-day supply of freeze-dried food, and explosives. Despite the fact they packed light for a short patrol, each pack weighed about 60 pounds. Besides the six grenades on his combat belt, JD carried twenty magazines for the M-16, five extra boxes of M-16 rounds, his Colt .32-caliber pistol, and three boxes of ammo for it. In his shirt pockets were other essential jungle survival tools: a compass, matches wrapped against the moisture, maps, and a multipurpose Swiss survival knife with a fork and toenail clipper.

In his jungle pants' utility pockets, he carried field bandages, a field surgery kit, pills, and morphine. After two patrols, he stopped carrying the Unit-1 medical bag issued to field corpsmen in the bush because it too easily identified him as a corpsman for bounty hunters. Plus, the bag gave the wait-a-minute vines another reason to embrace his body.

Each member of the team lugged along extra bandoleers for the M-79 and extra belts of rounds for the Pig, the 60-mm machine gun, which added another forty to fifty pounds to the burden on their backs. JD was just another grunt humping the boonies until someone got hurt. The word "grunt" came from the sound a Marine made when he moved with over 100 pounds of extra weight on his body. Every movement produced a grunt. "Humping" meant hauling the extra 100-plus pounds on your body through the jungle. Humping was just another form of grunting when you could move only 50 feet in an hour because of thick, heavy undergrowth. College men or officers called the bush or jungle the "boonies," but those who actually went out into the jungle called it the "bush."

JD boarded the chopper. He could tell the pilot hadn't been in Nam very long by his boyish grin and smooth face, his clean, bright-red hair and freshly pressed pants. His dirt-free helmet had "Jeff" printed on it. The pilot flashed a smile and gave a thumbs-up. Chopper pilots were cowboys riding metal horses in the sky.

He respected the air-cowboys that put the team in the bush because they always came back to get them. He'd seen cowboys die a few times saving the Valley Dogs' asses. He flashed a thumbs-up sign back to the smiling redhead.

The outside of the chopper was perforated with holes from bullets and shrapnel. When he stepped up into the chopper, JD noted dried blood stains on the floor. The chopper had obviously seen some hot fire zones, but he doubted the bright, smooth-faced kid made those trips.

The chopper took off and flew south from the base. Everyone sat quietly. There was usually very little talking during insertion flights because you had to yell. The *whump, whump, whump* of the chopper blades sounded like a chant that overwhelmed all other sounds.

After fifteen minutes of flying, the choppers turned west toward the highlands. This time of year, Khe Sanh was like northern California in the winter, with thick fog and cold, blustery weather. JD could feel the change.

The highlands of Vietnam were a spooky run of erratic mountain ranges, jungle-covered ravines, and unexpected plains. The jungle's high triple canopies of concealment conveyed a sinister gloom that kept everyone perpetually on edge.

The Khe Sanh Marine Base was on top of a round mountain traced with jagged trench lines. Choppers had to fly high and then drop quickly to land on the base because the surrounding landscape had 3,000-foot mountains. The choppers dropped down through the clouds into an impenetrable gray fog that surrounded Khe Sanh and enclosed the base in a wet fist that reduced both ceiling and visibility.

Khe Sanh's landing strip was considered enemy territory, so to land the choppers dove fast and at a steep angle. Small-arms fire opened up from the nearby jungle as the choppers came down. To avoid enemy fire, the pilots used a corkscrew action to land. Puffs of smoke popped from trees as the chopper passed. As their chopper's landing skids touched the metal runway mat, four mortar shells exploded around the airstrip.

"Jump! Jump! We've got to keep moving," the chopper's crew chief yelled. The team jumped from the chopper. As soon as JD's feet hit the ground, he scrambled to the nearest bunker. Shells fell all over the base, but most were directed at the choppers trying to take off.

A shell's scream ended in an earth-shattering explosion on the runway mat. JD peered out of the bunker. One of the choppers was in flames and on its side, split in two. The crew chief lay twenty feet from the back part of the chopper with only one leg, one arm, and his head intact on his body.

The front part of the chopper lay on its side facing him. One of the door gunners was trapped under the flipped chopper, his legs kicking wildly in the air. The pilots' faces had hard lines of desperation as they frantically slapped their chests to spring the quick-release buckle of the seat belts.

The redheaded pilot finally got free and scrambled to climb out of one of the chopper's small front windows. Men in the bunkers hollered, "Come on, come on, you can make it."

When he saw the look of terror on the redheaded pilot's face as he scrambled away from the flaming chopper, JD's corpsman instincts kicked in. He rolled out of the bunker and ran toward the pilot and the downed chopper. Jake and Mex tackled him. "Stay the fuck down, Doc," Mex yelled.

An explosion blew out from the chopper and the redheaded pilot's body was ripped into bits of flesh. Metal and plexiglas from the chopper, along with human debris and sand, spattered Mex, Jake, and JD.

A knot in JD's stomach rose up in his throat where it stuck with the sick taste of bile. "Take it easy, Doc," Mex said. "There's nothing you could've done except get yourself killed. Save it for patrol."

A shell screamed in and exploded close by, covering the three of them with dirt. Ham's yell broke through the thunderous noise. "Move to the right! To the right! Command bunker is on the other side of Charlie Med." He pointed to a bunker with multiple antennas on top.

Burning-shit stink hung thick in the air, greeting JD as it had the first day he'd arrived in Nam. His eyes scanned the base. Thick, black smoke billowed from fifty-five gallon drums in which diesel fuel burned rubbish, garbage, and human waste. The base was a trash heap. Helicopter blades, unhinged truck doors, shattered windshields, communications wire, and cardboard cartons lay scattered.

The team crawled from trenchline to trenchline toward the command bunker. A shell burst on JD's left. He dove to the right into a bunker and rolled in on top of four Marines. His eyes adjusted to the darkness, but his nose could not adjust to the smell. The bunker was a dank, stench-chamber, redolent of sweat and urine, diarrhea, vomit and panic-flatulence.

Exploding shells faded into the distance. He stuck his head out of the bunker. Ham and the rest of the team were already on the move. "Man, you're fucking crazy if you're going out there," muttered the Marines from the bunker.

JD glanced back at the four huddled men hiding in the dark hole, scared of being speared by hot metal, and worried about being buried in a collapsed bunker. The choice was to be crazy or be like them. "No shit," he said. JD rolled out of the bunker into the light of day.

The team had to crawl through garbage-filled trenches overflowing with torn ponchos, half-empty cans of beans, soggy crumples of paper, shell casings, boots without soles, and duds from the ammunition dump. They slithered over moldy bits of canvas, splintered fiberglass plates ripped from flak jackets, shrapnel chunks, and broken timber.

The noise of war was continuous. Its clamor erased any possibility of quietness. Fighter-bombers roared in low to hit NVA positioned a few hundred feet outside the base perimeter. Chopper blades thumped overhead. Enemy shells exploded on the steel plates of the runway. Truck horns warned of incoming. Machine-gunners fired clearing bursts along the perimeter. B-52 bombing strikes rumbled like heavy thunder in the distant, and not so distant, mountains.

A big red cross on a sign peppered with shrapnel holes marked Charlie Med's area. Charlie Med had three doctors and about twelve corpsmen. There were no operating tables, only stretchers. Doctors operated while wearing flak jackets and helmets to protect themselves from the constant shelling.

Two shells exploded behind them when they reached the command bunker. They flung themselves into the bunker's entrance. There were five officers in the bunker besides the commanding officer. The white-haired CO could have been forty- to sixty-five years old. It was difficult to judge his age because of the ravaging toll constant fear was taking on his facial lines and contours.

Ham had served with the commanding officer in Da Nang when he had been assigned to SOG Headquarters. "Colonel Dave," Ham said. "It's been a long time. What a shitty place to meet up again."

The colonel peered through the bunker's dim lighting. "Ham, you old dog. You're still beating the bush?!" The colonel shook Ham's hand. "Glad to see you," he said. "Shitty place to *be*."

The colonel gave a briefing on the situation as he saw it. He didn't add any new information to what the team had received in

Dong Ha earlier that morning. No matter how many ways it was said, it meant large forces of NVA ground troops were preparing to attack the base. No one knew how many or where the NVA were. They did know there were lots of them, and they seemed to be everywhere.

"Bring me back something I can use, Ham," the colonel said.

"Like a high-ranking NVA officer?" Ham asked.

"That would be a damn good start. You got any questions?" the colonel asked.

Jake's southern drawl broke through. "Yessir. I have a question, sir."

Irritation wrinkled the CO's brow. "Yes, what is it?"

Jake asked about the recon company that was supposedly operating out of Khe Sanh. "I have a friend in Bravo Company. Where can I find him?" he asked.

The colonel shifted his body and took a deep breath. "Your friend is not here. Bravo Company has been shipped out to Okinawa to regroup."

"Yeah, that's why you modern-day gunfighters and low-priced mercenaries are here," one of the officers chimed in. "I want to know how you're going to get to your recon zone. No one has been able to walk out of here more than a hundred yards without getting the shit blown out of them. How're you gonna do better?" he asked.

Ham faced the officer. "I do hope the gooks agree with you that no one can walk out of here. Make it easier for us to do it." Ham hooked a finger toward the colonel. "The colonel will brief you, if he thinks you need to know." He poked his finger into the officer's chest. "You just make sure *your* people don't shoot us when we come back."

Spooky kicked the mission off, standing on a column of tracers and tilling the earth outside the wire. The Army called it "Puff the Magic Dragon," but the Marines called it "Spooky." Whatever anyone cared to call it, the AC-47was a two-engined cargo plane converted into a gunship that hell on wings. Typically, it carried fourteen men, 17,000 pounds of armor plate, several tons of ammunition, a combination of two 40-mm automatic cannons, and two 7.62 mm or two 20-mm Gatling guns. It carried a flare launcher, a 1.5-million candlepower searchlight, a powerful computer, and various highly sophisticated sensor systems. It fired 6,000 rounds per minute and could fill every square inch of a football field with two rounds. For each red tracer you saw, there were four rounds you didn't see. A solid stream of violent red poured down from the sky when Spooky worked an area.

The Valley Dogs waited in a bunker next to the perimeter wire for Spooky to finish its rain of destruction. The Marines in the bunker couldn't believe the team of seven was going to walk into thousands of gooks on the other side of the wire in broad daylight.

"That's some crazy shit, man!" one of them said. "Every patrol outside the wire has been shot to pieces after a few yards. That's gook-land out there."

"Good! The gooks won't expect us to be out there. That's our edge," Jake drawled.

The Marine's fear was evident. "It's an edge all right. The edge of the knife they're going to cut your motherfuckin' throats with," he said.

Fading sounds of Spooky's gun-bursts still hung in the air when the Valley Dogs stepped through the wire. They worked their way across the firing zones beyond. Methodically, working as though with one mind, they made it through to the jungle without taking any fire. They slipped into the jungle's dense vegetation and began the next leg of their mission.

Spooky had taken out about twenty gooks 150 feet outside the wire; their stink hung in the air. The Valley Dogs tried to smell like the gooks, including their shit. In the thick underbrush of the jungle, you smelled a man's body before you even saw him. Since Americans ate red meat, the meat smell came out in their sweat and their heavy droppings. The rice-eating gooks' droppings didn't smell as strong and were a more natural odor in the jungle.

The Valley Dogs ate lots of rice and freeze-dried food packets that contained no beef, avoiding greasy foods especially. They never washed their bush clothes since soap was not a natural jungle odor. Small details like smell provided a split-second of uncertainty in the enemy, which could mean the difference between life and death. They'd proven it mission after mission.

The first dozen steps into the gooks' backyard were the most dangerous. The jungle was a collection of strange noises, confusing smells, and blurry green shapes. As he stepped into the bush, JD was just another blind and deaf American stumbling into unfamiliar territory. That's when the reality hit him that no matter how strong or powerful America was, he was the intruder on this turf. He was in a jungle full of people who wanted to kill him.

The team moved in silently, cautiously, and in single-file formation. The gooks would have mines in the area. Spooky's barrage should have detonated most of them. Still, JD's feet prickled at the anticipation of a landmine suddenly exploding in his face.

Mex walked point about twenty yards ahead of the team. He carried an M-14 rifle with a white phosphorus grenade, called a willy-peter, mounted on the barrel. When a willy-peter exploded, burning pieces of phosphorus splattered the area and burned as long as they were exposed to air. If a man's flesh became embedded with the burning phosphorus pieces he could jump into water and stop the burning by cutting off the oxygen, but the burning would burst out again as soon as free oxygen hit the phosphorus. Mex had broken up many ambushes with a well-placed first shot.

Mex was the best point-man in the company, reading the almost unnoticeable signs of a man's presence in the jungle: broken branches, grass pushed back in a different way, slight indentations in the ground, animal sounds (or the lack of them).

Ham followed Mex, then Vince with the radio, Mike with their M-79, JD, and Jake. Swene protected the rear with the machine gun. Gook foot-trails crisscrossed all over the area, but the Valley Dogs never followed trails. Trails were perfect sites for ambushes and booby traps. Recon teams moved in and through the bush. They worked their way through jungle undergrowth where other humans didn't go.

The Valley Dogs plunged into the dense undergrowth. There was a certain way to walk through this kind of jungle quietly. Ham taught JD to turn his foot outwards, step sideways away from his body and down to clear a small space for the next step.

Little yellow and green wait-a-minute vines with rows of small thorns wrapped around his arms and legs. Wait-a-minute vines seemed to be another device the jungle used to protest man's assumed right to be there. Hacking through them with a machete would make noise and the gooks would know exactly where you were. You had to carefully untangle them and push them from your body.

Ham stopped the team's movement to clear out the cluttered sounds of the base activity and to attune their ears to the bush. The jungle was both friend and enemy. It hid and exposed a man. Man moved through the jungle by colliding with it and trying to force his will on it—predatory man melded his will with the jungle to move *with* it.

Jake tapped JD on the shoulder and pointed toward a small pine tree. He smiled as they moved past it. You didn't see many pines in the jungle. The tree's presence meant someone relatively famous died there, and it had been planted in his honor so his spirit would live on. Most Americans thought pines were great to sleep under and used the needles to help start fires.

The jungle was quiet except for the periodic sounds of distant explosions, but even they gradually faded as the team moved further away from Khe Sanh. There were no animal sounds. The constant bombing drove most of the animals from the area.

JD crouched, his ears strained to pick up unusual sounds in the silent green covering. A small bead of sweat slowly made its way down behind his right ear, bouncing hair-by-hair down his neck. It dropped with a loud plop on his shoulder. Flies buzzed around his head, distracting his ears from sorting through the quiet for danger.

JD's loose fatigues bunched uncomfortably around his crotch. Sweat and grime coated his skin. The extra hundred pounds on his back caused the pack straps to bite deep into his shoulders. He had not totally adjusted to the extra weight on his back, but he knew his shoulders would be so numb in another hour the cutting pain of the straps would stop.

Ham raised his arm and moved it in a circle, a sign to mount up and move out. Hand signals, movement or non-movement, expressed directions. A good team did not talk on patrol except when absolutely necessary.

The team had been moving for over four hours when Ham suddenly raised his arm straight up in the air. The team froze. He moved his arm to the right, and the team moved to the right into thick undergrowth.

The high, melodic sounds of gook voices filtered through the still air. The team members lay on their stomachs, listening to the voices become louder and clearer. Twenty NVA troops walked ten yards in front of them. They were little people, around five-feet tall, with straight black hair, broad faces, and high cheekbones. Their eyes were dark, canopied with the typical Mongolian eyelids. Unlike most soldiers, recon teams got to see enemy eyes up close. The gooks vanished into the twilight zone.

The team crawled two miles through the undergrowth. They stumbled upon a camouflaged, well-traveled road wide enough for truck traffic. Ham checked his map; the road wasn't marked on it. He sent Mex down the road one way and Jake the other way. The rest of the team waited while they checked the road.

Jake returned first and reported that he'd followed the road to a large cave where he saw gooks, trucks, and stockpiled supplies. The cave also had large directional radio antennas sticking out all over.

Mex returned. "A shitload of gooks and two tanks are coming our way," he whispered to Ham.

"Tanks? Are you sure?" Ham asked.

"I've never seen a *gook* tank before, but I know what a tank looks like. It's a fucking tank," he said, nodding for emphasis.

A few minutes later everyone heard the hard, metallic clanking of the tank treads. The sound ripped through the silent green like a gasoline chainsaw. The team flattened on their bellies. Twenty-four gooks passed in four-man formations in front of them, and then two tanks with large red stars came into view. The metal monsters covered the team with dust as they rumbled by. The smell of gasoline and exhaust, and the sounds of metal clanking on metal lingered in the air after the tanks passed.

The team couldn't use the radio or move without being seen. They lay on their stomachs and watched large groups of gooks and trucks move constantly up and down the road ten feet in front of them. Finally, a break in the traffic gave them a chance to slip away. They moved back into the bush, away from the road, to face a cave Jake had spotted and observe the area.

The cave was set in a hill, about thirty yards off the main road. A road spun off the main one and circled in front of the cave. Machine-gun placements in sandbag bunkers guarded both sides of its entrance. Boxes of supplies were stacked in piles up and down the entrance road. The tanks were parked below the cave on the main road with guns pointed in both directions. Large numbers of troops moved up and down the road. Trucks were picking up and delivering supplies on the road to the cave. No building structures were in view. The road was as busy as a big city street, yet it wasn't on the map.

Ham radioed headquarters and reported the tanks and large troop movement. A couple of choppers were dispatched to pinpoint the road from the air, but it proved impossible because of high jungle canopy. At about four o'clock, the Valley Dogs settled in to await the dark.

Ham told Swene to set up the M-60 machine gun facing the cave while the rest of the team spread out in a circle. He told them to take off their packs and wait while he and Jake took a closer look at the layout and defenses of the cave.

JD propped his pack up against a tree and lay back on it. Vince sat across from him. JD closed his eyes. He didn't like waiting with his pack off. He knew the longer he kept it off, the heavier it would be when he picked it up again.

He heard the sound of movement and opened his eyes. Vince's M-16 was pointed at his head. Someone must be behind him. He shifted his eyes to the right and left, silently trying to question Vince as to what side the danger was on.

Vince's eyes were wide open. His mouth moved, but he didn't say anything. JD turned his head slowly to the right with his body tensed and coiled, ready to jump. He saw a red flickering movement out of the corner of his eye and froze.

A long, slender, split-tongue flickered from a triangular head right by his ear. He held his breath as the weight of the snake's coils pressed down on his shoulder. The fourteen-foot King Cobra's black, scaled body slithered across his chest, its tail still in the lower branches of the tree.

JD raised his brows and looked over at Vince. His M-16 was following the snake's head as it slithered down JD's body. Shit. Was Vince going to shoot the snake while it was on his chest?

Vince was scared shitless of snakes. He'd grown up in Detroit, a concrete jungle where people were the only wild animals. They didn't have snakes. It didn't matter to Vince if a snake was poisonous or not. In his mind, all snakes were to be killed as quickly as possible. If the snake went in Vince's direction, he would shoot, kill JD, and give the team's position away to the gooks. Vince was more afraid of snakes than gooks; was his fear stronger than loyalty and the urge to survive? Vince was worse about snakes than JD was about rats.

JD tried to lock eyes with Vince to plead for him not to shoot. The thickest part of the snake's body passed between his legs. The head moved toward Vince. *He's going to shoot the fucking snake while it's between my legs*, JD thought. *What a fucking way to die— shot in the nuts by a city nigger who's scared of snakes.*

The snake suddenly turned away from Vince and slithered into the undergrowth away from them. As soon as the snake's tail slid off his body, JD jumped in the opposite direction, his heart pounding. Vince finally whispered, "Snake!" and pointed the barrel of his rifle in the direction the snake had gone. JD stared at Vince, and through his parched mouth formed the silent words, *You mother-fucker!* Vince blinked, then shrugged and shot JD a glance that said, *just a thing, Blood, I got your back.* End of incident.

Jake and Ham returned. Not for the first time, the Valley Dogs' ability to understand and speak Vietnamese reaped rewards. They got so close to the cave's mouth, they overheard an officer giving orders for all units in the area to be on alert because the Valley Dog recon team was in the area.

"How in the fuck do they know we're in the area?" Mike said, "I thought this mission was supposed to be hush-hush."

"Who knows how they found out? They know we're here," Ham said. "Our immediate problem is that they're going to search for us tomorrow with every available man. Not a chance we get out of here. We have to do something tonight."

"What do you mean . . . do something tonight?" Vince asked.

"It's a slim chance, our only hope for staying alive tomorrow is to create a shitstorm of confusion tonight. Best way to cause that kind of confusion is to attack the cave," Ham said.

"Attack the cave?" Vince asked. Then got his mind around the thought. "You *must* be fucking crazy. There's tanks and a shitload of gooks down there. No way. We need to get picked up by the choppers—get flown the fuck out of here."

JD didn't like the idea of attacking the cave, but if Ham thought that was the only way to survive, he wouldn't question it. "Vince, think about where we are," Ham said. "This is gook country. The recon choppers couldn't see the cave from right the fuck on top of it—knowin' what they were lookin' for. What makes you think we'll be able to find a pickup point?" he asked.

Swene spoke up. "Doing what the gooks don't expect is the only edge we have."

"It's crazy; I like the idea," Mex said. "Go after the mother-fuckers. Take it to 'em."

Vince's fear started to break through. "Man, they got tanks down there—and snakes out here," he shuddered, "We ain't never gone up against no tanks, and what about all them gooks? We'll be outnumbered a hundred to one. No, I ain't goin' on no suicide assault."

"Vince, you think you're gonna live forever?" Jake asked. "If you're gonna go out, take as many little mother-fuckers as possible with you."

"I *am not* ordering anyone to commit suicide," Ham said. "The gooks wouldn't expect a recon team to attack the cave, especially at night. However, Vince is right, there're tanks and a shitload of gooks down there. It's a good bet some of us will not make it, but it's the only way I see for most of us to survive. If we wait for them to come after us—we're all fuckin' dead."

Ham's words quelled any further discussion. Each member of the team was alive because of Ham's bush survival savvy. They knew the best way to survive was to stay with him. They also knew he was right. The choice was simple: be the hunter or be the prey. No Valley Dog would ever choose to be the prey.

The team broke into two units. Mex, Swene, and Vince became one group, and Ham, Mike, Jake, and JD made up the other. The plan was simple: attack the cave from both sides of the road at the same time, making as much noise as possible. Hopefully, the confusion and surprise in the dark would give the impression a large force was attacking the cave. After the attack, the team would slip back into the bush and move south away from the cave and Khe Sanh. The gooks would take defensive positions to protect against another attack. They wouldn't care about searching for the Valley Dogs—at least not for a while.

The classic Nam standoff: no clear winners, just clearly defined losers. Death becomes a viable option in the absence of other options. The only thing to do is make the bastards pay.

JD had been in the same situation twice since being in Nam. Both times the gooks were trying to capture the team, and the team wasn't going to let that happen. They understood the embedded hatred gooks harbored for recon because they invaded their safe havens deep inside the jungle. Even in death, recon teams were worth more to the gooks than a live general. Recon created fear in the NVA and VC by striking at any time, day or night.

He had seen recon team members captured by gooks. One time, a recon team had been ambushed and the Valley Dogs, who were on patrol nearby, were ordered to assist the team. When they reached the site, everyone was dead except for one man. The gooks tied the man's hands and hung him upside down on a tree like a large piece of raw meat on a butcher's hook. The ground beneath him was soaked with his blood. Every bone in his body was broken from where the gooks had beaten the soldier with rifle butts. The gooks had slit his skin into thin strips, and then tore it from his body with wire pliers. His internal organs were exposed, trailing down from his body like bloody jungle vines.

Gooks believed that powerful enemies, when captured and killed, conferred special powers. Gooks would carry pieces of their enemies' bodies around to show their killing prowess. American men like Mex acquired that killing ritual—both as a way of understanding the enemy and as revenge.

Some would say it was a miracle the man was still alive. His only desire was to die, and he begged JD to help him along, begged JD to kill him. At first JD tried to figure out a way to save the man. But, it was impossible for a man in that condition to be put back together—especially under jungle conditions.

JD pointed his pistol at the bloody mush that was once the man's head. The soldier whispered his thanks just before JD pulled the trigger. The man was out of his suffering, but JD carried the memory of the man's grief and pain. He shuddered as the memories washed over him. If nothing else, JD wanted to die with his body whole. He didn't give a damn what they did with his body afterward.

The night sky was black. Clouds covered the stars and cut out the moonlight. A silent darkness surrounded every shadow. The green of the jungle added a thickness to the shadows; thick silence added tension to the air. JD, on watch, flickered his eyes from side to side, searching the shadows for movement.

Back in the bush! JD felt the rush in his head from the constant adrenalin pumping through his body. Living on the edge of death produced a high that made everything else boring. The base was boring. Waiting was boring. In the bush, he was aware of everything around him: the slight breeze across his eyelids, faint smells, and the presence of movement. Anything not existing in the moment did not matter. Fear was a truth he could deal with here in the bush—no longer the blurred anticipation of danger, but the certainty of it. Certainty of pain and death purifies fear into something useful: the motivation to do whatever it takes to survive.

The harsh, sputtered clamor of a generator startled JD. Bright lights flooded the area inside the cave. He moved to touch Ham, but Ham was already moving to peer through the leaves and vines at the cave. He saw gooks putting up a bamboo screen in front of the cave's entrance to hide the light from the surrounding darkness. Ham said he saw a generator, which was probably powering the lights, to the right of the cave entrance.

Ham signaled it was time to move. They dug holes and buried their packs. Jake booby-trapped the holes and packs with grenades and trip wires. "If they find our packs, this will slow them down," he said.

The team members looked into each other's eyes and nodded their heads. "Let's do it," Ham whispered.

The team crawled down to the road. Mex and his group needed to get across the road and move within twenty yards of the cave without being spotted or the attack plan would mean nothing.

They started to cross the road. A searchlight beam sliced through the blackness onto the road. They dove back into the undergrowth. The heavy clanking of tank treads battered the dark silence. Two tanks rumbled down the road toward the cave. Mex's group jumped behind the last tank as it passed and followed it for about twenty-five yards. He set a delayed explosive charge on the back of the tank and jumped to the other side of the road.

The two new tanks pulled up to the two other tanks in front of the cave. The tanks in front of the cave repositioned themselves so the new arrivals could pull off the main road. As one tank maneuvered past the other two, Mex's charge exploded and knocked out three of the tanks. The other tank was trapped behind the three burning tanks and blocked from the road.

The explosion signaled their attack. "Rock and roll," Jake yelled out.

Mike dropped M-79 rounds around the mouth of the cave and walked them down to the burning tanks. Whump. Whump. Men screamed. More explosions. A burning tank's ammo and fuel tanks blew up. Mike fired the M-79 so fast it sounded like a mortar team was working the area.

"Where're the fucking gooks?" Mike asked. "We saw a shitload of them pass by us. Didn't see them leave," he said.

"If they're around, we'll see them soon," Jake said.

They moved toward the cave. They could hear gook voices, but didn't see any gooks. Ham halted the team to listen. The voices were coming from the ground. The area had to be interconnected with tunnels.

The ground slowly rose four feet in front of JD—a trap door. He lay flat on the ground and pointed his M-16 at the opening trap door. A gook's head popped up. The gook's eyes widened when he saw JD.

The gook struggled to get his rifle out of the hole. JD squeezed the trigger of his M-16, sending four bullets into the gook's small, yellow face. Blood and brain matter burst from the back of the gook's head. The body jerked and fell back inside the hole.

JD dropped two grenades down the hole. The hole erupted with smoke and fire. Four or five secondary explosions rumbled underground; then, the ground in front of JD erupted like a volcano.

Swene's machine-gun opened up on the other side of the road. The mad minute started. JD could hear small explosions and screams on the other side of the road.

"The generator," Ham yelled. "Take out the generator." There was a machine-gun placement twenty feet in front of the generator, but the two gooks manning the gun were leaning over sandbags trying to see what was happening on the other side of the road. Ham raked the gun placement and threw a grenade, killing the gooks as they looked in the wrong direction. Jake ran to the generator and put a plastic explosive charge on it.

Ground troops came down the road from both directions, firing toward the front of the cave. Bullets zinged over and around JD's head. He dove into the sandbagged machine-gun placement, into the arms of the gooks Ham had just killed. Jake's bomb blew the generator out and the cave went dark. The shadowy jungle became a background for the yellowish-red flames shooting up from the burning tanks.

The gooks firing at JD from in front of the cave were blinded by the flames. They didn't see Mex and the others work their way across the road through the darkness. Swene's Pig barked out its death call. Mex rolled next to JD. "Guess we found those gooks Vince was worried about," he said.

"Everyone make it?" JD asked.

"Vince bought it," he said.

"The radio?" JD asked.

"Dead with Vince. Let's get the fuck out of here," he said.

Ham, Jake, and Mike had thrown grenades and fired M-79 rounds into the cave and were going in when JD and the others reached them. Mex, Swene, and JD stayed at the mouth of the cave sniping the gooks around the tanks.

In a few minutes, Ham and the others rushed out of the cave, hollering, "Get down! Get down!"

An explosion blasted out the mouth of the cave like a giant gun. Black smoke from the cave and the burning tanks billowed into the sky.

"Mex! Point! Get us the fuck outta here," Ham barked.

The explosions burned through the jungle canopy and lit up the sky. Choppers and jets would be on the scene soon. They may be on your side, but that doesn't count when bombs fall from the sky into your lap. The gooks were firing at everything that moved, including each other.

The team moved in a big circle and ended up facing the cave again. Rockets and bombs rained from the sky. The burning tanks acted as a homing beacon. The cave was now totally exposed to attack from the air, and the air-cowboys were making the most of their chance to take it to Charlie.

The attack was a tremendous loss-of-face for the gooks. The cave was not General Giap's headquarters, but a communications base that coordinated all the NVA radio transmissions around Khe Sanh. The camp was exposed and destroyed, an ammo dump blown up, four tanks taken out of action, and lots of troops killed. The gooks had only one dead body to show for the loss. It was an embarrassment, a dishonor, a loss-of-face. They had to make someone pay.

They didn't know where the Valley Dogs were, so in retribution the gooks shelled Khe Sanh all night. The team knew the gooks' number-one mission the next day would be to find and kill the Valley Dogs.

When you are being hunted, your instinct is to run. But Valley Dogs never reacted as expected. They spent the night in a big tree watching the cave. The next morning, JD awoke sore and stiff. It took a certain talent to sleep in a tree if you weren't a monkey. He tied a rope around his body and then to the tree to keep from falling. While he slept, the rope sliced into his flesh and cut off his circulation.

The problem with sleeping in trees was that things fell out of your pockets. One scary moment during the night, Mike dropped an M-79 round from his pouch. Gooks were probing the area. Everyone's heart skipped a beat, but the gooks never detected them. Gooks moved around all night on the ground beneath them, so close the Dogs could have leaned down and touched their heads.

The last time JD had slept in a tree, the team took along an SOG officer as an observer. The gooks trapped them, so they decided to wait in the trees until things cooled off. The officer was a young, blonde kid whose fear turned him into an old, white-haired man overnight. Things got so hot getting him out the next day that Ham had threatened to shoot him to even out his panic. Ham was good at making men more afraid of him than of the enemy to distract them from fouling a mission or getting his team members killed.

When he got back to headquarters, the young officer reported that the Valley Dogs were the most ruthless killing force the world had ever seen and that he would never enter enemy territory again without them to save his ass. What happened in the bush stayed in the bush—including fractured protocols.

The team watched gooks clear the wreckage from the night before. Two jeeps pulled up, and two gook officers got out of one. They looked at the dead American's body. One leaned over, pulled out a knife, and cut off Vince's ears and two fingers. He turned and said something to a group of gooks standing close. They pulled out knives and started cutting pieces off Vince's body. The other officer refrained from any cutting. He walked off to look at the damage in the cave.

JD's stomach stiffened against the intense anger flowing down his throat. He watched the gooks hack at Vince's body. "You mother-fuckers," he whispered.

The two officers got into the jeeps. "They've got to come down the road where we were last night when they leave," Ham said. "Let's get the bastards. Mex, you're on point. Get us down to the road."

Mex led the team back to the road close to where they'd been the day before. "Jake, you and Mike take out the lead jeep. Swene, cover the road toward the cave." Ham pointed at Mex. "You're with me on the second jeep. We want one officer alive," he said, "we all know which one."

In the lead jeep, a gook sat behind a Russian 50-caliber machine gun, and two other gooks sat in front. Jake and Mike threw grenades into the lead jeep as it passed. The gooks were blown out of the jeep as it flipped upside down in the middle of the road.

The driver of the second jeep tried to avoid hitting the first jeep, ran off the road and crashed into thick brush on one side. The officer with Vince's cut-off fingers and ears was thrown through the jeep's windshield. The other officer flew from the back seat over the windshield. The driver was killed instantly from being thrown chest-first into the steering column.

Jake grabbed the first officer. He pulled Vince's fingers and ears out of the man's pockets. Jake jammed his shotgun into the officer's mouth. Ham and Mex collared the other officer. Ham twisted the officer's head so he could see his fellow officer with the shotgun in his mouth. Ham nodded. Jake pulled the trigger. The gook's head jerked backwards as the shotgun blast ripped the top of his head off.

"Do you want to die like that?" Ham asked the officer in Vietnamese. Tears streamed down his cheeks as he shook his head violently from side to side. "No, no," he cried. JD jerked a strip of black tape across his mouth.

The gooks at the cave heard the explosion and ran down the road toward the team. Swene's Pig started spitting lead. The gooks fell like clay pigeons at a shooting gallery. Then Mike's M-79 laid three rounds on the road, creating a death-wall of explosions.

The remaining gooks ducked for cover, surprised at the intense fire. They had no idea how many men they were facing. This gave the Valley Dogs time to disappear back into the deep underbrush.

CHAPTER 14

"Kill that son of a bitch!"

The thunder of thousand-pound bombs dropping from B-52s flying high in the sky reverberated through the jungle. The explosions were miles away, but the thick jungle canopy seized the sound and echoed it. The deep rumblings overwhelmed the familiar cries and calls of the jungle.

The gooks' presence was so thick there was no way for the team to get back to Khe Sanh. They crawled on their bellies most of the day, hiding from the gooks in dense jungle nooks and crevices. Gook patrols constantly moved through the area searching for them. The Valley Dogs knew there would be no mercy if the gooks caught them.

Jake kept his knife pressed on the gook officer's throat even though his hands were bound and his mouth taped shut. The officer's uniform was drenched with sweat from jungle heat and fear. Jake's brutal killing of his fellow officer left him with no doubt that Jake would kill him without hesitation.

They climbed a hill that rose to a peak of nearly 1,500 feet. A narrow strip of level ground, treeless with only knee-high grass and small shrub growth, ran along the top for several hundred feet. The team took positions on a tiny, rock-strewn knoll with the bright sun beating down on them. Passing clouds provided moving patches of shade, which gave momentary relief from the fierce heat.

Small foxholes dotted the ground. Obviously, gooks had occupied the area before. Jake and Mex set up Claymore mines in an arc facing outward and down the hill.

The gooks were well aware of the Valley Dogs' presence. A fresh, well-equipped, highly trained battalion of enemy assembled at the base of the hill, and, during the late afternoon, hundreds of gooks started to climb toward them. Only one order was given— *kill the Valley Dogs*.

Jake, Mex, and JD were lying in a shallow depression. "How we gonna get out of here without a radio?" Mex asked. "I'm tired of crawling on my belly," he said.

"Walk out; 'less you know another way," Jake said.

"I might," Mex said. He casually propped himself up on his elbows and placed his M-14 on his shoulder, pointed the barrel toward a bush twelve feet away, and fired.

Jake jumped from the loud crack of Mex's rifle. "What in the fuck's wrong with you? Every gook around for miles will hear that," he yelled.

The white phosphorus grenade hit the bush and exploded. A man screamed, and the bush pitched backwards and started thrashing. Other bushes on the hill moved. A jolt of adrenalin shot through JD's body. He jumped up on one knee and started firing his M-16.

"Grenades, throw grenades," Jake yelled. They threw grenades at the other moving bushes and scrambled up the hill.

The NVA made no noise while climbing the hill. They were less than twenty yards away when Mex noticed them and opened fire. They attacked from all directions. The Valley Dogs were surrounded.

Swene swung his M-60 around in a circle, mowing down the first line of men that stood up. The gooks tossed grenades at them. Everyone except Swene hit the ground. He stayed on his feet firing the M-60 at the swarming mass of brown uniforms. A grenade landed at Swene's feet. He looked down at it and kept firing, growling defiance. The explosion threw Swene's body up in the air. He landed twenty feet on the other side of JD. The right side of Swene's jungle uniform was peppered with holes that dripped blood. JD crawled over to Swene's body. He turned Swene over. Dead, vacant eyes stared up at JD. Swene was gone.

"Bring the 60," Jake hollered to JD.

The gook officer stood up and started to run. "Kill that son-of-a-bitch!" Ham screamed.

Mike twirled and shot his M-79 at the gook officer running toward him. The 40-mm shell exploded in the man's chest, splattering the gook's body into the air. His upper torso was nearly severed at the waist, and the stark, white bones of his ribcage looked like the hull of an ancient, beached ship.

They started to hear shrill whistles and clacking bamboo sticks. "Here they come!" Mex hollered.

Ham, Jake, Mex, and JD flopped on their stomachs facing outward like four points of a compass. Mex grabbed the M-60 machine gun from JD and kept the gooks' heads down. Mike, down on one knee, was in the middle of the compass bombarding all directions with the M-79.

Enemy swarmed the five men firing automatic weapons, throwing grenades, and screaming. Green tracer rounds from machine guns streaked in, mortar shells smashed rocks and added rock splinters to the metal shrapnel whining through the air. The ground jerked beneath them as explosions ripped into its surface.

Ham grabbed the Claymore detonator and pushed the firing lever. The back blast of the mines was absorbed somewhat by the slight overhang of the hill slope. The jungle area directly in front and to the sides was devastated by a swarm of ball bearings from the curved mines.

The first lines of enemy skirmishers were cut down seconds after they stood up and exposed themselves. The surprise, swift charge failed. Gooks blundered out of the sparse undergrowth into bullets that ripped through them. Puffs of dust flared up from the tan uniforms as the bullets smacked into twisting bodies.

Explosions and sharp cracks of rifles filled the air. Bullets zipped around, hitting trees, rocks, ground, and human flesh. The noise of battle was overwhelming. Bluish-white smoke draped the hilltop like a fog.

Mike's M-79 held the attacking enemy at a distance. Then his head jerked back as it exploded backward with the impact of a high-caliber rifle shot. The impact slammed him out of the circle into the bushes fifteen feet away.

"Mike's hit," JD yelled. He crawled over to Mike. Blood and brain matter drained from the jagged hole in the back of his head, soaking the ground.

A gook grenade landed next to JD. He rolled Mike's body over onto the grenade, then coiled himself into a fetal ball. The grenade exploded; a bright, white light blotted everything from his mind. He slipped into darkness.

CHAPTER 15

"Good show."

Consciousness slowly, painfully came back to JD. His temples pounded loudly like a deep bass drum. His tongue felt parched and thick in his mouth. His lips were cracked flakes of dried skin. A high-pitched ringing bounced between his ears as waves of nausea rippled through his stomach. His head seemed to float above his shoulders. Painfully, he forced his eyes open. He was naked. He didn't know how he'd gotten that way. He couldn't move his arms; he was tied to a tree.

He raised his head and saw four NVA soldiers sitting on their haunches in front of him, going through his pants' pockets. One of the soldiers looked up and noticed that JD's eyes were open. He walked over to the tree carrying JD's knife in his hand. The hard look in the soldier's eyes told JD he was not alive to become a *guest* at the Hanoi Hilton.

JD had found men tied to trees before. Their skin was peeled off, their penises were jammed into their mouths. They were left in that condition to spook other Americans—it worked. No one wanted their body cut up while they were still alive.

The gook stood two feet in front of JD and looked intensely into his eyes. "You, Valley Dog," it said. The gook slowly pulled the knife across JD's chest, leaving a shallow trail that dripped blood.

A tear slowly joined the sweat running down his cheek. He knew they were going to cut his body up. It would be these shallow cuts first to keep him horrified, then deeper ones to keep the agony going, then a stripping of skin to muscle. . . .

Waves of pain coursed through JD's body. His knees sagged, but the rope tied around him and the tree held him upright. He tried to spit in the gook's face, but his mouth was too dry. "You mother-fucker," he whispered dryly. His head fell to his chest.

The gook laughed and slapped him across his face with the knife, leaving a welt and a scratch about four inches along his lower jaw. Then the gook grabbed JD's chin, forced his head up and back so he could look into JD's glazed eyes. "You, American dog, will die slow," he said. The gook smiled and put the knife between JD's legs with the sharp edge pressing against his scrotum.

The hardness of steel and his fear of being cut up made JD's body shake. He shook his head side to side. Tears dripped down his face. He stared in the gook's eyes and made another feeble attempt to spit in its face—

The gook's face and head exploded suddenly into JD's face. Blood, brains, flesh, and bone chips covered JD's naked body. He saw a blurred vision of Ham and Jake in front of him. Someone cut the rope. JD crumbled to the ground.

Ham's voice came from a distant place in the darkness. "Doc, come on. You're alive. You're alive. Understand? You're alive. JD, do you understand?"

JD opened his eyes and saw Ham's big black face in front of him.

"That's it, let me see some eyeballs. How in hell you gonna take care of us if you ain't around?" Ham said, helping JD dress himself.

Moving his body hurt. But he was alive; nothing else mattered. "Can you walk?" Ham asked.

JD's voice was no more than a whisper. "Yeah. Let's get the fuck outta here." They moved out—Mex on point, followed by JD leaning on Ham's shoulders, and Jake covering the rear.

There were too many gooks to defend a position on the knoll, so they played hide and seek. They popped in and out of the gooks' ranks, shooting and then quietly melting into the bushes. The Valley Dogs didn't run, but stayed in the middle of the gooks around the top of the hill.

They came upon a dry streambed filled with an overgrowth of bushes and vines and crawled down it for a few yards to hide. They heard the crunch of leaves, snap of twigs, and shuffling of feet. The gooks couldn't see them, and they couldn't see the gooks, but gooks on both sides shot down into the streambed.

Bullets zipped past JD's head, making holes in big, broad leaves only six inches from his nose. One bullet went through the brim of his bush hat and kicked up a puff of dirt as it slammed into the ground only inches from his right foot. He didn't flinch. If he got hit, he didn't want to holler out; that would give the team's position away.

An Army Cessna Bird Dog flew through the area, gathering aerial reconnaissance in a widening circle around the cave where all hell had broken out. The scuttlebutt had it that the Valley Dogs had gotten the shit started and been wiped out in heroic fashion. Heightened to the situation and hoping to find such signs, this plane's pilot thought he saw enemy movement on the hill. The sun was going down, blackness descending over the jungle floor. He called in an Air Force "Puff" to drop flares and illuminate the area.

The valley floor looked like a ripped apart anthill. NVA troops ran in all directions. The pilot quickly radioed for attack jets and helicopter gunships.

The jets got there first and concentrated their firepower on the valley floor to keep the enemy from escaping down the hill. Mushrooming black clouds erupted in the dusk-covered jungle as the jets dropped napalm. Boiling columns of liquid fire splashed through the trees. Its searing jelly coated the ridgeline.

Then the choppers arrived—Huey Cobras. They zoomed down ninety-degrees at 200 MPH unleashing rockets, 20-mm cannon fire, and miniguns. The barrage ripped up earth, trees, bushes, and men.

The Dogs huddled underneath a rocky overhang in the dry streambed while the earth was battered around them. Twigs, tree bark, and leaves cascaded down on them. Bullets tore trees into fibrous pulp. Planes dropped 250-pound bombs; hot blasts of air carried by the shock waves pushed the temperature up ten degrees. The team cringed and hugged the ground with each blast. SPADS and gunships pounded the hill throughout the night, darkness making it unsafe for the jets after that first strafing run.

Marine infantry tried to land on top of the hill at daybreak, but intense enemy fire blocked them. The choppers circled for forty-five minutes while jets and artillery blasted a secure landing zone.

In nearly catatonic shock, the team crawled out of the streambed. A rocket exploded barely fifteen yards in front of them, throwing dirt and debris into the air. Whirling shards of metal flayed the trees around them. Smoke and dust riding air currents slid slowly down the slope over the splayed and tattered thickets of grass.

When the smoke cleared, they saw trees ripped apart and large, black clumps of dirt strewn all over like giant bird droppings. The bittersweet smell of cordite permeated the air, so hot-damp it was like the sky itself was sweating.

The main column of Marines climbed straight upward to the crown of the hill when they landed. Ham, Jake, Mex, and JD met them just before they got to the top. The Marines were surprised the team was there and alive with all the firepower pouring down on the hill. They immediately called in choppers to evac the team.

On the way to the Huey, Ham came up and rubbed JD's head. "Now, let's get your ass home," he said.

"I'm fucking ready to get out of here," JD sighed. "Thanks! You saved my ass back there," he said.

Ham laughed. "Yeah, that should be worth a good drink in Springfield, Illinois on you."

"I'm looking forward to that day," JD said.

"It won't be any cheap affair," Ham said. "Make sure you have some money. I'm going to be mighty thirsty when I hit town—and you know that Peoria dog piss ain't gonna do it."

They climbed into the chopper. Ham sat across from JD with a big smile on his face. JD looked out of the chopper at the grunts heading into the bush. *It's yours, thank God*, he thought.

Thwack! JD heard the familiar sound. A vapor of red burst from Ham's head. His big, black body jerked, slammed into the chopper's wall, then fell forward, landing head-first into JD's lap.

Stunned, JD stared at the blood gushing out of the wound. The chopper rose in a sudden convulsion of power. The wind blew rivulets of blood in a scarlet wake trailing out the door.

"No!" JD screamed.

He fought the weight pushing down on him from the upward rush of takeoff. He turned Ham's lifeless body over and saw a black, jagged hole where Ham's left eye should be.

"God damn it, Ham!" he yelled. Just like that. Ham was dead.

Ham's warm, sticky blood and brain matter soaked JD's pants and flowed into his boots. Nothing he could do. He knew it. Ham was dead. JD rode all the way back to Dong Ha cradling Ham's bloody head in his lap, unconsciously rocking and crooning a spiritual learned a lifetime ago in another world.

The whole recon company waited for the Valley Dogs at the chopper pad. Men lifted Ham's body from JD's lap. "No! No, Jesus Christ, no!" Masters' shout could be heard over the roar of the chopper's whine.

Jake, Mex, and JD stepped out of the chopper and walked through a sea of eyes and whispers. The company of men stared at the three blood-soaked Dogs who had survived the hell in and around Khe Sanh.

JD's body was so sore, stiff, and weak that he leaned on Mex and Jake to walk. A corpsman came up to examine him. "I'm okay," JD said. The corpsman insisted JD be carried on a stretcher. JD angrily waved him off. He would walk, though in pain, with Mex and Jake.

Masters walked up to meet them. They walked past him as though he didn't exist. "It's okay, Doc. I understand," Masters said softly as they went by.

JD spun around. "What's fuckin' okay?" He pointed to Ham's carcass being put into a body bag. "That's okay?" he asked.

Mex stepped between JD and Masters. He jammed his finger into Masters' chest. "The fucking gooks came looking for us. How did they know the Valley Dogs were there?" he asked. "This was supposed to be a fucking secret patrol."

"It was a suicide patrol. The gooks knew . . . every-fucking-body knew . . . except us," Jake said. "Our asses were offered to the gooks as bait."

Masters backed off. He knew better than to push them. "Take it easy," he said. "Go get cleaned up. We'll talk later."

General Scott's chopper landed. He jumped out and walked to the three men. The general was beaming. "You men did an outstanding job," he said.

"There were no prisoners," Mex said.

"SOG thinks we've broken their backs and stopped a pending ground attack on Khe Sanh. We're getting a hell of a body count from that hill. We needed a high body count, and you got it for us," the general said.

Jake had a sharp edge in his voice. "The gooks knew we were out there. They were waiting for us," he said.

The general ignored Jake's words. "All of you will get a decoration for this action. I'll make sure of that personally," he said.

Ham, Mike, Swene, and Vince were simply four more men lost on a mission. The general's only interest was the gook body count and that it outweighed the American KIA numbers. "I'll take these three men back with me in my chopper for debriefing," he said. "Good show."

"Good show?" Jake asked. His anger boiled over. His face became flushed. "I'm not going anywhere for any fucking debriefing until I get some sleep—and Doc's orders for home are in his hands."

The general was surprised by Jake's attitude. He softened his words. "I understand, Marine. Corpsman Douglas will be on the next plane out of country after the debriefing," he said.

He walked over to JD and said, "I hope you realize that you saved the lives of a lot of other good men."

JD turned and walked away from the general. He didn't care about good men he didn't know. He cared about the good men he knew and loved. He cared about the Valley Dogs. And they were no more. Even though the Valley Dogs were the best, they were no more. Vince was left dead and hacked up in the jungle. Swene, Mike, and Ham's bodies would be shipped home in body bags. Jake and Mex were alive, but still trapped in hell.

JD would ride the freedom bird out of hell. He was too tired and miserable to be happy about it. Ham kept him alive to get home. The pain of losing Ham dulled any importance going home might have had—or should have had. He wanted to go back to the bush and kill gooks. He wanted to kill gooks—go back to the bush and kill gooks—make them pay for the red stain covering his pants.

CHAPTER 16

". . . you've made it, man."

JD erupted from sleep twenty-four hours after he had closed his eyes. Pulsating pain deluged his mind. The knife cuts on his chest and face, along with small welts from scrapes and bruises, sent searing messages of hurt to his brain. Stiffness and soreness in his knees, hip, back, and shoulders warned him not to move quickly.

Slowly, he swung his legs over the edge of the cot. His body reeked of sweat and funk, as well as dried gore. He moved sluggishly and awkwardly to the back of the hooch and pushed the back door open. The bright sun forced him back inside. He covered his eyes and fell to the floor. He sat on the floor a few minutes looking blankly out into space. *Damn. Being alive can be terribly painful sometimes.* He looked down at his legs; they were covered with clumped islands of caked blood.

He finally dragged his body off the floor and made it out the door, stumbling in a daze to the showers. He stood in the shower with his eyes closed and let the water pour down over his head. Cold water washed the dirt and blood of the mission off his body; but nothing could wash it out of his mind.

A hollow pain shot through him, freeing something inside his chest and stomach. The mission whirled through his head. What could've happened. What didn't happen. What did happen.

The vision of Ham's head with a bullet hole in it lying in his lap made his body shudder. He felt tears well up inside of him, but the tears didn't make it to his eyes. He washed the streaks of camouflage grease from his face. The soap—he could use it now that he'd never be in the bush again—brought his face back from spotty green patches to something recognizable.

Mex walked into the shower while JD was drying off, inspecting the cuts and bruises on his legs that had mingled his blood with Ham's. He wondered when they'd happened, having thought the gooks had put most of those rips in his shredded pants while they had him tied to the tree—

"Shit, Doc, you got a back full of leeches."

A spasm shook JD's body. "Ugh . . . Just what I needed to hear. Get those fuckers offa me!"

Mex lit a cigarette and pushed the burning end against the fat parasites. When the hot cigarette embers touched them, they fell to the concrete floor. "We've been waiting for you to join us. We have to go to Da Nang for debriefing with General Scott."

"Da Nang? Oh, fuck." JD curled his lips as if he had swallowed a live bug. Debriefing in Da Nang could go on forever with some of the stupidest questions asked over and over. What type of underwear did the team members wear? They should know by now they wore none. Did they bury their feces? Ham always told them the Valley Dogs didn't have time to shit when they were in the bush.

Then there were the questions that had no meaning whatsoever. Were there any streams or prominent terrain features not shown on the map? Usually, the green of the map and the jungle were the only similarity. That was the joke. The map wouldn't indicate the ridgelines they had walked over and the gook roads they found on patrol.

"Hang loose, Doc. It's your last one." Mex slapped him on the back. "You're on a freedom bird as soon as debriefing is over. You've made it, man."

"What do you mean, I've made it?" JD asked.

Mex laughed. "You're homeward bound, amigo."

JD stared at him blankly.

"Want any meat for the trip?" Mex asked. "I got plenty to spare from that little Pathfinder-by-fire we did."

CHAPTER 17

"Fuck you, Charlie! We're going home!"

After the debriefing, JD was assigned to a group of men leaving the next morning on the freedom bird. When the night set in, they sat together between the barracks to smoke dope in celebration. Music blasted from a tape player. Men kept hollering over and over, "We made it, we made it!"

The music and the men were loud. The few MPs milling around the edge of the crowd weren't going to bust anybody who was in the bush for a year and was on their way home the next day. They knew how dangerous that could be. These men were survivors—they were walking away from hell after making a long and horrifying walk through it.

There was a difference between the bush grunts and the clerks going home. The grunts looked rumpled and used, with a year's worth of dirt deep in their pores. Their stares came from somewhere far behind and beyond their eyes—the same look as the thousand-yard stare of weary WWII soldiers.

The clerks were the overweight ones wearing new fatigues with decorations on them. Grunts didn't have any decorations sewn on their jungle shirts. Clerks wore spit-shined black boots. The black dye had worn off the grunts' boots a long time ago. Their boots had turned the color of the dirt they'd fought in— either brown mud or red clay.

A tall, slender black Marine standing next to JD handed him a long, fat joint. The Marine wore a floppy bush hat decorated with a John Wayne can opener and a dozen grenade pins. His big smile seemed to fill up his whole face. "Home boy," he said. "Take a hit of this shit. Make you sparkle like a star. It'll make you feel special."

JD took a deep hit off the joint. Once smoke hit his lungs, he knew he'd taken too much. He coughed the smoke back up; his throat felt like the smoke was dragging dull razor blades up with it.

JD gasped when he was able to talk again. "God damn, man. What the fuck you got in that thing?" he asked.

"Told you, it'll fly you to the moon," the smiling face said. "I carried it through the war zone for fourteen months." He nodded his head. "It's been wet, dry, I don't know how many times. Never took it out of the bag. I saved it for this special night." He took a long drag from the bomber. JD waited for him to start coughing. He didn't. He just grinned as the smoke slowly escaped between his teeth.

The smiling face started to say something else, but the rumble of machinegun fire on a distant perimeter stopped him mid-sentence. The men froze. They turned off the tape player so they could listen.

"Gooks must be in the wire. Gooks in the wire," voices whispered to one another. The firing wavered, almost died, and then erupted again.

JD was about to tell the smiling man he was going to go into the bunker before the rockets started, when some of the men began to cheer. At first it was just a few voices, but it quickly became a roar from all the men. "Fuck you, Charlie! We're going home!"

JD grinned as two smoldering joints were pressed into his hands. Yeah, he was going home. For the first time in a long time, it wasn't him who was fighting, caring, or keeping anyone alive. Someone else would do that job now! He felt peaceful. He felt the queasy sensation of being homesick.

The next morning at the airport, JD watched the fresh meat imported for the Nam meat grinder. They were baby-faced boys wearing clean uniforms soaked with sweat and had eyes that weren't yet trained to see everything in one glance. New meat. "So that's how dumb and scared I looked my first day *in-country*," he said to no one in particular.

On one side of a tarmac, shiny aluminum coffins were stacked on top of each other with their tags flapping in the wind. "Fuck you," he muttered.

He greeted death on his arrival, and now he was saying goodbye to it. The only claim of victory for him in the past year was the fact that he'd survived. In spite of himself and others, he'd made it. He was leaving Nam alive and whole. He wasn't going home in a closed-lid coffin. Nor were his dogtags—those small pieces of metal with name, religion, blood type, and serial number—going back with a note. Death touched close to him and claimed many men around him, but it didn't get him.

He boarded the TWA Boeing 707, which looked like any other chartered civilian airliner. The men and their duffel bags were not checked closely for drugs or weapons. He had his .32-caliber pistol in the waistband of his pants, and his curved-blade knife strapped to his leg. He was comfortable and ready to go home.

A round-eyed, pretty blonde stewardess greeted him at the door with a professional smile. He had not been this close to an American woman in a year. The pleasant sensation of desire rippled through his body. Her eyes met his. He wanted to smile, but he couldn't. He walked down the aisle to find a seat.

He stopped at an empty row of seats and sidestepped the two outer seats to sit by the window. He wanted to see Nam fade from his sight. However, he closed his eyes when the plane started down the runway. It was really happening—he was leaving Nam. Still, he felt something could go wrong. It always did in Nam.

He felt for his seatbelt and tightened it as the engine began to roar for take-off. The plane's acceleration pressed him back into the seat. Its tires made muted clunking sounds as they rolled over the tar seams of the runway. Finally, the *freedom bird* lifted off the ground; everyone raised their voices in a ritualistic scream of joy. He emptied his lungs with the other winners, squeezing the last drop of drama out of leaving Nam. As the plane climbed over the bay, he sagged deeper into his seat. His forearms and fingers hurt because he gripped the armrests so hard.

He slept for most of the fourteen-hour flight from Nam to California. He awoke just as the California coastline came into view. The sunset in the west hung halfway into the horizon. The blue sky was a canvas covered with light brush strokes of reddish, wispy clouds.

The skyline of tall buildings looked curious. Except on R&R in Hong Kong, he'd seen only jungle landscape in the sky for the past year. A tingle of fear ran up his spine. Those buildings were full of people. The thought of so many people in one place made him uncomfortable.

When the plane door opened, a cool breeze blew through the cabin. The air was full of unrecognized odors. His first whiff of American air, untainted by the smell of decay and shit, smelled strange to him.

When his feet touched the ground, his knees almost collapsed from the thought that he was home. Some of the men fell on their knees and kissed the sweet California concrete. Ground crews and other people standing around stared at them and laughed. No one cared about the laughing. They were home.

A bus met the plane, and most of the men were taken to barracks where they would stay the night prior to processing their orders the next day. A hot meal of steak and french fries was laid out for them in the mess hall. The strong smell of grease overwhelmed his nose.

One of the cooks told him men from Nam were always fed steak and eggs for breakfast, or steak and french fries for lunch and dinner. The military thought every American fighting man coming home must want a meat and potatoes meal.

JD spent most of that first night in the bathroom throwing up. His stomach couldn't handle or digest the greasy food after almost a year of eating like a gook.

Free telephones were available for returning men to call home and let their loved ones know they arrived safely in the United States. JD didn't call home. He decided to surprise his family since he was a week and a half earlier than expected. He would go to Detroit first, pick up the new car he ordered through the PX in Nam, and drive it home.

His orders were processed more quickly than most of the other men, probably because they were personally issued from General Scott's office. He received six weeks leave before he needed to report to Bethesda, Maryland for Radioisotope Nuclear Medicine School.

A Marine jeep dropped JD at the Los Angeles International

Airport two hours before his flight left for Detroit. He found a quiet corner away from the streams of travelers rushing through the terminal. He put his back against the wall and watched people and planes come and go.

A group of Army men, obviously just in from Nam by the look of their rough, rumpled uniforms, and faces with hard-drawn lines and hollow eyes, sat on the floor of the terminal sharing a bottle of booze among them. They were drunk. They were hugging each other and kept shouting out, "We made it! We made it!" People walking through the terminal made a wide berth around the drunken, loud men and shook their heads.

The group talked about fucking every girl who passed within or out of hearing range. "Round-eyed, white girls walking around with short skirts and see-through blouses . . ." one said loudly, "pussy-heaven!" They probably had not seen so many women since they left for Nam, at least not in colors other than yellow.

Other men returning from Nam, like JD, kept aloof and made no outward gestures at all. These men sat or stood with their backs against a wall, their eyes nervous and darting, watching every movement around them.

The terminal was full of soft people who smelled sweet and walked with clumsy footsteps. They were strange creatures to JD. They seemed to stumble along with no purpose to their walk.

Three Marines were surrounded by a group of long-haired white kids dressed in strange, bright-colored clothes. They were yelling at each other. He walked closer to them to see what it was about. A blonde girl with beads around her neck and a bright yellow top was yelling at the Marines, saying they were baby killers who killed innocent people in an unjust war. "Only the dumb and poor—or black people—are being sent to Vietnam to fight a phony war for rich people!" she told them.

The Marines yelled back, saying that the others were nothing but a bunch of dirty, drugged-up, hippy antiwar protestors, and, if they didn't like America, they should leave.

The hippies started chanting, "Baby killers, baby killers." The Marines tried to ignore them until the blonde girl and two boys started spitting on the Marines. One Marine became so incensed he slapped the girl. The two hippie boys attacked the Marine. Then, the other two Marines tried to pull the boys off their buddy. Other hippies jumped into the fight. JD moved toward them to join the Marines, but before he got to them, the military police waded into the fight swinging their nightsticks at the hippies. JD eased back into his corner. The three Marines were escorted away while the hippies kept yelling, "Baby killers!"

What did hippies know about what those Marines had been through to make it home? They didn't care. Whatever was in their heads about the war was not the truth. Instead of coming home as heroes, the Marines were attacked as though they were criminals. He was coming home to be called a "baby killer"? To be spit on? It wasn't the Marines' or his fault there was a Vietnam War. They were just soldiers doing their duty and trying to stay alive—like any soldier in any war. Nam was crazy. Now it looked like home was crazy. He slipped into the bathroom to get away from the people in the terminal.

The terminal bathroom's indoor plumbing caught his attention for a long time. He stood in front of the toilet, pulling the handle and flushing it over and over again. He listened to the sound of swirling water and watched it circle and disappear, then fill the bowl again. Water took the "fecal matter" away in hidden pipes. They didn't burn *shit* in 55-gallon drums like back in Nam.

He turned on the faucet in the face bowl and let it run. It didn't run out of water like the showers in Nam. It kept flowing. He turned it off and back on. *Back in America, running water at my fingertips,* he thought. *Wow!* That's when it really dawned on him he was back in America—back in a pussy heaven of white, round-eyed girls and flushable toilets.

Outside the terminal windows, he didn't see one green jeep among the parked cars, and concrete roads ran as far as his eyes could see. Different types and different colored cars zipped by.

People were dressed in a deluge of different-colored and strangely styled clothes. He was used to seeing only one color—green—in Nam. The moving whirlwind of hues bewildered him. He closed his eyes periodically to adjust them to the swirl of bright colors that surrounded him.

All his efforts in Nam had been to blend with the green of the jungle. Anyone who cared for his own ass didn't wear anything in the jungle that would make him stand out. Officers hid their bars, sergeants ripped their stripes off, and corpsmen tore off the medical symbols. These things identified you as a target.

He looked at the many types of bright-colored shoes, loafers,

Stacy Adams, and gym shoes. Soldiers were easy to recognize—
they wore boots.

The air terminal was air-conditioned. The cool air felt thinner
in the large, open space of the building. A constant hum hung in
the air from the mix of so many people talking and walking with
hard-soled shoes on tile floors. He couldn't hear any silence in the
air to recognize sounds that inferred danger. The assorted sounds
he did hear were odd to his ears. The sound of a woman's voice, a
car horn beeping, loudspeakers blaring, or doors closing were
new, disturbing sounds. He stood with his back to the wall until his
flight left.

JD slept during most of the flight to Detroit. Clouds hid the
ground throughout the flight. When the plane dropped below the
clouds on its descent, he saw snowflakes whipping against the
window. The snow was heavy when the plane's wheels touched
the runway.

He stared out the plane's window in a trance. A furious winter
snowstorm raged outside. Snow, ice, and cold winds were a year-
old memory. He had forgotten snow during his tour of duty. Winter
had become merely a picture imagined in his mind like *Alice in
Wonderland*.

CHAPTER 18

*"I see by the way you're dressed you just returned
from overseas. Were you in Vietnam?"*

JD had not been issued winter clothing for his overnight stay
in California because General Scott's office wanted to make sure
there would be no delay to his returning home. The Nam jungle
uniform was not the uniform for traveling in the United States, but
no one questioned him when he left the California base.

The uniform he wore offered no protection against the winter
cold. When he stepped outside the terminal, the icy wind cut
through him like a razor blade. The wind hammered ice particles
into his face. His body shivered and shook from the shocking cold.
His insides felt like barbed ice crystals were moving through his
bloodstream.

He caught a cab to the General Motors factory to pick up his
new car. The driver, a white-haired old geezer, talked during the
ride about how he served in the Big War.

"I see by the way you're dressed you just returned from
overseas. Were you in Vietnam?" he asked.

"I served my time in hell," JD answered.

"Hell. Let me tell you 'bout hell. In the Big War, being trapped
on a beach while the big guns pounded the shit out of you was
hell. That was hell, buddy boy. What you kids call hell can't
compare to that," he said.

"All wars are the same size when people are shootin' at you. What difference does the size of the war make when you get killed? It's all crazy shit," JD said.

"Ya got a point there. That war's driving our boys crazy. They're over there killing kids and burning down villages. Killing innocent folks ain't no way to fight a war. That ain't right," he said.

"I don't know what's right or wrong about war. I know you kill anyone trying to kill you," JD said.

"You Vietnam boys are killin' *kids*," he said. "That's sick."

JD felt anger blow from his stomach to his head. What the fuck did this old man understand about Nam? Probably only something he read in the newspaper and took to be the truth. JD refrained from response. He didn't want to talk to the old man about war or Nam. He sat back and looked out the taxi window at the swirling snow.

The driver was determined to make sure JD understood how important and different the Big War was.

"Yeah, buddy boy, that was a war." His voice dipped lower for a moment as he held some faraway thought. "The way you kids are fighting this war brings disgrace to the country," he said.

JD squeezed his hands into a fist. His voice carried a razor-sharp edge. "Why don't you shut your fucking mouth old man? Just drive me where I want to go. Okay, *buddy boy*," JD said.

The driver didn't say another word the rest of the trip. He kept his eyes on JD in the rearview mirror.

The roads were clear despite the heavy snowfall. The snowplows piled the snow four feet high on the sides of the roads. He felt like Alice in Wonderland, except he was not sucked up into a whirling black hurricane; rather, he was sliding through a white tunnel.

His car had been ready for a week, so the paperwork didn't take long. He slid into the 1968 GTO and twisted the key in the ignition. The engine roared to life. He ran his hand over the dashboard. He slammed the Hurst shift into first gear. The engine whined as he gunned it. He fishtailed out of the parking lot onto the snowy road.

His stomach buzzed with excitement as he started the thirteen-hour drive home. It had been over a year since he was behind the wheel of a car. The people at the factory warned him to take it easy for the first hundred miles since a new car needed to be broken in at low speeds. They told him not to drive faster than fifty miles per hour.

He restrained himself, content to watch the spears of sunlight reflect off approaching car windshields in the snow. The sound of the engine was intoxicating, and the sensation of speed soothing. He wanted more. He punched the speedometer up to seventy, keeping it there for only twenty minutes, and then dropped it back to fifty-five. It was a long drive home, and he didn't want anything to happen that would put him out into the snow. He decided if the car got stuck in a snow bank, he would just stay in the car with the motor running until it ran out of gas.

He pulled out a joint, lit it, and turned on the radio. Smoky and the Miracles' "Baby, I love you," came across the airwaves. He turned the volume up. "Baby, baby . . ." he sang along, and settled into the routine of driving.

The snow-covered road didn't hold his attention. His mind wandered. He was back in the United States, and 12,000 miles from Nam, yet he didn't feel relaxed. The distant cold and snowy landscape intensified his feeling of being dropped into a foreign place he didn't understand.

Vivid memories of the past year begin to bubble up in his mind. He lit another joint. Thoughts of R&R in Hong Kong came back to him. He took $1,500 in cold cash with him to Hong Kong, along with an attitude and the energy to party and drink all week.

He remembered the plane's approach to Hong Kong. He was watching the sky when suddenly a huge cliff emerged from the ocean. The city seemed to be sitting on the edge of an island. He thought the plane was too low when he saw white-capped waves crashing into the rocky cliff.

Updrafts from the cliff caused the plane to bounce up and down. The plane abruptly hit the runway. He never did see a landing strip. The plane bounced several times. He remembered thinking had he lived through seven months of hell in the bush to die in an airplane crash? When he stepped off the plane, he was so high on the realization he was on R&R that he felt like his head was floating twenty feet above the ground.

Military personnel on R&R were loaded on buses and taken to a large auditorium that was part of the Hong Kong Municipal Center. Army medics gave lectures and cautioned them about VD.

JD couldn't help but laugh. The only VD he had cared about for the past seven months was the Valley Dogs. They were given names of hotels that catered to R&R servicemen and turned loose.

Hong Kong! Neon lights glowed purple and red, turning people's skin into the color of raw meat. Soldiers, sailors, bar girls, prostitutes, money changers, beggars, and old women selling flowers mingled in the street. There was a hurried intensity to the people moving along the sidewalk.

JD had met a Marine named Jim on the plane to Hong Kong. They became R&R running mates. The first night it was clear they were not there to drink for enjoyment. They were drinking to get drunk. Jim got so drunk he threw up and wet himself. They were only out for a few hours before they needed to go back to the hotel and sleep it off. After sleeping seven hours, they showered and hit the streets again.

Jim started talking to a streetwalker a few blocks from the hotel. He left JD to go with her. JD walked down a street off the beaten path to smoke a joint. He stopped in an alleyway and sat on some boxes. He remembered looking up through the canyon walls of buildings at the night sky. It was a strange sight seeing stars above buildings rather than through leaves.

Prostitutes in tight clothes stood in small clusters, saying, "Come with me" to passing GIs. JD waved them off. He was a corpsman and had treated enough men who returned from R&R with the clap and syphilis. There were too many women in this city to just pick up one from the street. He ignored the pussy calls until he found an entrance with a sign for massages and steam baths.

Inside, a momma-san greeted him with, "You want a girl?"

JD was embarrassed by the woman's blunt question. He felt a warm blush on his face. "Yes," he said.

She led him into another big room, where behind a glass wall were eight or nine girls covered only with small pieces of cloth across their breasts and between their legs. The momma-san pointed toward the glass. "Pick one you like," she said.

His first thought was to find one that looked like Jan—tall and slender with long hair. None measured up to that standard, though. Most had long, black hair and were short and skinny. The women made erotic movements, opening and closing their legs, rubbing their breasts, and licking their lips to get his attention.

The one girl that did catch his eye was the one not trying to get his attention. She acted shy compared to the other women. She had smooth, light-yellow skin and blue eyes. He pointed. "That one. I want to see her closer." Momma-san took JD back through a twisting hallway to a small room and brought the shy girl to him. The blue-eyed girl walked in the room with her head bowed and eyes staring at the floor. "You want her?" Momma-san questioned him again.

"Yeah, I want her. What's her name?" he asked.

"We call her Suzie."

Momma-san left the two of them alone. JD hadn't been with a woman in over seven months. He just stared at her for a few minutes. The soft look of the woman's body was so different from the hard bodies he was used to being around. It made him slightly nervous. She stood in the middle of the room with her head bowed.

His voice sounded harsh, something he had not noticed before. "Turn around," he said. She turned quickly like he'd barked an order.

He walked over to her and ran his hands through her long hair. She was trembling. "I like your hair," he said.

Her voice was sharp with fear. "I brush it every day. You want me?" she asked.

"Baby, how much I want you," he said. He placed his hand on her shoulder. "Not just tonight, for the whole week." His voice became softer. "Let's leave this place."

"Okay, you have to pay Momma-san to take me out."

JD paid five dollars to take her out of the place. Back in his hotel room, they agreed on thirty dollars a night for a week. She was good in bed. They fucked all night.

Suzie left in a hurry when morning came, but promised to meet him later that night in his room.

After a bath and a change of clothes, JD walked the streets most of the day, darting in and out of shops and the massive crowds of people.

That night, Suzie took him to a disco filled with dark-skinned Chinese girls and black GIs. He bought some dope.

She didn't leave in the morning, but instead stayed in his arms. It was noon when they finally got out of bed. She took him to several shops and bargained with the owners for whatever he bought. Later on, he found out he paid half the price that Jim paid for the same things. He also found out later he was the first black man she had been with.

At the time, he thought it was a week of pure bliss. In retrospect, he wasn't sure it was all that good, but it was better than Nam. Although he was away from the bush for a week, Nam never left his head.

Hong Kong was a weeklong party, the same as Da Nang, or in-country R&R. In Hong Kong he didn't expect incoming rounds in the hotel room, but he dreamed about Nam every night—unless he drank so much he went to sleep in a stupor.

The sight of a jackknifed truck on the side of the road brought JD back to the snow-covered road. Snowflakes jumped out of the darkness at him. He tried to focus on a single snowflake hurling toward the windshield. He watched it hit, stick, and then turn into a trickle of water.

He pulled over on the side of the road several times during the long drive to take short naps. Most of the time he kept the motor running, but he was always scared he would run out of gas. During one of his breaks, the car was almost hit by a sliding semi-truck, so he decided not to sleep roadside anymore. He would pull over on an exit ramp if he needed another nap.

The snowy landscape stretched for miles, making him feel small and out of place. He was alone. Which way was home?

CHAPTER 19

"I'm home, Momma. I told you I'd be back."

Eight inches of snow plunged Springfield's landscape into a white winter wasteland. The swirling, white haze concealed commonplace shapes and forms, turning them into unfamiliar objects. The heavy snow destroyed JD's anticipation of returning to the streets and buildings he missed while in Nam.

Old-fashioned concrete streetlights with brown-stained bulb covers threw rings of stiff, yellow light into the street, creating small islands in the white flurry. Only three cars crept slowly on South Grand Avenue, a major east-west road in the south side of town.

He drove to Eleventh Street, where the majority of black joints were located. Most of the bars were empty. He didn't expect a parade because he was home, but he expected to at least see people. Home, in his mind, meant people out in the streets. The cold snow and howling winds kept people in their own houses.

He turned left onto Stuart Street. The wind's fury whipped snow past old streetlights, creating strange light shapes that lunged at his windshield. The street where he'd spent most of his life became an unrecognizable road. He wasn't even sure he was on the right street.

Finally, he pulled up in front of his mother's house. He sat in the car looking at the house, comparing what he saw to the thoughts he carried of it. The blowing snow rounded off the edges of the house and blended the walls into the surrounding darkness. The light above the front door seemed to turn the entrance into a mysterious, shadowy hole.

Winter's dominance erased the elm tree's summer green and multicolored fall leaves in front of the house. Its stark, leafless branches reached upward with grotesque, bony, knotted, twisted fingers into the dark, white-specked sky. In his mind, he'd always pictured it as a green shade tree.

Across the sidewalk from the elm tree was a pine tree. It was taller and fuller than he remembered. At least it looked natural covered by snow. Neither tree reflected his memories.

JD stepped out of the car and sank to the top of his boots in the deep snow. He took short, unsure steps, like a mechanical man, walking between the car and the house. The light from the front room formed a quilted weave of shadows on the porch's undisturbed snow.

He knocked softly, at first, like a visitor, three times. Then he said to himself, "I'm home," and banged hard on the door.

His sister, Judy, cracked the door and peeped out. She saw who it was, flung open the door, and stared at him with her mouth open. Her voice trembled. "Johnny?" she asked.

"Who else looks like your brother? It's me! You gonna give me a hug or just stand there with your mouth hangin' open?"

"You're okay," she said. "We were told . . . we thought . . . you were missing in action."

"I'm standing in front of you, ain't I? Here, touch," he said, grabbing her hand to place it on his shoulder. "Don't I feel real?" he asked.

When she touched his shoulder, she burst out crying and threw her arms around his neck. "You're okay, you're okay!"

The racket at the front door and the chill that ran through the house brought his mother to the front room. "What's all the noise about? Close that door, girl. I don't pay to heat the outside."

"Momma, Johnny's home. Johnny's okay!" Judy said.

When Judy stepped away from the door, Johnny's body appeared. His mother, Ruth, froze in the middle of the room. "Johnny?" she asked.

"I'm home, Momma. I told you I'd be back," he said.

"Johnny! Oh, Johnny." She ran across the room and hugged him.

"My baby's home. You're all right! Thank you, Jesus. Thank you, Jee-sus," she repeated over and over.

"Let's get out of the doorway so I can close the door and get out of the cold," Judy said.

JD's mother clung onto her Johnny as they stepped inside. "So glad you're home safe. Thank you, Jesus. The nightmare is finally over. I can touch you, feel your heart beat, hear your voice again."

"I told you I'd make it back home." Being safe felt foreign. He shifted his feet and stiffened his back, straining against the unusual feeling. He unwrapped his mother's arms from around his neck.

"Where's Jan?" he asked.

JD's mother pulled him over to the couch. "Sit. Jan had a dance show tonight at school. She should be home soon. She's gonna be so glad to see you." They sat on the couch. "We thought you were missing in action. We've been worried out of our minds that something terrible happened to you. Praise the Lord, you're home safe," she said.

He was confused. "I wasn't MIA. Who told you I was MIA?" he asked.

"We heard it on television. They said that team . . . the Valley Dogs . . . you wrote you were a member of, was missing around Khe Sanh. What happened to you?" Judy asked.

JD looked at the soft faces of his mother and sister. They wanted him to tell them what happened in Khe Sanh? How could he tell them about the killing and dying? He couldn't tell his mother all the sins and transgressions he committed—sins that violated all of her training and beliefs.

"A lot happened. It doesn't matter now. I'm home," he said.

"We're so thankful you're okay," she said.

He laughed. "I want to see my son." He touched his nose. "See that Douglas nose that takes up a third of his face."

"He's got the nose and your face. He's a quiet baby like you were," she said.

"I bet you've spoiled him already. Where is he?" JD asked.

"Come on, I'll show you. He's sleeping in my room," JD's mother unconsciously put a finger to her lips. "Don't you wake him, he just went to sleep."

"How did you get here?" Judy asked.

He smiled. "Walked."

Judy laughed. "You didn't walk across the water from Vietnam, at least not in this weather."

"No, I drove. I've got a new car," he said.

"You can't get a car in Vietnam," she said.

"I didn't get it in Nam. I flew to Detroit, picked it up, and drove here," he said.

"You went to Detroit and got a car? No way. You're just kiddin' me," Judy said.

"No, I'm not. Look out the window."

Judy ran to the front window and looked out. "There is a car out there," she said. "I can't tell what kind because of the snow."

"A brand new 1968 Pontiac GTO," he said.

"Oh, wow! Can I drive it, big brother?" she asked.

"Don't worry, you'll get a chance, I promise," he said.

"This is great," Judy squealed. "I'm going to call Ida and tell her you're home with a new car, and I'm going to drive it to school." She hopped off toward her room.

JD's mother took him to her bedroom, where his son, Jimmy, lay on his back, his arms open like he was reaching for a hug. He made a smacking sound as he sucked on the nipple of a milk bottle propped up on diapers. His small, doll-like hands curled and uncurled. His smooth, relaxed face had no wrinkles or lines. JD's baby looked so soft, so tiny, so defenseless. Looking down at his son for the first time, he felt the full realization he was a father.

"That's my son," JD whispered softly.

He had delivered babies before and saw the special glow in mothers' and fathers' faces when they saw their new babies for the first time. He had wondered what they were feeling at the time. As he watched the quiet rise and fall of his son's small chest, a warm, soft sensation flowed through his body. JD had brought life into the world.

He reached out to pick Jimmy up and wanted to touch him and feel the life he created. He wanted to swing him around in the air, and tell him his dad was home. They were going to have fun doing the things dads do with sons. Play ball, go places, see things, and do things together. When he touched Jimmy, the baby opened his eyes briefly and made some small sounds. JD's mother grabbed his arm.

"Don't wake him," she said.

JD stiffened at the touch. "Okay, tomorrow my son will get to know his daddy." JD quietly backed out of the room.

"I got a hot pot of coffee on. Want some?" she asked.

"Okay. Sounds good," JD said. "It was a long drive." JD sat at the kitchen table.

"I know you're hungry," she said.

"Momma, even if I wasn't hungry, I'm ready to eat just so I can taste all your good home-cookin' I've missed."

JD's mother beamed and pulled out an old black iron skillet. "I'll make some breakfast. Tomorrow I'll make you a special dinner. Fried chicken, french fries, and a whole sweet potato pie just for you," she said.

"The sound of those words makes my mouth water. Ain't been to any place where they cooked better than my Momma," he said.

She blushed. "You've tasted something you liked in all those places you've been."

"No matter what the taste, the food had strange-sounding names. I never knew what I was eating. I understand what fried chicken is and what it tastes like, and how a good sweet potato pie should taste. You're still the best cook in my life."

Her cheeks flushed again. "Ain't nothing better than home cooking when you've been away from home." She started humming. When JD's mother was happy, she hummed.

Watching his mother move around the kitchen reminded him of when he would sit at the table as a kid, fidget in his seat impatiently, and wait to devour his dinner.

The sizzling aroma from the bacon in the pan drifted throughout his Momma's house. Judy popped into the kitchen. "Oh, goody! That smells so good."

He laughed. "I see my little sister's nose is working as hard as usual. I bet you can still smell food cookin' in your sleep."

"I can't help it," she said. She put her hands on her hips. "I got a Douglas nose just like you."

"Yeah, but you're a girl. A big-nosed girl. The guys like big noses on their girls now?" JD said.

"Momma, Johnny's messin' with me! I got a pretty nose like Momma," Judy said. "Momma, Johnny's saying you got a big nose."

"You two stop. You both got big noses 'cause I gave 'em to both of you," JD's mother said. "Don't you worry, baby. If the boys like you, your nose will be the last thing they notice."

She turned back to the stove and flipped the bacon over.

"Did Momma tell you about the television program she saw?" Judy asked.

"No. What was it, Momma?" he asked.

She told JD she saw a news program about the Valley Dogs recon team missing in action around a place called Khe Sanh. She remembered how he wrote in one of his letters that he belonged to a team called the Valley Dogs. She and Jan went down to the Marines' recruiting office to find out if it was his team. An officer lectured them about the press causing confusion by reporting directly from the combat zone and creating unnecessary drama. The officer wrote down JD's name, social security number, service number, and said he would send an inquiry through the proper channels.

They went to the American Red Cross. A man there told them how painful it must be for a family to discover on television that something terrible happened to a loved one so far away. He said he would try to contact JD's commanding officer through the Marine Corps.

"What happened, Johnny? Were you missing in action? What does that mean?" Judy asked.

JD laughed. "We weren't missing. We knew exactly where we were. However, nobody else knew, which is exactly what we wanted," he said.

"Why didn't they know where you were?" Judy asked.

"Things and people were always getting lost in Nam. That's the way it was," he said.

"Why do you call Vietnam, Nam?" Judy asked.

"It's shorter and easier to say. I haven't been asked this many questions at once in a long time. Must be a little sister thing."

Nam, the word brought a flashback to his mind's eye of that last moment with Ham before the stray bullet and its *thwack*. His stomach tightened with the memory, his breath suddenly catching in his chest. He closed his eyes and focused on his present moment—the *real-world* aroma of bacon.

"Too much to tell in one night."

JD changed the subject. His voice carried a slight, sharp edge to it. "It's going on eleven o'clock. When is Jan's dance show supposed to be over?" he asked.

"They might have gone to the Corner Disco afterwards. I'll call and find out." She reached for the telephone.

"No, that's alright. After I eat, I'll go on down there. I want to see this place. A disco in Springfield? They didn't have anything like that when I left. What street's it on?" he asked.

Judy spoke up quickly—a little too quickly. "Eighteenth Street, just north of South Grand Avenue. They have live music, fancy lights, and a *big* dance floor."

"And how is it you know so much about it, young lady? Is that where you go when you stay out so late with those boys?" their mother asked.

"I *have not* been there. I just heard about it." Judy muttered. "All the kids at school talk about it. They must've heard about it from their older brothers and sisters."

"What kids are you talkin' about?" JD's mother asked.

"Oh, Momma, you know. Just kids around school," Judy said.

"These kids got names?" she asked.

JD broke into the bickering between them. "Is Jeff still around?" he asked.

The high-pitched sound of their voices reminded him of gook voices. Their squabbling back and forth irritated him. He felt like little red ants were running underneath his skin. He needed away from them.

Jeff and JD attended the same schools from kindergarten to high school. "I saw him a few days ago. He asked about you. He told me to tell you to give him a call when you got in. His number's in the telephone book. Judy, get the telephone book for your brother," she said.

JD dialed the telephone and Jeff answered. Jeff sounded surprised to hear JD's voice. JD's mother had told him about the program she saw on television concerning the Valley Dogs. Jeff asked when they were going to get together; JD said he wanted to see him tonight.

"You mean this cold, snowy night? Nigger, please!" Jeff's whine was the same as ever.

"I'll pick you up. You can check out my new ride," JD said.

"You got a new ride? What're you drivin'?" he asked.

The mention of the car revved up Jeff's excitement. "I drove a '68 GTO out of the factory door. It's a real bad mother—" JD said, catching himself from finishing.

"A GTO? That is a bad ride! Yeah. A mighty bad ride. Pick me up in a half-hour." Jeff always needed to be talked into doing something. But once you got something in his mind, he didn't think about it anymore, he just did it.

JD gobbled his food down quickly, too quickly for his mother, and she fussed at him for shoveling food. He started to tell her it was his mouth and his business how he put food in it, but then he remembered he was talking to his mother. He teased her instead. "It's just too good, Momma. I'll eat slower next time." He left for Jeff's house.

Jeff was dressed except for his boots. They were the same age, but Jeff had been married for six years and had a five-year-old son named James. Pictures of Jeff's family sat on a table in the living room. A picture of Jeff pushing James on a tricycle at the park caught JD's eye. He was smiling from ear to ear, and his eyes looked happy, clear, and bright. JD imagined having moments like that with his son someday. They would do all the things a father does with his son.

CHAPTER 20

*He was home. No more sneaking through the Nam jungle
with little yellow people trying to kill him.*

Jeff had some dope, so they smoked a couple of joints on the way to the Corner Disco. This dope didn't step on you like dope in Nam, but got you enough of a buzz to feel light and easy.

Jeff was high, fumbling for words, trying to tell JD everything he missed while he was in Nam. Most of what Jeff said didn't make sense. JD would mutter "Uh," to everything, and Jeff would start talking about something else, thinking he got his point across. It didn't matter to JD if he understood what Jeff was saying. This was his first night home—plenty of time to go over it again later.

When JD got out of the car, he patted the pistol in the back of his pants. His knife strapped on his leg, he felt fully dressed. They walked into the Corner Disco. The polished dance floor reflected rotating lights off the tall mirrors. A bright, white spotlight centered on a large crystal ball revolved above the dance floor. The ceiling, walls, floor, and dancers echoed the moving circles of light. Oversized speakers hung from the ceiling, pounding a heavy bass beat.

A couple of people he knew slapped his hand and welcomed him home when he came through the door. They pulled him into the bar and told the bartender his drinks were free for the night.

This was what he expected to happen when he came home. He felt good. The dope high mixed with the drinks to make him float with the music. He was home. No more sneaking through the Nam jungle with little yellow people trying to kill him.

He stood with his back to the bar looking for Jan among the tables. He didn't see her. The DJ played a slow song he didn't know. People rushed to the dance floor. He watched the dips and grinding motion of dancers on the dance floor. He remembered how good he felt when he held Jan close to his body while swaying to music. He wondered where she was. He had expected her to be at home waiting for him.

Finally, he saw Jan on the dance floor. His body tensed. Her arms were wrapped tightly around a man's neck, and his hands were on her ass. A flash of hot anger pierced JD's chest, ripping away the nice buzz he'd been floating on. His eyes narrowed, took on a hard glint. He walked onto the dance floor, shoving dancing couples aside as he worked his way toward Jan. Her head was buried in the man's shoulder. She didn't see JD when he tapped Willy on the shoulder.

Willy ignored JD and kept dancing. JD tapped his shoulder harder. Willy spun around, faced him and shouted, "Nigger, please! Get off my back! You must be crazy trying to break in on a man in a slow grind. What's your fucking problem?"

"Your fucking hands," JD said softly.

Jan's voice cried out above the music, "Johnny!"

Willy was only five-feet-eight and 120 pounds, but he was a professional dancer and his small, tightly-packed body was powerful.

"You worried about my hands? I'll give you good reason to worry." Willy swung at JD's chin.

JD ducked, spun, and mule-kicked Willy in his chest. Willy's punch froze midair. The kick was so hard Willy flew backwards across the room.

The other dancers' eyes followed Willy's flight across the dance floor. He fell among a group of dancers on the other side of the floor. Willy stood wobbly on his feet and shook his head, trying to clear it.

JD ran across the floor, jumped in the air and kicked Willy in the chest again with both feet. Willy slid across the dance floor on his back. JD jumped, his knees on Willy's chest. The air flew out of

Willy's lungs. He grabbed Willy's hair and forced his forehead back, exposing and extending his neck. His hand poised in midair, ready to deliver a crushing blow to Willy's neck.

Tears flooded Willy's eyes. He realized he was about to die—this man was going to kill him. Paralyzed with terror, he looked up wide-eyed into JD's hardened, emotionless face and begged for his life. "Please! Don't kill me. I'm sorry."

"Too fucking late. You're dead meat," JD said.

"Johnny. You're alive!" Jan screamed, "You're alive!" Her voice stopped JD's deathblow. He stood up and turned toward her. Jan's body was shaking. The color drained out of her face. "Johnny, you're home. Thank God! You're alive!"

"Yeah. I'm home." JD turned around, and pulled Willy up from the dance floor. He grabbed Willy's shirt collar and pulled his face close until their noses almost touched. Willy's body hung limp in his hands. "I'm home, mother-fucker, and you're dead meat if I ever catch you sneaking around my wife again." JD shook the limp body in his hands. "Understand, nigger?"

"Yes—oh Jesus-God—yes! No harm meant, man! No harm," Willy blubbered.

"Yeah, we'll see," JD muttered as he dropped Willy to the dance floor.

He turned and faced Jan. Anger pounded his temples. He was in a surreal world with the loud music and revolving multicolored lights. People left the dance floor, leaving only JD and Jan on it.

Tears streamed down Jan's cheeks, her arms were wrapped around her body as she tried to hold herself together. The pain and shock in her eyes soothed the anger burning within him.

"I made it home like I told you, baby," he crooned in softer tones. He put his arms around her and pulled her close. She hugged him tight. They stood in the middle of the dance floor holding each other.

People started clapping and cheering. The music got louder and suddenly a fast beat blared down from the speakers. Jan and JD realized they were the only ones on the dance floor. People yelled, "Right on!" and "Welcome home!" Jan blushed. JD waved to the crowd and led her off the dance floor to a table. He ordered drinks. They sat close, side-by-side, their bodies touching. She laid her head on his shoulder.

Her hair is so short, he thought. *Why did she cut it so close?*

In Nam, all thoughts, his mental images, were of her with long hair. He looked at her eyes. She still had those enchanting eyes that captured him years ago.

"Oh, Johnny. I'm so glad you're home!" She buried her head into his chest. "We thought something terrible happened to you. Momma saw a television program and we thought you were—"

"Mom told me about it," he cut her off. "I'm glad I'm home, so you can know I'm alright." He kissed her forehead. "I saw our son for the first time. He's a beautiful baby, and has a Douglas nose."

Jan snuggled closer to him. "He'll grow up and be like his daddy."

"Like his daddy? I hope not." The waitress interrupted them and put their drinks on the table.

Friends joined them. It became a joyous reunion. They stayed until the place closed at 1 A.M., then went to a couple of after-hour places. Dawn was breaking when he pulled up in front of his mother's house, followed by two carloads of friends.

JD's mother opened the door. As they piled in, she went into the kitchen to make a pot of coffee. Live, vibrant bodies were spread around on furniture and the floors, from the front door in the living room to the back door in the kitchen. JD watched his mother move among his friends. She was enjoying her house, now so full of laughter and people.

JD's friends talked more to each other than to him. That was okay. He didn't understand half the things they were talking about, and they didn't seem to care if he did. The group was loud, but no matter how loud everyone got, he didn't raise his voice.

A few people commented that he seemed different because he was so quiet and he had a faraway look in his eyes. He laughed and told them perhaps he was not who they thought he was. They laughed. He was gone only a year. That was not enough time to completely change a person.

"You were born and raised in Springfield, Johnny. We know you. You'll be okay, you just need some time to get that Vietnam shit out your head," Jeff said.

They told him all the things that happened to people he knew during the past year—old friends who were killed in car accidents, those who left town, where they were, and what they were doing.

They also told him stories they had heard about how crazy and fucked up guys were who returned from Vietnam. They couldn't understand how someone could forget their roots. They heard most of the returning veterans were badly wounded, and they figured that was the reason. JD didn't have any visible mutilation from being wounded, so they figured he was okay and didn't have a reason to be crazy. The only marks they could see were the days-old scratch across his jaw and a few older scars no worse than he could have picked up in Springfield.

JD didn't care about the gossip and didn't see it having any direct effect on his life. His friends' conversation turned to the times when they were kids and what they were doing now. Nothing changed in their lives, and they were still doing the same things they did as kids—going skating, dancing on Friday and Saturday nights, chasing the same girls. His friends hadn't gone anywhere or seen anything new since he left a year ago.

Their drivel bored him. He looked over at Jan and saw she was staring at him. He walked over, grabbed her hand, and pulled her up out of the chair she was sitting in. "I'm glad to see all of you my first night home, but, hey . . . since I haven't had any time with my wife for a year, I'll talk to you folks later. Stay as long as you want to. We're leaving," he said. They left the room and walked up the stairs to his old bedroom.

"Finally, it's just you and me," he whispered in her ear. He took her into his arms and kissed her. "Let's take a shower together." Jan didn't answer. She just held onto him.

He stood behind her under the hot shower and watched the water bounce off her body, fully exposed before him, not in a dream, not as a thought, but in the flesh.

She stood with her arms hanging at her sides. He slowly rubbed a soapy washcloth over her neck to her breasts, paying extra attention to her nipples. He made long strokes on her stomach leading to her pubic hair, down her long legs, then back up the back of them.

They smiled as they dried each others' wet bodies. His body tingled as she rubbed the thick towel over it. They lay across the bed while JD caressed her body and ran his hands over her as if she were thin porcelain. His hands explored the dips and curves of her body with delicate touches. He explored her breasts with his mouth, sucking and flicking his tongue across her nipples. She moaned. He left wet traces of his tongue along the long lines of her legs. Every dip in her body he touched with lingering kisses.

Liquid warmth flowed through Jan's body, building pressure between her legs, forcing her pelvis to thrust up to his mouth. He ran his tongue slowly up and down between her legs, stopping for a few moments at special places that made her groan. She grabbed his head and opened her legs wider. "Oh, baby," she said. He slipped his hands underneath her, pulling her tighter to his mouth. A small scream escaped her lips, and she wrapped her legs around his shoulders. The excitement exploded between her legs.

Her body jerked with spasms as he planted kisses on her thighs. His tongue left a wet trail as he moved up her body over her stomach. When he reached her nipples, he kissed first one, then the other, making little sucking motions with his lips. He lay on top of her, without moving, as her warm, moist body twisted and turned beneath him.

"Ooh, baby, your body is so hot!" he groaned. "I've dreamed about this moment for a year." He kissed her forehead, her eyebrows, the tip of her nose, and then sucked on her ear lobe. His hand slipped down between their bodies until he could grab his penis. Her legs parted. He rubbed the head up and down between her legs. She was so wet. Her juices flowed, anticipating his first thrust. He slipped inside her. Her knees came up to her chest, and she locked her ankles around his back.

"Johnny, Johnny, you feel so good!" He slid more of his hardness into her—buried it all inside. She nibbled at his neck, making little sucking sounds. He didn't move, just held her with his hardness deep inside. Her body twitched with little jerks as spasms shot through her. She squeezed her thigh muscles tight against his sides while her locked ankles straightened above his back. Her head snapped up and she sucked, bit, and licked his neck as her juices flooded his throbbing penis.

He plunged deep inside her and out. Their bodies jerked with little spasms of pleasure. His body was wet with sweat as he thrust harder and faster. "Oh, Johnny, I'm coming. I'm coming." Her body arched up off the bed. "Yes, Yes!" His body jerked hard as he climaxed inside her.

They lay in each other's arms, feeling spent and weak for a long time. Jan finally moved; she got a warm washcloth and wiped their mixed moisture from her body. They touched and hugged for hours, making up for lost time. Finally exhausted, they fell into a deep sleep.

The next day started for JD around four o'clock in the afternoon. He came downstairs to the aroma of fried chicken, french fries, and sweet potato pie drifting from the kitchen. "I heard you moving around and figured you'd be down soon—and hungry," JD's mother greeted him as he walked into the kitchen.

"I'm hungry enough to eat a water buffalo!"

"Eat what?" she asked.

"A water buffalo." He searched for a way to describe it. "It's like a huge bull with big horns that likes to lie in the mud all the time." The things he had become so familiar with for the past year were nothing but strange-sounding names to his family and friends. He didn't like having to explain things all the time.

"They say water buffalo taste like shit," JD said. "I've killed the fuckers, but never ate one." After he spoke, he realized he'd cursed. His mother didn't allow cussing in her house. She obviously heard the slip, but she didn't say anything.

Jan joined them in the kitchen, beaming with a mile-wide smile. She kissed JD. "Mmm, I'm glad you're home. I missed you." She lowered her eyes when she noticed everyone looking at her and smiling. "What can I do to help?" she asked.

"Nothing dear, you just sit next to Johnny. Got everything under control," she said.

JD, his mother, Jan, and Judy sat around the table talking after eating. "Reverend Cleo lost his church. He was the pastor for over ten years," JD's mother told him. "They caught him in bed with the wife of one of the deacons. It really caused a stir."

"I don't see why. Everyone knows he's been doing that kind of thing for years," JD said. "What made them get so upset this time? Couldn't be just 'cause he got caught?"

"It was the head deacon's wife, his contract was up, and they finally got tired of him and his foolishness," JD's mother summarized. "Old man Karl died, and Louise, who lived down the street on the next block, had a heart attack."

Reverend Cleo married Jan and JD, but it didn't mean anything to JD if Reverend Cleo was the pastor of the church or not. He lit a cigarette. He tried to catch passing memories of the other people she mentioned. Vague, faceless images floated through his mind. It just didn't mean that much to him that Karl died or Louise suffered a heart attack.

JD's mother left the room and came back with a big box and

two smaller ones filled with photo albums. She spread pictures and albums over the table. "Do you remember this picture?" she asked him and passed a picture to him.

It was a picture of him when he got his first bike. "I'll never forget that day. I broke my arm riding that new bike the day this picture was taken," he said.

He looked closer at the picture. The kid was smiling. He didn't remember that. He remembered pain and being told he couldn't ride his bike for two weeks because his arm was in a cast.

"Here's one of you when you got out of boot camp," she said, passing a picture to him.

The boot camp shot was taken only three years ago. A young, fresh face with hair cut so short his head seemed bald, stared at JD from the picture. "That was a long, long time ago," he said. The skinhead in the picture looked like him except for the smaller body and the softness in its eyes. The face was that of a stranger. The person in the picture no longer existed.

They spent a couple of hours walking down memory lane. JD's mother beamed as she showed pictures of her family. She pulled out an old, faded brown picture of two women in their teens.

"Momma, I've never seen this picture before." He held it up to the light. "Some good-looking women in it. Who are they?"

"Me and your Aunt Kathryn in our younger days. We were a couple of high-spirited gals during those days." She took the picture from her son. "Yes, high-spirited." She caressed the picture. "Your Aunt Kathryn is still high-spirited," she said, with a thin smile.

"That must explain why I dig her so much," JD said. "She's high-spirited."

The next pictures she passed around were of his father, Thomas, and the family doing different things together. Some were posed, but most captured surprised faces.

Thomas Douglas had died suddenly when JD was young. One morning his father was there, that night he was dead and gone forever. JD looked over at his son. *At least I came back,* he thought.

The ritual began to bore JD. The folks in these pictures were from a time in the past. The pictures of him were of a stranger, despite his ownership of memories attached to them. The JD in those pictures had died in a world of shit called Viet-Fucking-Nam.

Several times, JD's mother and Jan asked him what happened

during the past year. He tried to tell them about the Valley Dogs, and Ham, Jake, and Mex and what happened to them. They had funny looks on their faces, and they said they couldn't believe something like that could really happen. JD stiffened and changed the subject.

Women didn't want to hear about violence, killing, and death. The only other male in the house was his son, who couldn't understand even if he cared enough to listen.

JD glanced around the room at his mother, sister, and wife. He was in the middle of a roomfull of women who didn't want to hear his story—his survival. A week ago, he was in the middle of men whose only concern was surviving at any cost. *What a hell of a change,* he thought.

CHAPTER 21

Living on the edge in Nam and coming home so suddenly was like driving a car off a cliff, then slamming on the brakes.

People at home changed some while JD was away, but the differences were insignificant. In contrast, JD had changed—a lot. What he had seen and done in Vietnam over the past year made him radically different from anyone at home.

The people at home had Johnny Douglas in their memories. He was the kid they knew and loved a year ago. But, JD, not Johnny, came back from Nam. Vague traits of Johnny remained in him, but the forced birth of JD was carved into his soul.

Being home failed to meet JD's expectations. He had looked forward to going home to see the people and places he imagined while he was in Nam. He had dreams and expectations of his future at home. But home was different—or was it?

JD felt like a stranger in his hometown. He knew the faces and names that surrounded him, places and events that happened, and vague memories of being there. He couldn't hold the thought of being Johnny very long because gruesome visions of Nam pulsated continually in his mind. The recollections captured his sanity and flung him back into the hell of Nam.

JD's pace was quick, short, abrupt, and unpredictable for no reason his friends could understand. Johnny's pace was slow and one-tracked for reasons with which none of them could identify, or even imagine.

Every night his sleep was plagued with graphic, bizarre nightmares of Nam. He cried out, "Oh, no, please, oh God, no!" in his sleep. His body tossed and turned, fighting the bed as he fought the assaults in his mind. He awoke drenched with sweat and trembling with chills.

One recurring nightmare, the same nightmare, one recurring nightmare . . . In Nam, he is tied to a tree. A smiling gook, staring into his eyes, slowly draws a sharp-edged knife across his chest. Intense pain clenches his stomach, twists it so tight that foul-tasting bile is forced up into his throat.

In desperation, he kicks at the gook. The gook grabs his leg and cuts it to the bone. "No!" he shrieks. The gook grins, then plunges the knife deep into JD's stomach and slowly slices across it. He looks down at his stomach to watch his intestines slide slowly out of his body.

"Kill me! Kill me!" he screams.

The gook smiles and slashes the knife across and into his intestines. "Oh my God," he mutters. He raises his head level with the gook's face. "Kill me," he begs. "Please."

The gook lets out a high-pitched laugh. He forces JD's head back against the tree and cuts an arc into his chest. A thick slab of JD's torso falls away from his body.

"Kill me! Kill me!" he screams. The gook looks into his eyes and laughs.

Suddenly, Ham's scarred face, dark holes for eyes, filled with congealed dirty-dark blood, replaces the gook's face. Blood seeps from Ham's hollow eyes. Ham's voice booms in his head. "I can help you, Doc. Stop my bleeding."

"I can't, I'm dying," JD says.

"You're not dying, Doc. You're looking for a quick death. You're praying for it. You're frightened of dying slow, so you want to rush death. You want someone to kill you," Ham says.

JD looks at the blood-soaked ground beneath him. "My life is draining from my body; I can't stop it. My hands are tied."

Ham's voice booms in commanding tone, "your hands aren't tied." JD's arms hang at his sides. He hovers in mid-air, face to face with Ham.

"Your hands aren't tied now. Stop my bleeding," Ham says.

His mind fights to find some explanation of what is happening to him. How can Ham's face replace the smiling gook's? Ham is dead. How can he speak to him? If Ham is alive, he must try to save him. Ham has two small holes dripping blood in his head where his eyes should be. Perhaps, he should plug the holes with his fingers. He sticks his fingers into Ham's eye sockets to stop the flow of blood.

His fingers slip into the oozing holes. They grow larger. He sticks his fists in to plug the holes. They grow wider. His hands slip deeper into Ham's eyes. *Oh God*, he thinks. *I'm being sucked into Ham's head. He's dead. I don't want to die like this.* "No. You're dead. Let me go! Let me go!" JD screams.

The first time, his screaming awakened Jan. She leaped out of the bed and ran to the other side of the room. "What's the matter? What's wrong?" she shrieked. Her eyes were wide and her body trembled with fear.

"Nothing is wrong. Just a bad nightmare. I'm alright now," he said. But, his words couldn't calm Jan.

They sat up the rest of the night. Both were scared to close their eyes. Jan was terrified he would harm her. JD was scared of the haunting death-visions that lurked behind his eyelids.

Home was a strange, gray world that made JD edgy. What used to be normal and common for him was suddenly an extreme adjustment. The soft bed felt mushy after sleeping on stiff cots and hard ground. Nam had trained his body well to adapt to uncomfortable sleeping positions, to be prepared to leap from them, to fight. Sleeping in a soft, comfortable bed felt dangerous. It was too spongy, and provided no leverage to jump up if attacked.

Scents in the air here were either sweet or perfumed to cover up real odors. In Nam, it was important to smell your surroundings because so often it was the only way to know when the unseen enemy was near. A faint odor foreign to your surroundings could save your life. He constantly sniffed at the air, trying to sort through the camouflage of perfumes that hid the smell of people.

Since he had not been in a heated building for a year, furnace heat felt strange to him as well. Sometimes, the heat flowing up from the floor felt so thick he had to step outside for air.

Everyone was noisy and awkward when they moved. They would not have lasted long in Nam's bush country, where quiet and precise movement kept you alive.

Alien noises bombarded his ears. The cluttered background sawed across his nerves. These unfamiliar, non-Nam sounds kept him skittish. He could not identify which sounds were harmful. Sounds of his childhood, such as dogs barking, became strange to his ears.

Before Nam, he never noticed the sounds of stiff shoes on the sidewalk or the roar of car engines. He did not hear a train whistle in Nam, church bells ringing, or babies crying in the night. Footsteps above his head were a scary sound. Wind rattling glass-plated windows made him jump to see if someone was sneaking up on him.

He had spent most of his life listening to his mother's old clock in the front room. Now it was no longer a caller of time, but a queer noise that caused disorder in his ears every hour.

Creaks and moans of the house that provided comfort and safety when he was growing up became nuisances in his mind. His body would tense up, poised to react to possible attack every time he heard a floorboard creak.

The most awkward sound was high-pitched female voices in the night. In Nam, high-pitched voices talking to each other usually meant gooks. He would wake up and peek into the next room whenever he heard voices, only to find that it was his mother or Jan he heard.

Continually alert for an ambush, he walked down the streets searching for movement in bushes along the sidewalk. He kept his eyes on dark corners and scanned trees for hidden enemies. He watched windows above the second floor since they were a perfect place for snipers to launch an attack.

People with quick, jerky motions put him on edge. He never turned his back to them. Even when he was sleeping, his survival instincts were on full alert for sneak attacks. Living on the edge in Nam and coming home so suddenly was like driving a car off a cliff, then slamming on the brakes.

He needed to talk to someone about the fears he carried inside. But to whom? His experiences of fear and triumphs of survival held little meaning in the lives of the people around him. The only things his hometown friends could offer were smart quips and dumb questions. They were absurd questions: How many people did he kill? How did it feel to kill?

He told them, "Killing was a hell of a lot better than being killed."

They would laugh and slap hands. "Yeah, right. You killed mothers and babies to keep your ass safe."

They did not have any idea of what it took to survive in Nam. They couldn't understand that "why" stopped being a question or even a thought; it didn't help your chances of survival.

Their questions contained implied answers they thought were true, like, "Man, where was your head when you were blowing away people? Did you get high first?" Their view of Nam was TV-generated. "Yeah, I bet you mowed them down just like on TV."

JD would laugh. "Mowing them down wasn't the problem. Seeing them was."

He was alive and didn't lose any body parts. He didn't run off to Canada or fake some headcase to go 4-F. He went to Nam. He did what he needed to do to stay alive.

Their questions grated on his nerves. They were running their mouths about something they knew nothing about. In Nam, fools were the first to become dead meat. Death was the payout for foolish mistakes. Just the fact he was home and not dead meant he was a survivor of Nam. He'd lived through his mistakes.

Some of his hometown friends with reputations of being *bad* sounded like little kids when they bragged about what they would have done if they were in Nam. They thought being bad on the streets of Springfield would carry over. They didn't grasp the reality that everyone was a stranger in Nam. No one knew or cared about your hometown street reputation.

So what if people were scared of you back on the streets in your hometown? It didn't mean anything when exploding shells rained from the sky. Your constant prayer was that someone else got the call from God. Listening to foolhardy bombast from street punks of what they would do if they were in Nam bored him. They'd just be new meat for the grinder.

Who could he talk to? His son, the only other male in the household, couldn't talk or listen. Jan and his mother tried to listen to him, but they didn't want to hear about the terrible places he had spent the past year. Yet they would say they were family and he could talk to them about anything. He didn't trust their words. He trusted men who could do a job. He didn't know how to trust women. They were soft and helpless, with no understanding of the brutal ways of war.

He needed to talk to a man who survived the hells of combat like he did. He needed someone he trusted enough to talk about the terrible things he saw and the terrible things he did. More importantly, he needed to talk about the terrible things that happened to him—a father who saw the horrors of war, survived at all costs, and came home to live a normal life. Who could help him find a way through the confusion and madness that twirled inside him?

His father had died at such a young age that JD didn't have many memories of him. He remembered a man in the house whom he called father, who played with him and made him laugh, and drove the family to the store and other places. After his father was killed in a car accident, his mother raised them without a man in the house. She told JD that he was the man of the house. He may have been the man *in* the house, but that wasn't the same as being the man *of* the house.

Home at times seemed irrelevent. Thoughts of signing up for another tour of duty in Nam took root in his mind. He started to think he should go back to the things he understood, with the people who understood what was real. But the only people he trusted there were dead.

He didn't miss—or maybe he did—the smell of shit, funk, and death in the air, the brimstone stink of cordite and napalm, piss and the honesty of fear-sweat dripping from unwashed bodies, and the natural decay smells of the jungle. The more he tried to forget Vietnam, the more he thought about it. The memories of Ia Drang Valley, Ashaw Valley, Dong Ha, Hue, and Khe Sanh, wouldn't fade from his mind. He knew too many men, and too many friends, who died in those places. People at home didn't care what happened in strange-sounding, faraway places. They cared about towns like Springfield, Peoria, East St. Louis.

He drove up to Peoria every week to spend time with Kareen. Although Kareen hadn't served in Nam, he was different than JD's friends in Springfield. He was serious about everything he did or said, and he took the time to at least listen to JD's stories without judgment. He was a warrior for the Black Revolution. According to some people, he was fighting a losing battle. White people were scared of Kareen's black militant stance. Black folks believed it was dangerous to be around Kareen because they thought someday white people would surely kill him.

One afternoon, sitting on Kareen's back porch smoking pot, JD told him about questions his friends would ask him.

"Sounds like a bunch of assholes that don't know and never will," Kareen said.

JD shrugged his shoulders. "People deal with what they know."

"Listening to what you've told me about Khe Sanh and those other places, I wouldn't have made it back. I would've just gone crazy," Kareen said.

"I've been crazy. It's not all it's cracked up to be. I can deal with that. But—the fucking nightmares are beginning to get to me," JD said.

"What do you mean, *getting to you*?" Kareen asked.

JD took a long drag off the joint they were sharing. "A couple days after I got home I started to have these dreams about men I knew who were killed," he said.

"Damn. That's got to be a bitch. Havin' that shit replayed over in your head."

"I could handle it if that's all it was about. One bizarre nightmare repeats itself over and over. It starts off with me swimming in a big barrel full of shit. I'm struggling to keep my head above it. Men's faces I've served with pop up on the surface. Faces without eyes, just dark holes where their eyes should be, with little waterfalls of blood flowing out of them. Arms, legs, intestines, and other organs are floating around in the shit. Their mouths are open toward me and rifles with yellow fingers on the triggers stick out. All the guns fire at the same time at my head."

JD sucked deep on the joint, held the hit deep in his lungs a long moment, then continued. "I wake up, and I'm sitting straight up in bed. I jump out of bed and turn on all the lights in the room, force myself to stay awake the rest of the night."

Kareen's body shook like he felt a chill. "Jesus! That's the strangest shit I ever heard. I get goose bumps just hearing you talk about it," he said.

They passed another joint back and forth between them in silence. JD looked up at the stars peeking through the cloudy sky. *The sky is the same everywhere*, he thought, *but the views are so different.* The same sun, moon, and stars were above him in Nam. They seemed different at home. In Nam, they felt closer and bigger. At home, they seemed farther away and smaller.

"Johnny. We need men like you," Kareen's voice broke into JD's thoughts.

"Who needs me?" JD asked.

"The Black Panther Party needs you. We have lots of members who served in Vietnam. The brothers came back no longer scared of the white man. That's why the white man tries to put so many black brothers from Nam into prison," Kareen said.

"Prison?" JD asked.

"The prisons are full of black Vietnam veterans. Those brothers know too much about killing and hurting people. They stand strong and take no bullshit from anyone, including white people. Man, this racist country can't handle that. Think about it, black men not scared of white America and knowing how to fight. One of the basic expectations of white America is for niggers to be scared. If niggers aren't scared, then white people are," Kareen said.

"White people are the ones who shoved all this killing bullshit into my head. I never wanted to kill anyone," JD said.

"They didn't want you to just kill; they wanted you to kill non-white people. That's why you were sent to Nam, to kill yellow people. To white people, yellow people are just another shade of nigger." Kareen acted like he was preaching to a crowd, waving his arms and poking his finger in the air for emphasis. "Yeah, they sent black brothers to Nam to fight yellow niggers. White people trained you to do their killing in faraway places. However, when you come back to America, you're supposed to remember your lowly place and forget what they taught you. After all, they damn sure don't want you to think you can kill white men. They have to make sure you understand a nigger is a nigger in America no matter what you do for them in another country," Kareen said.

"I guess it'll never change. Once a nigger, always a nigger. I've fought side-by-side, back-to-back and would have died with white boys who wouldn't let me live on the same block with them. It's fucking insane, dying with white people in foreign countries while fighting America's enemies, then coming home to be a nigger. Even worse, some white people here want to kill you just because you aren't white."

"Yeah, crazy shit. I tried to tell you that before you left, but you were so hyped up about going to war, nothing else mattered." Kareen leaned forward in the chair toward JD. "Why don't you attend my next Panther meeting? Check the brothers out."

"I don't know." Even though JD understood and agreed with most of what Kareen said about whites in America, Kareen really didn't understand what he said about the Valley Dogs. Everyone from the Valley Dogs was from different backgrounds, but they were a team, one of the best in the bush. The men he saw killed in Nam were of different colors and hues. They believed in different things. When they were dead, their differences didn't show. Dead meat was dead meat, no matter what color it was.

"I'm not ready to join anything right now. I've been a part of enough heavy shit," JD said.

"I can understand that," Kareen said. "Take your time. Think about it. We'll talk another time. You're home—that's the most important thing you have to deal with."

"I'm not sure how to deal with home. I've changed, but it's changed, too. Maybe it's just my expectations of something different. Fuck, I don't know," JD said.

"Nothing has changed here. People are still narrow-minded. Everybody is scared of their own fuckin' shadow. Everything's just as fucked-up as when you left," Kareen said.

"So why do you keep on trying to show them the light?" JD asked.

"I don't have a choice anymore. I've made my destiny, and I have to follow it," Kareen said.

"You gonna save black folks from themselves? No way. You better be trying to save your own ass. The way you're fuckin' with the man, he's gonna take you out. He sure doesn't need another big-mouth nigger in his life," JD said.

Kareen laughed. "At least I've given him a reason to take me out. The man kills niggers when he has nothing else to do. Anyway, think about attending one of my Black Panther meetings," he said.

"I'll think about it, but I'm not sure I'll be here long enough to do anything. I've got to report for duty in three weeks," JD said.

They shared a ritual handshake.

"Wherever you go, you'll find one of us. At least fighting at home is better than being in Nam."

"I'm not sure about that," JD said. "I'll talk to you later."

During the drive back to Springfield, JD rehashed his conversation with Kareen. It added another twist to his confusion of what home was supposed to be.

CHAPTER 22

JD didn't feel like he was a hero.

"You received a letter from that place," his mother said.

"From what place?" he asked.

"That place you just left, Vietnam. I hope they don't want you to come back," she said.

"A letter from Nam! Where is it?" He couldn't think of anyone who would write. He knew Jake and Mex weren't the writing type.

It was from Masters, his old CO.

Initially he was surprised by everything about the letter. It took a moment to tear it open because his stomach coiled into tight ball at the most likely possibilities and he had to wait out several waves of nausea and flashbacks before his hands quit trembling enough he was able to open it.

JD had only gotten a handful of letters from men in active duty, and all but one had been the worst kind of news—death or dismemberment, he wasn't sure which was worse but thought he'd take death with his body intact over the grueling life of a mutilated veteran. He stopped himself from pursuing such thoughts and tore open the envelope.

Dear Doc:

Hope you are doing well. I'm really enjoying writing this letter. It isn't often I get a chance to write to a man's home and he gets to read it. So, this is a pleasure.

I have put your name in for a Silver Star and a Purple Heart because of your last patrol. I just wanted to drop you a line so you know you're a hero and to say thanks to the best Doc I've ever served with.

Mex and Jake have been promoted to team leaders. They're the best recon team I have in the bush. They are almost as good as the Valley Dogs were.

I'm glad you made it home. Got to go. This correspondence will not shorten the war. I hope the best for you, your mother, wife, and new baby boy.

Take care of yourself.

Colonel Ed Masters, USM

MACV-SOG, Da Nang, Vietnam

Masters had made colonel and was out of the bush. Jake was an assistant team leader, so it didn't surprise him that he was now running a team. But, Mex, the meat man, leading a team? That surprised him. Mex was the best point man in recon, and JD would follow him anywhere, but Mex wasn't very good at planning or thinking very far ahead.

He felt good that Masters had taken the time to write to him. His feelings were mixed about the medals; why should he get medals? JD didn't feel he was a hero. He'd gotten out of Nam alive because of Ham—Ham saved him. Now, if he could only figure out why.

JD read the letter over and over, like he'd done when Jan wrote him in Nam. *Me a medal? What the fuck? Ham pulled my ass out of that clusterfuck; I just did what any man does to save his own ass. Give the fuckin' medal to Ham—Ham don't need a medal. Ham's dead! Medal my ass!*

"Going out," he said to his mother, then took his car down to the store.

"You got Johnnie Walker?"

"Sure thing, brother," said the clerk. "You want the red or the black label?"

"What's the difference?" JD asked, perplexed.

"Black's twelve years aged—s'posed to be a lot better. If price is tellin' then it's the best on the shelf far as scotch goes."

"I'll take three bottles, thanks." JD paid and drove out to Bridgeview. There he listened to the night away from the people and looked up at the stars. And tried to sort out his tangled thoughts.

He raised the bottle of Johnnie Walker into the air. "Here's to your fuckin' medal, Masters." He drank, then spit it out.

"Here's to you, Ham." He drank several drinks, repeating the toast each time, interspersing it with toasts to the Valley Dogs and to each Dog individually, until the bottle was gone.

Later, as the cold cut into him and his bladder grew full, JD pulled his business from his pants, "Here's to you, General mother-fucker."

CHAPTER 23

". . . People get killed. You didn't, you made it back home,
and that's all that counts."

The next weekend Jan and JD took a train up to Chicago to
visit his Aunt Kathryn. He was glad they took the train. The seats
were firm enough that the swaying and rocking put him to sleep.
The ride was too short, though.

He looked forward to getting away from Springfield and into
the different, faster pace of Chicago, into a pace more attuned to
the beat in his head. Something's always going on in Chicago. He
could scream out and not be different. Taverns stayed open until
four o'clock in the morning, and after drinking all night there was
always breakfast at Gladys'.

Chicago was a dangerous place to most people from
Springfield. But he was comfortable being on the alert, poised to
spring into action. Before he left for Nam, all he saw in Chicago
were hardened, black faces sporting scars. On Sixty-Third Street,
between Cottage Grove and South Parkway, where his aunt lived,
pimps and street hustlers seemed huge and mean. On this trip, the
faces on the streets were smaller, softer, and non-threatening.
Their street gestures of intimidation were like the clumsy huffing
and puffing of a broken-wing bird.

Kathryn was his mother's younger sister, but Kathryn was taller and had lighter skin. She traveled quite a bit around the country, and had seen and done a lot of things. She liked big cities and had lived in New York and Los Angeles.

She had never married and vowed she never would. She had an unwritten rule that no man would live at her house; and she never stayed in a man's house longer than two days.

She owned a tavern on Sixty-Third Street, between Cottage Grove and Lake Park. She possessed an insight into people's nature because she was around so many types and kinds of people in her business. JD wanted to talk to her about the problems he was having at home.

He finally got a chance to talk with her when Jan went out shopping with a friend. They were sitting at her kitchen table. "Now, it's just the two of us. Perhaps you'll tell me what's got your face twisted up like you've been chewing something sour?" she asked. "Something got hold of you and is burning holes in your mind. You've been jittery and jumpy since you been here. You going to tell me what's going on, or do I have to figure it out?" she asked.

"There *are* some things bothering me," he said.

"Baby, I knew you before you knew yourself. I can tell when something's wrong. It's dripping all over you. Come on. Tell me what the problem is. There a problem between you and Jan?" she asked.

"It's not just a problem between Jan and me. It's a problem I'm having with everything and everyone since I've been back from Nam," he said, his words shot like M-16 rounds strafing the room.

"Whoa, slow down. What do you mean a problem with everything and everyone?" she asked.

"I told people some of the things I did in Nam," JD said quietly. "I told them that I and six other men went on missions in Laos and North Vietnam. That, ah, a lot of people got killed."

"So?" She fiddled with her cigarette. "It was war. That's what happens in war. People get killed. You didn't, you made it back home, and that's all that counts."

"That's what they all say. Nam was something that happened in the past, something to forget. Trouble is, I can't forget. I'll never be able to forget. I was there," he said.

"Johnny." She tapped her long fingernails on the table for emphasis. "Listen, I watched men come back from World War II and Korea. I saw them go away, and I saw them when they came back." She fumbled with the pack of cigarettes. "I watched my Johnny go—" her voice grew raw with a kind of needful despair, "but I don't know that you've come back yet." She lit the cigarette, then looked at it as though it were a snake that had just bitten her. She stamped it out studiously and then looked into JD's eyes to say softly, in an injured voice, "You act like your time over there is more important than being home."

CHAPTER 24

Home seemed to get in his way.

During the trip back to Springfield on the Amtrak, Jan was excited and sparkling. It was the first trip she had taken since Johnny had left for Vietnam. She was spilling over with chatter.

He kept his eyes closed like he was sleeping. He wasn't in the mood for talking. His mind kept replaying Aunt Kathryn's words about him not being back from Vietnam.

He pondered over what Kathryn meant about "being back." He was at home, away from Nam, yet in his mind everything he thought or did was based on something about Nam. Home seemed to get in his way. *Momma said the same thing last night,* he thought, *what's that mean?*

Why would he want to go back to Nam? He fought to survive—and to come home after he survived. None of the thoughts swirling in his mind made sense.

Jan finally drifted off to sleep. He opened his eyes and watched the snow-covered landscape. It lulled him into himself despite his vigilance against thinking too much.

He wished he had a joint with him to still his own internal voice, a voice composed of many voices. He heard everyone he ever knew inside his head, especially his team members in Nam. The Valley Dogs vied the most noisily for his attention, cutting at him and clinging to him like wait-a-minute vines in the bush.

These were just memories—not hallucinations—but JD was trapped by them. He tried to reason his way through their jungle of nonsense. He'd survived Nam on gut instinct. That's what it takes in the bush with numberless enemy gunning for you. So why was it so hard at home?

Home. The very word took on a cardboard sound, a foreign echo in a high-pitched voice. It no longer carried distinct images. It carried only an empty sense of longing. Longing was a threat to survival; you had to get that shit out of your head, out of your heart. But he shouldn't have to here. . . .

He drifted into something like sleep.

Ham was there. His eyes were soft this time, and whole. He motioned JD to join him. They sat at a table in a Hong Kong bar and shared a bottle of Black Label Johnnie Walker.

"You know you got ta think different at home, JD."

JD stared at him, distantly wondering how he could be here, how it might be possible for this to be happening. Even within the dream it seemed impossible.

"Ain't you figured it out yet, Blood? Nam is about what you do *to stay alive; the* real world *is where you stop yourself from doin' shit to manage," Ham lifted his glass, "here's to your ass intact!"*

JD awoke, startled. *What the fuck was that supposed to mean?* he asked himself. He rubbed his eyes and focused on the white prairie outside the train window. He fought his mind to silence several times before losing again to the incessant speculations rolling around there and wrestling for dominance. He chose the survival line and followed that meandering thought.

Nam was about killing men with no emotions. Home was about killing emotions to keep from hurting human beings. Human beings had no place in the jungles of Nam—or at least being human had no place. Being human was the key to survival back home. But how could JD live as a human being; a human being should feel guilt and shame for those things kept in JD's memory. Guilt and shame were cripplers of direct action, and direct action the only tool that worked against the madness for any length of time. Sure, weed and booze could salve the wounds, but they could never fill that aching hole where his atrophied heart should have been.

JD felt his heartbeat pulse harder and faster with the thoughts streaming through his mind. *The heart is an organ*, he thought. *The brain is an organ. Humans are organisms, systems made of blood, bone, epidermis, pancreas, gall bladder*—he pointed to his torso as he named the parts with the medical terms he knew as though the incantation of science words might push unreason away—*stomach, duodenum, kidney, kidney, lung, lung, carotid artery, brachial artery, femoral artery. . . .*

Pictures stormed through his mind along with the words. Some were faded memories from his medical training and local ambulance experience. More were from Nam. The two collided in a maelstrom that threatened to overwhelm him completely, their contrast blinding his senses from the inside-out. Each of the names represented two worlds to him: one of taking life, one of saving life.

What sense did it make to save a man from death just so he could go back out and die? Was that his *purpose*? To save people so they could go out and die? It meant nothing. *Death will get you when he's ready*, JD thought. Nam or home, it didn't matter.

Springfield landmarks beat against his eyes and dragged his attention from within. The long train ride was over.

CHAPTER 25

"Johnny, stop! What are you doing?"

Kareen demanded an answer from JD about becoming a member of the Black Panther Party. JD drove to Peoria to talk to Kareen about why he couldn't commit to becoming a member. If he wanted to fight a war, he would return to Nam. Even though he was on his way to school, he knew if he requested reassignment to Nam he would be on the next plane out.

He didn't find Kareen and left Peoria under the glow of a full moon that turned the highway into a dark, twisted ribbon cutting through a barren, white landscape. Jagged-edged creatures created by wind-whipped snow appeared at the edge of the headlights' glow. Snow converted the flat farmland into a desolate, chalky terrain. Nothing looked familiar.

He floored the accelerator. The speedometer shot up to seventy miles per hour. The car fishtailed on the snow-packed road. He eased his foot off of the accelerator. The roads were too slippery for that kind of dumb shit. The car radio blared out Steppenwolf's "Magic Carpet Ride," a song that reflected the distorted view whirling past his windshield.

His memory didn't include images of snowy countryside, although he'd missed the change of seasons when he was in Nam. In his mind, seasons meant the liveliness of spring, hot humid days of summer, and multicolored trees of fall. Winter meant Momma cooking a big meal on Christmas and going over to a friend's warm house to talk and listen to music. His winter remembrances were fun and warm.

He did have faint winter memories of his younger years with his father, like sledding down a hill and his father pulling him up to the top. JD and his father were two of the three blacks who ice-skated in town. He loved watching his father ice-skate because he was so graceful. His large body glided lightly above the ice and he never fell.

He didn't remember being cold or a winter view without being surrounded by family and friends. He didn't remember this frigid strangeness and the barren, hazy view of shapes blurring past the car.

When JD got home, his mother told him Jan went out for a drink with Mary at the Corner Disco, and she wanted him to join them when he got back.

He walked over to the couch, picked up Jimmy, and tossed him into the air. He laughed at the surprised look on the baby's face.

"Surprise is part of being a man. Now that your dad is home, I'll teach you those things and a lot of other things women can't." He laid the baby down on the couch. Jimmy kicked wildly in the air for a few minutes. "You liked that. You're a strong baby." He tickled the baby's stomach. The baby's little hand reached out and grabbed JD's finger. "You got a man's grip."

"He's a good baby. He's got more than your nose," JD's mother said. "As your daddy said when he played with you, he's a boy-man."

"I'm glad he's a boy," JD said. "I can teach him the things I know, can teach him how to be a man. It doesn't matter to you if he's a boy. You just like to spoil babies."

"You're just like your daddy. You want a boy so you can talk man-to-man stuff. I have to agree, he was right about that. Sons hold back when talking to their mothers—like the way you've been acting," his mother said.

Her remark surprised JD. "The way I've been acting? What do you mean?" he asked.

"You're upset all the time." Her voice softened, "Is there something wrong with you?" she asked.

"Nothing is wrong with me. I just haven't figured out what's right with everybody else," JD said.

"I don't understand what you mean, 'right with everybody else'?" she asked.

"I can't tell you. It's a feeling I can't explain. Things seem out of whack. I don't know why." Just talking about how he felt made him nervous. "I've got to get going. I'll talk to you later."

He put his coat on and was walking out the door before she could say another word. A blast of cold air rushed into the house. She called out his name as he shut the door.

There weren't many cars parked in the disco parking lot when he pulled up, which was not surprising since it was the middle of the week and a cold night. A long, yellow Caddy, packaged in chrome bumpers and chrome wheels—a full-blown pimpmobile—was parked by the door. A Chicago city sticker was prominently displayed in the windshield. You didn't see cars like that in Springfield; it was probably a Chicago hustler on the prowl for young country girls.

He got out of the car, put his lucky pistol, his most personal link to Nam, in his back pocket and walked into the disco. Jan and Mary were sitting at a table close to the dance floor. He went over and joined them. "How're you ladies doing?" he asked.

"It's cold in here. The drinks help keep my insides warm at least," Mary said.

"I can't get used to this cold weather. My blood's too thin," JD said and kissed Jan on the cheek. "Now, that's warm."

He had smoked a joint during the drive to the disco, so his insides felt warm and fuzzy. Jan's green eyes, with the deep bass droning in the background and the flashing disco lights, engrossed him. He sat and stared at her with a grin.

"Why do you have such a silly look on your face?" Mary asked.

"Thinking about Jan," he said.

His mind wandered back to the first time he saw her at the beach. She was the sexiest girl he ever saw. Her bright, green eyes and long, black hair overwhelmed him.

A waitress asked him what he wanted to drink and he ordered a scotch on the rocks with water on the side. Jan and Mary still had fresh drinks in front of them.

JD glanced casually around the room. He saw Willy sitting with two other men across the dance floor, whispering and pointing toward his table. "This place is dead tonight. It's too damn cold to be out, except for some all-weather animals," he said.

JD glared at the men. Mary nudged Jan under the table and pointed at JD. Jan grabbed her coat. "Let's go Johnny. I'm ready to go home," she said.

Mary stretched her arms up in the air and yawned. "Yeah, it's too quiet in here, and I'm about ready to go to sleep. I'd rather sleep in my own bed than in this chair."

JD turned and stared at Jan. "What's the rush? I haven't gotten my drink yet," he said.

"Oh, there's no rush. I'm sorry, I didn't realize you haven't gotten your drink."

Jan's nervousness was apparent to JD. He looked in the direction of Willy's table. "What's wrong? Why are you so jumpy and uptight?" he asked.

"Nothing's wrong."

JD knew Willy and his friends were upsetting Jan with their whispering and pointing. Something was going on, but he didn't know what. "Something got you on edge. Did I get back from Peoria too soon?" he asked.

"What do you mean?" Jan asked.

He pointed at Willy's table. "You know what I mean. Did I get back sooner than you thought I would?"

"Johnny. I told your Momma to tell you where we were and to come join us," she said.

"Why is Willy here?" he asked.

"Why ask me? I don't know. I didn't ask him to come here," Jan said.

"Who cares about what Willy does? He don't mean anything to anyone at this table," Mary said.

"He don't mean anything, but he needs watching just like you keep your eyes on a snake crawling around your house," JD said.

Mary saw the waitress coming to the table. "Here comes your drink. Maybe that will help your attitude," Mary said.

The waitress sat a round of drinks in front of them. "I only ordered one drink," JD said.

The waitress pointed across the dance floor to Willy's table. "The man over there sent a round of drinks to the table," she said.

JD looked across the dance floor. Willy raised his glass as if he was giving a toast.

"Fuck you and your drink," JD yelled. He turned back around and faced Jan. "I don't need your chicken-shit friend to buy my drinks."

"Maybe he's just trying to say *no hard feelings*," Mary said.

"I have hard feelings toward him and sending a drink over ain't gonna change that. He's playin' me. The son of a bitch creeps around with my woman and now he wants to buy me a drink? I should go over there and kick his ass again," JD said.

"Johnny, he ain't done anything to you. Why you want to make trouble?" Jan asked.

He could feel the rage rise up in his chest. "It ain't what he's done to me. It's what he's done to you," JD snapped.

The tornado of anger swirling inside of JD erupted. He picked up one of the drinks on the table and threw it across the dance floor. The glass shattered against the wall a few feet from Willy's table. The men at the table jumped up from their chairs and glared at JD.

JD stood up. "You want some of me? Come on mother-fuckers!" JD yelled.

"Hey, no trouble in here, take it outside," the bartender shouted from behind the bar.

Willy and his two friends started toward JD's table. He egged them on. "Come on," JD shouted. His heartbeat pounded in his ears. "Yeah, you slope-head mother-fuckers, come on. I'll kick all your asses. You puke-face wimps."

The three men rushed across the dance floor to accept JD's challenge. "I'm gonna cut this mother-fucker. Cut his fucking liver out and feed it to him," said one of the men. He had a long scar from his ear down his neck. He whipped out a long knife. "Crazy nigger doesn't know who he's fucking with."

The bartender stepped in front of Willy and his friends. "Take it easy, Willy. You know the man ain't right," he said.

The scar-faced man pushed the bartender out of the way. "Get the fuck out of my face or I'll cut you."

JD watched the three men advance across the dance floor.

He shook his head slowly side-to-side. The three men were almost upon him when he laughed out loud. The men stopped.

"You're going to cut me?" JD asked. He laughed. "Cut this," he said, pulling the pearl-handled pistol from behind his back and pointing it at the three men.

"He's got a fucking gun!" one of the men yelled.

All three of them dropped to the floor. JD pulled the trigger. The shot went over the men's heads. They crawled on their stomachs and covered their heads with their arms.

"Don't shoot, don't shoot. Please, man. For God's sake, don't shoot me," the scar-faced man pleaded.

JD leaned down and put the gun next to the scar-faced man's head. "You want to cut someone? I should make you cut yourself," he said.

JD moved over to the huddled figure of Willy. He knelt down and put the gun in Willy's crotch. "Told you, you Jody-mother-fucker, your ass was dead meat if I caught you sniffing around my wife. You didn't believe me? You think I'm a fucking punk to be played with?" he asked.

"No, man. We didn't mean you any harm. I'm sorry," Willy pleaded.

JD pointed the barrel of the pistol at Willy's head. "I'm gonna blow your fucking head off. You're dead meat," he hissed.

Jan tugged on his arm. "Johnny, stop! What're you doing?"

He jerked his arm away from Jan's hand. "Don't touch me. You trying to protect your boyfriend?" he asked. "It's too fucking late." JD put the pistol next to Willy's face and pulled the trigger.

Jan screamed and jumped back with her hands covering her face. Willy recoiled as if he got shot.

"Oh my God, don't kill me," Willy sputtered out between sobs. "I'll stay away. I'll stay away. Please don't kill me," he begged.

"Stop, Johnny," Jan cried out. "Don't shoot him." She dropped to her knees. "Please, Johnny, stop. This is crazy."

JD could see the look of Jan's fear in her eyes as she watched him brutally attack Willy and his friends. He understood fear. He was used to feeling it and seeing it in others. But he never saw this kind of fear in Jan's eyes before. She feared *him*.

"The cops will be here in a few minutes," the bartender yelled from the bar.

JD stood up. "This is all bullshit," he said and backed away from the dance floor, keeping his eyes on the men still lying on their stomachs. When he got to the door, he shot into the air. "If anyone follows me out this door, I will kill them," he said.

Jan was on her knees crying, asking him, "Johnny, what's wrong with you?"

"Every-fucking-thing is wrong," he said. He backed out the door.

CHAPTER 26

He wanted to go faster—to fly and zoom up into the sky
above the confusion that clouded his mind.

In Nam, Willy would have been dead. JD would have shot Willy without hesitation. But, he didn't in the club. He did not want Jan to see the horrible demon inside him turned loose.

JD slammed the Hurst shifter into first gear and jammed the accelerator to the floor. The GTO's tires screamed as the car shot out of the parking lot. He didn't look to see if there were any cars on the street. He didn't care.

The car slid on an ice patch and spun around twice. He straightened it out of the spin and floored the accelerator again, causing the car to fishtail wildly.

He wanted to get far away from Springfield, away from the hurt of being home. When he finally noticed where he was, he found himself on Route 66 driving toward Peoria. He turned the radio up as loud as it would go. A song with a hard-driving beat blared from the speakers. He whizzed past blurred forms—cars, trees, and buildings, flashing splashes of multicolored lights. He rolled down all the windows. Cold, stinging air whipped through the car. All he felt were hot spasms of anger wracking his stomach.

"Fuck!" he yelled at the top of his lungs and pressed harder on the accelerator. Faster. He wanted to go faster—to fly, to zoom up into the sky above the confusion that clouded his mind.

It didn't take long for Springfield to fade into the distance. The only lights were car headlights and the dim rays he could see from the windows of farmhouses. The icy air blasting through the car finally pierced his veil of rage.

His body shuddered and his teeth chattered as chills ran through him. He rolled up the windows and turned on the heat. The jangled distortion blaring from the radio jarred his nerves. He turned off the radio. The only sound left was the straining hum of the engine and the periodic thumping of the car's tires on the road. He lit a joint and sucked the smoke deep into his lungs.

How could he have been so far off track about home? His wife didn't look like the woman he remembered. His mother and sister did not—or could not—understand the other world he lived in and what it took to survive there.

His friends thought he should act differently. Why? What do they know? They believed they would have behaved differently if they'd been in Nam. *How in the hell do they know what they would have done? No one knows until their time comes—and when the time does come, would they really know how to survive?*

JD's family and friends considered him fortunate for surviving Vietnam with no visible scars. He looked whole and fit on the outside. However, on the inside he carried festering sores on his soul from deep wounds that would never heal completely.

His family and friends were scared of him, harboring suspicions that he was crazy and would hurt or kill them. Every week, the local newspaper carried an article about crazy Vietnam veterans going on killing sprees. People who were interviewed in the stories were shocked because the veteran had been considered a nice boy when he was growing up. They blamed Vietnam and drugs for messing up his mind and making him do such horrible deeds. There was nothing mentioned about how he learned such horrible things or that he did those horrible deeds for his country.

He came around a curve, and the low skyline of Peoria popped into view. The streets were deserted. He pulled up in front of a black tavern close to downtown. Despite having smoked a couple of joints, he had a taste for the fire of alcohol. The place was empty except for two couples huddling in a booth and two men at the bar.

He recognized one of the men at the bar as LA, a friend of Kareen's. JD didn't know his real name and never heard anyone call him anything but LA. People called him LA because he was from Los Angeles. He was always a good source to score dope, and reasonable to talk to most of the time. JD remembered him as a straight-up brother.

He waved for JD to come over and join him. JD walked over to the bar. The man sitting next to LA wore a battered bush hat on his head, faded jungle greens, and boots. His eyes, clouded with yellow and red around each dark iris, constantly flickered around the room. JD knew he was a Nam survivor.

LA gave JD his stool so JD could sit next to the man. "I just left Kareen," LA said. "He heard you were up earlier and went back to Springfield."

"Yeah, I did, but I'm back. Where is Kareen?" JD asked.

"I don't know. He's supposed to call me later. Johnny, I'd like you to meet Hank," LA said. "You have something in common." LA put his arms around JD and Hank's shoulders. "Both of you just got back from Vietnam."

Hank lifted his glass. "Congratulations." He threw the drink down his throat.

"Same," JD said. "You made it home." The bartender came over, and JD ordered a drink.

"I'm going back to Nam next week. Wish it was today," Hank said.

"I say he's nuts. Why would anyone want to go back over there?" LA asked.

The bartender brought JD's drink. He watched as JD swallowed the drink in one gulp. JD pushed the glass toward the bartender. "Another one."

He turned to Hank. "How long you been back?" he asked.

"A week."

"Who were you with?" JD asked.

"Third Marines, Ninth Regiment. Spent most of my time up by the rockpile," Hank said.

JD smiled. "I've been that way a few times. I was a doc with Third Marine Recon out of Dong Ha."

Hank's face brightened. He laughed. "I bet you did. Who'd believe that two fuckin' bush monkeys would be in Peoria at the same time? Ain't that somethin'? I would offer you some hospitality, but I've been giving my homeboys the high of their lives and my stash is all gone."

"I've got a little of my stash out in the car. I'll provide the hospitality," JD said.

Hank flashed a big smile. "Lead the way, Blood. Feels good to have real company," he said.

"Where there's one, there are all of us," JD said.

"We can go to my place and cool out," LA said. He was finally getting a chance to join in.

LA lived in a small, one-bedroom apartment on the second floor. Bold posters proclaiming black power hung on the walls with pictures of defiant-looking black men. Black Panther pamphlets were piled on the floor. LA put music on.

JD rolled a big joint and gave it to Hank. "You start this one while I roll a few more for the night," he said.

Hank took a long drag on the joint and held the smoke in his lungs a few minutes. "Shit. This is the real stuff." He took another drag. "Damn, Doc, this is some good shit."

JD laughed. "Yeah, from the other side of the world, just for you."

They smoked and passed joints between them for about two hours. LA couldn't handle it any longer. He closed his eyes and crashed.

"You belong to the Black Panther Party?" JD asked Hank.

"No." He pointed to LA sleeping on the couch. "He's been working on me, trying to get me to join before I leave. Hell, I'm going back to Nam. They can't help me there, and I can't help them here. How long you been back, Doc?" Hank asked.

"About a month."

"I couldn't handle this shit for a month." Hank's face wrenched into tight lines. "I've never stayed longer than two weeks before I go back to where I belong," Hank said.

"How many tours you done?" JD asked.

Hank stared out into space. "This'll be my third. People here are too unreal. I have to go back where I know what's going on. I don't fit in here with these people," he said.

"Yeah, I know the feeling. *Being* home is different from the thought of *going* home," JD said.

"Shit. Home left you the same time you left it, Dorothy," Hank said. "Home's just a thing your mind fucks you with—you leave a place it changes. Just like in Nam, Blood. Different day, different jungle. No matter it's the same square foot of ground you sniffed around yesterday, it's a different jungle." He pulled on the joint. "A body can never go home, Blood; home's just a fairytale anymore. Even going back to the bush is different—but at least it's the kind of shit-stink you know is comin'. This so-called *real world* just don't work right. Even the air smells funny here," Hank said.

JD laughed. "You don't smell shit all the time. Your nose miss the smell of shit, Hank?" JD asked.

"It's more than that, Doc. If that's all it was, I'd just stick my head in a toilet once in awhile. No, I don't fit with family or friends. They're strangers." Hank took a drag of the joint.

"My best friend jumped in my face about being a baby killer. Ain't that a bitch? He heard on TV that some American soldiers killed kids in Nam. He couldn't remember where he heard it, and he jumps in my face? He was my best friend at home. I started to rip his fucking tongue out of his head, but LA and a couple other guys stopped me." Hank's head dropped down. His voice seemed like he was talking from his stomach.

"What the fuck do they know? Yeah, I blown away kids," Hank said. He took a long drag from the joint. "They were trying to kill me. The first time, a kid threw a grenade in a truck that nine guys and I were riding in. Three of us jumped out before the grenade exploded. Four guys were killed instantly, the other two were torn up so bad they might as well've been dead. Yeah, I blew the little fucker away. What the fuck was I supposed to do? I damn sure ain't gonna let a little fucker kill me so these dumb sons of bitches back here feel better. These people don't understand. How the fuck do they know what it takes to survive in Nam?" Hank asked.

"Hell, we didn't know what it took. You damn sure found out quick or you were dead. It was no fucking game, it was war, and your ass could be blown away at any time. After awhile, you figure your ass don't mean anything, but neither's anyone else's ass. So, everybody's ass is up for grabs—the last ass standing survives. Hank, you can only go back so many times. One way or another you have to come home," JD said. "Unless your ass ends up dead, and your body's left to waste away in the jungle."

"I didn't stay alive in that shithole to come home for this kind of dumb shit. Rather die in Nam than die here. They can ship my body back home," Hank said.

JD sat quietly looking at Hank. He shared the same thoughts as Hank about going back to Nam. "Are you married? Got any kids?" JD asked.

"I got two ex-wives and three kids. The ex-wives don't want to see me, and I don't care if I ever see them. The kids, well, they live with their mothers."

"You think about not seeing your kids grow up? Not being there to help and teach them about the world they live in?" JD asked.

The hard lines in Hank's face relaxed. He put his hand on JD's arm and locked eyes with him. "I miss my kids. They're the only good things I have in my life. But, what do I have to give them? Nothing. What can I teach 'em? What I know? How to survive in the jungle? As a father, you want to give your kids a chance for a better life than yours. The only thing I can do is make sure they'll be taken care of when I die."

Hank couldn't live anywhere comfortably except Nam, and he knew that meant death sooner or later. The madness of Nam turned a man into suicide-bait or a junkie hooked on killing and dying. Hank had nothing to look forward to except his own death.

Was death what JD wanted? He'd killed and done other terrible things to stay alive and go back home to mom's cooking, laughter, a loving wife with long hair, being a father, and raising a family—at least he thought he'd stayed alive for those reasons.

A queasy weakness penetrated JD's stomach and flowed down to his knees. His head felt hot, beads of sweat popped out on his forehead. The room seemed to close in on him, pressing the space and air into a suffocating blanket. He needed to get out of the room, get away from Hank and the feelings he stirred up.

JD struggled to his feet. "I've got to hit it. Tell LA bye for me. Keep your head down," JD said.

"For sure. Any messages you want me to take back?" Hank asked.

"Jake and Mex, Third Recon. Everyone knows them in the unit. Just tell them we met and shared time together. They're good people. You ever need anything, they know how to get it," JD said.

"Will do. Glad our paths crossed. Take care, Doc."

JD stumbled down the stairs. His body felt small, but his feet were still the same size. He leaned against a wall on the landing between the first and second floors and took several deep breaths.

He went to his car and took more deep breaths before he could drive.

Insanity was the price for survival. He knew the look of death and hopelessness that Hank carried. Hank's empty look forced the memories and nightmares to resurface in his mind.

Men ripped apart from exploding shells. Blood. Gunshot wounds. Blood. Mines and booby traps. Blood. Nam's red dirt. Blood. Ham's head with a hole blown in it, his brains and life spilling out onto JD's lap.

His stomach tied itself in knots, his head ached as he drove back to Springfield. Hank had stayed alive in hell to come home. He'd made it back home; now he couldn't get back to hell quick enough.

The real terror of Nam was that it planted a seed of madness inside a person. It gave sanction to that madness, so it grew and was accepted as normal. However, the madness left long tracks of memories. It meant recurring nightmares that live within a person for a lifetime. Only through death would the madness leave. Johnny died so JD could be a survivor. Would JD have to die for the birth of another?

Ham was right when he said he couldn't live at home like he did in Nam. But, how could he change? Who could help him? His father and Ham were dead. He didn't know anyone else he could turn to for help.

When he pulled up in front of the house in Springfield, he saw the downstairs' lights on. He looked at his watch. It was two o'clock in the morning. He wondered why his mom was still up. Jan probably came home crying and filled her head with a lot of worry about what happened at the disco.

He stepped out of the car into a cutting wind and walked slowly up the steps to the porch, his head bent down, braced against the howling wind. He opened the door.

His mother sat in a chair in the front room. Jimmy was lying on the couch.

"Hi, Mom." He moved quickly through the room.

"Johnny," she said, just as he started upstairs.

"Yeah, Mom," JD said as he took another step up.

"The police were here looking for you," she said. "Do you want me to come upstairs and tell you about it?"

JD came back into the room with her. "What did you tell them?" he asked.

"I told them what I know—nothing. I didn't know where you were. They said they'd be back."

"I'll go down to the police station tomorrow and take care of it," he said. "Don't worry about it."

"My days and nights are filled with worry about you," Momma said. "I think it's time we finished the talk we started earlier."

"I'm tired, Mom. Let's talk in the morning."

"No. Now, Johnny. We'll talk now," she said in a stern tone. "No use putting it off."

He walked back into the living room and sat on the couch next to Jimmy. "I know Jan told you what happened at the Corner Disco, and you're upset. Don't worry, Mom, nothing's going to come of it," he said.

"You're telling me not to worry. The *police* were here looking for you because you were going to kill a man. I worried myself sick when you were over in that place, and now, you're home and I'm worried about how you've been acting toward your family and friends. What's the matter with you? What's making you act so funny?" she asked.

He sat quietly for a few minutes before he answered. "Nothing is wrong. Things are just different. I can't explain it." He touched his son's hand. The baby stirred. "It will get better, don't worry," he said.

"Telling me it will get better don't tell me anything. How am I supposed to understand what's going on inside of you when you don't talk to me? You can't treat Jan the way you have been and expect her to stay with you. You know that, don't you?" she asked.

He caught the anger that bolted through him in his throat before it spewed out at his mother, but his voice snapped, sharp-edged anyway. "What has she been telling you? How bad your son has been to her? I'm sure she didn't say it all."

"She didn't have to tell me how you've been acting toward her. I got ears. I've heard you yelling at her and beating on the walls."

"She can't say I ever hit her," JD said.

"You haven't hit her body," her voice changed from reasonable to compassionate mother-protector, "but you're beating up her heart and mind, Johnny."

JD tugged at Jimmy's feet. The baby was on the verge of waking up. "Stop, don't you wake him up, Johnny," she said.

"He's my son. His daddy can wake him up to talk."

"He's your son, but when he wakes up crying, there ain't gonna be any talkin'."

JD got up from the couch and walked toward the stairs. "I've had enough talkin' today. I'm going to bed."

She was not ready to drop the conversation. "Wait a minute. If you can't talk to your mother, who can you talk to?" she asked.

"I don't know."

"If you don't talk to me, baby, how can I understand?" JD's mother said.

"I don't know," JD said.

She looked at her son and took a deep breath. "Baby, I know you been through hard times—I know you have—but, don't you remember the good times you had before going over to *that place*?" she asked.

"What I did before I went to Nam is vague memory," JD said, "and blown to shit with this . . ." he spread his arms to take in everything—the one person in the world who could have seen behind the rage in JD's eyes was there to see Johnny inside JD.

"Let me tell you about some times I remember," Momma said in her bring-you-to-Jesus sing-song so full of compassion it hurt to hear. "You were such a happy baby, a good baby. Oh, you had your moments, but you slept at night and didn't cry too much. You were so smart in school they let you skip seventh grade and go straight to eighth. When you graduated from grammar school, you were one of the top five students in your class. You gave a little speech. I was so proud how smart you were."

"Being smart didn't mean anything in Nam. Smart men died same as dumb ones. Dead is dead, no matter how much you know," he said, sealing himself against his own confusion.

"But you're *home* now. Your time *over there* is over and done, Johnny," she said. The way she said his name was some kind of plea he couldn't seem to grasp.

"I'm trying to understand what that means. People are telling me how I should feel or how I should think because I'm *back*. They never had to come back from where I came from. What they don't understand is that I needed to forget what was important in my life so I could survive *over there*. I was alone there—and now, I'm alone here," JD said. "I can't talk to them."

"I'm always here for you to talk to," she said.

"I can't talk to you about the things I've seen, the things I've done," he said. "You wouldn't understand—how can you? You shouldn't have to."

She sighed. "If your father was here. . ." Her voice trailed off.

"I don't know much about my father," JD said. "I don't know what kind of man he was—and that jive about gramps Jackson ain't doin' for me either!"

"I can tell you what kind of man your father was. Thomas Douglas was a hard-working man." She smiled. "He was a little wild when I first met him, but he was a good man. Like most of the black men back then, he made money however he could. But he settled down when we got married." Her voice cooed with nostalgia, "he got a job with the Trailways Bus Company as a porter handling luggage and worked as a janitor at the bus station. Then he got a job driving a bus between Quincy, Illinois and Keokuk, Iowa. He was the first black bus driver down there."

"How did he become a bus driver? I thought black folks couldn't ride in the front of buses, let alone drive 'em," JD said.

"I think some wealthy white folks he did odd jobs for, like cutting grass and fixing things around their houses, helped him. He experienced rough times with some of the white bus drivers. He drove the last bus between the cities. The white drivers didn't like to drive black folks filled with corn liquor late at night. There was always trouble. There was less trouble once he started driving the route. Your father was a big man. He was six-foot, five and well-known as someone you didn't mess with. White folks even started riding on his bus." She shook her head side-to-side. "The white drivers didn't like that. No, sir. Some came to the house one night and threatened him with guns. Another night, a few of them put sheets on like the Klan and burned a cross in front of our house. He knew who they were. He wasn't scared of them."

"They burned a cross in our yard?" JD had never heard these stories before. Anger rose in his chest. "They did that to stop him from driving a bus with white people on it? That doesn't make any sense. It wasn't his fault white people bought a bus ticket."

"Oh, that happened before you were born." She laughed. "You weren't even a thought. It was just the two of us, your father and me. When you were born, we left Quincy and came to Springfield. He didn't want his son growing up in that kind of town—that kind of hostility. He wanted *community*. We got that the minute we got to Stuart street." Her eyes glistened with sweet memories.

"It ain't much better here," JD said.

"It was better in some ways. At least you could get a good job with the government. He started as a janitor, and then as an elevator operator. He was working in the Secretary of Education's office when he died. God always seemed to provide a way. That's why we kept close to the church."

JD remembered how much the church was a part of his younger life. If he didn't go to church on Sunday, he couldn't go anywhere for the rest of the day. He remembered Bible studies, church summer school, and his father cutting the church lawn. He seemed to be in church every other day doing something. He had liked being there and felt he was part of something special. Back then, he had a clear idea of what was right and wrong.

He looked at his mother. She was the most beautiful woman in the world to him when he was younger. Her smooth, medium-brown skin felt soft and warm when she held him. She was tall for a woman—five-feet, seven-inches. Her bright, brown eyes seemed to be watching him all the time, and she always knew when he was doing something he shouldn't be doing. As she aged, she gained weight and somehow didn't look as tall as he remembered. Her eyes dulled over the years, and her skin became wrinkled and tough. But, he still thought she was the most beautiful woman in the world.

"We tried the best we could to raise you right. Respect people, be kind, believe in God, and stay away from trouble. Your father didn't want you to have to face hard times like he did," she said. "He worked odd jobs to set aside money every month for you to go to college. He could see how smart you were. He believed you'd be the first doctor in the family."

"At one time, I thought I was smart," JD said. "I had dreams of going to college and being a doctor. I don't dream about it now."

"You're still smart, son," she said. "You're just confused from being over in that place. You can still go to college and reach for your dreams."

"I don't know where those dreams have gone," he said. "They're not any dreams I have now. They don't *mean* anything. I'll stop your worrying about me."

"How're you going to stop my worrying?" she asked.

"I know how to end the worry, but tonight I'm tired and I'm going to bed."

He moved again to go upstairs, but Momma stopped him again, "What was that you said about my Daddy?"

JD sighed, "Nothing, Mom. I was just spouting off." He wanted the talking to stop.

"That was an accusation, John Douglas," she said with authority, "and I deserve the chance to answer any accusation you throw my way—especially in my own house with your gramps's memories all around."

"It was just a slip, Momma."

"You feel you been jived? Tell me what you know."

JD told his mother about telling the story to Ham and Ham's response. The thought of it wrenched his guts tighter. He could taste the edge of bile crawling up his throat.

"American soldiers never marched into Paris in 1918, Momma, especially black soldiers," he said wearily.

"Listen up, John Douglas. You think just 'cause the facts are a little tilted the whole story's a lie? No. Your granddaddy was a lot of things Jesus might not like, but a liar he was not. He was in the Argonne with our soldiers fighting for the French in Champagne. I checked the facts, Johnny; Thomas Crawford Jackson of DeSotto County Mississippi was never conscripted because he volunteered in Spartanburg, South Carolina under another name. Seems there was some trouble in Mississippi he needed untangled from, but I can't find anything out about that.

"I can tell you that the Indiana farm boy came by here last summer looking for your grandfather. He was a nice man, a gentleman, and he'd been trying to find the black boy who'd pulled him out of the frying pan in the hills of Champagne, France in October of 1918. He told me the same story you know, just with a few different details like you 'xpect from anyone telling a story from another point of view."

"Why didn't you write and tell me?" JD asked.

"I had too many questions, I guess," she said softly. "Point is that your granddaddy was a hero. He came back from a war, and like you said—a war is a war."

"Thanks, Momma," JD said, kissing her on the forehead as he stood and walked to the stairs, resolution visible in the lines of his posture.

Jan was asleep on the bed with her clothes on. He woke her, and told her to take off her clothes and get under the covers. She stumbled to the bathroom. He took his clothes off and got into bed.

When she came out of the bathroom, she turned her back to him and lay on the bed as far away from him as she could.

He looked at her back. "What's this shit? You don't want to sleep with your husband?" he asked. His voice was rough, sharp-toned. "Maybe you would be more comfortable sleeping with the fucker that took that half-naked picture of you there hangin' over my bed?! Did Willy take it?" he asked.

Jan looked up at the picture. "You wouldn't understand," she said, and turned her back to him.

"I wouldn't understand. What the fuck's to understand? Some clown took a picture of you without your clothes on. I understand that. Don't give me that I-wouldn't-understand shit."

His anger was an attempt to bait her into argument. Jan lay quietly, not responding.

"You don't have anything to say? If I blew that little mother-fucker away, you'd have something to say."

She turned and faced him. "Johnny, what happened to you? You're a different person entirely. You've changed so much. I don't know you."

"I've changed?" He ripped the bed covers off and sat on the edge of the bed. "What about you? You're nothing like I remember." He lit a cigarette. "You cut your hair. You prance around half-naked in front of crowds. I come home and find some man rubbing your ass. Talk about changes." He stood up and slammed his hand down hard on the night table. "God dammit. You gave away all the things I looked forward to coming back to when I was in that hellhole." He slammed his fist into the wall. "The things I thought were being saved for me are scattered in the fucking wind."

"That's not true. I ain't ever done anything against you. The things I've done were because I wanted to do them for me—*for me*. Yes, I cut my hair. It's mine. I'm the one who combs it every day. I took dancing lessons because I wanted to do something; otherwise, I'd go crazy staying in the house waiting for you to come back. What was I supposed to do? Just sit on my ass and feel bad while I waited? And let me clear up another stupid thing rooted in your head. There is nothing between Willy and me. We dance together, *that is all*."

She pulled her knees up to her breasts and wrapped her arms around them, then laid her head on her knees and started rocking.

"Johnny, did you sleep with other women over there?" she asked.

He couldn't speak. He'd never expected that question. He didn't answer her. He just sat on the bed. She finally drifted off to sleep.

His mind flooded with confusion. What was he supposed to do? Ham said living at home was different, but he didn't say what it took to live differently.

In Nam, he learned it took a team to survive. There, he had Ham, Jack, Mex, Vince, Mike, and Swene—the best team to stay alive in that hellhole. And before the Valley Dogs there'd been others. Some whose names he recalled and others he'd forgotten.

Who would help him survive at home?

He looked at Jan's balled-up figure. His anger was not her fault. She waited the best way she could, just like he stayed alive the best way he could. Both of them did things that could never be explained to the other and they carried regrets for what they did. Combat taught him that every person lived with his or her pain differently. Coming home made that knowledge real to him.

CHAPTER 27

A single tear slid out the corner of JD's eye.

JD went down to the police station the next morning. The desk sergeant put him in an interrogation room until a detective was available. Two old, metal chairs with frayed, torn seat covers faced each other at a small table in the middle of the room. He sat in the chair that put his back to a wall-size mirror and faced the door. The grimy, dirty room reminded him of the small interrogation rooms in Nam where gook prisoners were grilled. He remembered how frightened the prisoners looked as they got bombarded with questions.

He understood their fear. It punched into your body suddenly like a striking snake's fang; other times it draped your body in a slow-creeping darkness. Your legs turned into melting rubber bands. Your body covered over with grimy sweat. Your hands would shake uncontrollably.

The room's drab, dirty walls were covered with soundproof material. The wall behind him had a one-way mirror so people on the other side could watch the interrogation. He'd seen a few gooks interrogated in Nam and knew the lucky ones made it to one of these rooms. The alternative was getting thrown out of a chopper or tortured to death.

A tall, big, ruddy-faced detective came into the room. He had big, flat feet and walked with a limp. He wore a white shirt and a tie with ketchup stains on it. He practically fell into the metal chair across from JD, put a clean file folder on the table, and opened it. "My name is Detective Thomas," he said. "Are you Johnny Douglas?"

"Yeah."

Detective Thomas shuffled some papers in the file folder. He kept his head down and looked at the papers as he spoke. "Do you know why you're here?"

"Couple of police officers came to my mother's and told her they were looking for me. I came to the police station to find out why."

The detective locked eyes with JD. "We have witnesses that say you attempted to murder a man. Is that true?"

"Murder?" JD was surprised to hear the word. "I've never murdered or tried to murder anyone." In Nam, the killing he did was not murder. "If I wanted to kill that man, you'd be talking to me about him being dead. I didn't try to murder him. He came after me with a knife; I defended myself."

"You don't understand how much trouble you're in, do you? You're accused of attempted murder. You could go to jail for a long time."

JD laughed at the thought of being in trouble for trying to kill someone. For the past year, all he did was kill people—he even got medals and commendations for doing it. What he did to Willy would have been considered rough-housing in Nam. "At least no one will be shooting at me," he said.

The detective's eyes took on a hard glint, then softened. "I understand you just got back from Vietnam," Thomas said. "Seems like a lot of you boys go over there and come back with problems."

JD read the newspaper and heard people talk about how crazy Vietnam veterans are when they return home. "Only dead boys come back from Nam," JD said. "Everyone else is a survivor."

"What did you do in Vietnam?" Detective Thomas asked.

"I'm a Navy corpsman. I served with a Marines' long-range recon team," JD said.

"I served with the Marines in the second World War. Recon is tough duty—but you're home now. You have to let that part of your life go," Thomas said. "I know people don't understand what you've been through, and there is no way for them to know." The detective dropped his head. "I know how hard it is, I went through it. When I came home, I couldn't talk to my family or friends about what I went through during the war. Only the guys I served with understood. They helped me get back home."

"Most of the men I served with are dead. The ones alive are still in Nam. That's why I'm going back for another tour," JD said. Why did he say that? The thought was inside him, but he never said it aloud.

Detective Thomas stared at JD for a few moments. "Why are you going back to Vietnam? You made it home."

"Guess I'm just crazy," JD said.

Thomas wrote something in the file, then said, "Look, I'm not going to pursue these allegations because I believe you were defending yourself. Where is the gun?"

"I don't know," JD said. "I threw it away."

"I'm not sure I believe that, but you're free to go," he said. "You can't go around shooting at people here. You're not in Nam."

"I won't be around town very long. You'll have no more trouble with me."

JD stood up and walked around the table. At the door, he turned and said, "If that man had stabbed me, I would be just as dead as being killed in Nam."

JD left the police station. He figured Detective Thomas let him go because he said he was going back to Nam, which was worse than going to jail.

Two days later there was a police raid on the Black Panther's headquarters in Peoria, and Kareen was killed in a shootout. JD was halfway to Peoria before he got control of his anger and turned around.

He drove out to Bridgeview Beach. It was covered with snow and ice. Only his memory could see the sand and water where his life with Jan began. He remembered her long hair gently fluffed by a warm breeze while the sun created a bright glow around her head. He sat in the car with the motor running, looking out over the frozen lake. Ham's words flooded his mind. "You can't act at home like you do in Nam."

Ham was dead. Kareen was dead. The two men in his life whom he trusted with his thoughts and, more importantly, who could listen to him, were gone. He took a deep breath to stop the flow of tears collecting behind his eyes. A single tear slid out the corner of JD's eye and rolled down his cheek.

He once told Kareen he didn't live through the hell of Nam to come home and go to fight a war. What he didn't tell him was how scared he was of losing control, and of the madness within him surfacing to hurt or kill someone.

Jan left him and went back to Peoria to be with her family. She said she'd call him once in awhile. She said she loved him, but couldn't live with him. She didn't want him to come to Peoria and visit. It didn't matter. Since Kareen was killed there, he didn't want to be in that town anyway.

JD drank, smoked dope, and stared at the walls in his room most of the night. He wouldn't go out of the house. He was fearful someone would say something, and he would lose control. His friends stopped visiting. His mother and sister stayed in their rooms. His mother would cook for him, but it was a quiet affair. No one could find anything to talk about with him.

A few mornings later, he got up and looked in the mirror for a long time at the grotesque face staring back at him. He saw a black-bearded stranger with dark, hollow eyes who didn't look like Johnny or JD. Who was he?

Johnny was dead. JD was dying because he wasn't Johnny in people's minds or lives. Johnny couldn't be saved, and the only way to save JD was to go back to Nam.

JD signed up for another tour of duty in Nam.

When Jan heard he was going back, she called him. She couldn't live with him, but said he had no right to take Jimmy's father away from him. Why was he going back? It didn't make any sense to her. Why go when he didn't have to?

JD couldn't answer her. The answer deep inside him couldn't be fully shared. He needed help and didn't see how he could get it at home.

His mother was full of pain when he told her. She didn't understand, but he felt she was relieved to have him out of her house. His crazy actions in the small town where she had lived all her adult life were too hard on her.

CHAPTER 28

"Why in the fuck would you want to come back here?"

On the flight to Nam, JD was in a plane full of clean-shaven faces and close-cut hairlines. They were young men filled with possibilities.

A smooth-faced kid in a sharply pressed Marine uniform sitting next to him tried to start a conversation. "You have any idea where you're going?" he asked.

"To Nam, with the rest of the dumb fuckers on this plane," JD answered roughly.

"I mean what outfit?"

"My old outfit, Third Recon."

"Wow. You've been in Nam? They're sending you back to recon? I heard they're crazy. You must have really pissed somebody off," he said.

"What outfit are you going to?" JD asked.

"Second Battalion, Third Marine Division," the kid said proudly.

"Fresh meat for the grinder," JD said.

The kid had no idea what he was talking about. "What do you mean?" he asked.

JD looked at the young face. He didn't want to tell the kid that grunts were the primary feeders for the Nam meat grinder. "Nothin'. They'll be glad to see you."

"Why're you going back?" the kid asked.

The kid's questions were grating on JD's nerves. "Ain't got anything better to do." He closed his eyes. "You better get as much sleep as you can. You're going to need it."

JD didn't want to talk to the young face any longer. He didn't want to know about him, how his girlfriend looked, or if his mom cooked the best apple pie in town. JD wanted him to stay a passing face in the crowd. That way, he wouldn't care if the kid lived or died.

On the ground in Nam, the heat and smell of shit didn't shock him like it did the smooth-faced kids that stumbled off the plane. He looked forward to it. Shining aluminum caskets were piled on the tarmac. They would always be there. Death demanded an expression to the world, of the world, from the world. Caskets fulfilled death's symbol. Everyone knew death's claim when they saw a casket. *I'm back*, he thought as he looked at the caskets. *Maybe that's the only way to go home in peace.*

The new commanding officer of JD's old company said he'd heard of him. He was glad to have a man with JD's bush experience. He commanded a lot of new people with very little bush time, and they kept getting killed before they could get any experience. JD was assigned to a team going out in two days.

JD was still the highest ranking corpsman since no one had replaced him when he left. He was assigned to the medical hooch. He felt like he was back home. JD was sitting on his cot cleaning his M-16 when he heard footsteps in the front room. He looked up just as Mex and Jake pulled back the dirty blanket that hung between the two rooms.

"Didn't get enough meat, so you came back?" Mex asked.

"Fuck no. You're the meat man," JD said.

They hugged and slapped each other on the back. Jake threw his large arms around JD.

"I see the gooks still haven't figured out what to do with you two yet," JD said.

"Oh, they know what to do *to* us. But they have to get us first," Jake said in his southern drawl.

Mex pulled out an oversized joint. "Let me be the first to welcome you back," he said.

"Shit. How many of you did it take to roll that big mother?" JD asked.

Mex and JD smoked the joint. Jake brought beer since he still didn't smoke dope. JD knew that meant he still got his high from killing.

Mex had a silly grin on his face. "We're all fucking crazy here, but only fools come back. I thought you were smarter, Doc. What the fuck happened? Couldn't make it at home?" he asked.

JD lied. "Couldn't get in the school I wanted for at least a year. Figured I might as well do the time here and make money while I wait."

"Bullshit. But, what the fuck—don't mean nothing. You're here. Light another joint," Mex said.

"You're a crazy nigger, Doc. Why-in-the-fuck would you want to come back here? You made it. You were home, man," Jake said.

JD laughed. "What can I say? Next thing you know, I'll be listening to your redneck music. How would I explain that?" he said.

"You finally got good taste. Well, what the hell, you're here. What team you get assigned to?" Jake asked.

"Cal Johnson is team leader. What's the story on him?" JD asked.

"He's trying to make rank in the bush. He's not smart, but so far he has been lucky," Mex said.

"Mex and I will get you out of his team. We'll get you with one of us so we can watch your crazy ass," Jake said.

"I'm supposed to go out on patrol with him in a couple days. Wait until I come back. The CO wants me to go with them," JD said.

"Watch your ass. Those people don't have much bush time. Because they been lucky, they think they know what's goin' on. They don't know what it means to be in real shit yet."

"Seriously, amigo," Mex said, locking eyes with JD, "Johnson's not just another lucky FNG. He thinks he knows things—he's on a real power trip. Cover your ass and remember you're a Valley Dog—and they ain't!"

"Gotcha, amigo," JD said. "I'll watch my ass for the whole team, then. I know where my ass is and how to lug it home."

They talked deep into the night, curious about the changes in each world, fascinated with personal accounts of things they'd only heard rumors about. JD was not very generous in his descriptions of *the world*. Jake and Mex spoke of events in the bush just as they always had, dismissively and in utilitarian terms.

"Need some starter meat," Mex asked JD, holding out a shriveled, reeking nose on a lanyard. "Lucky one to start you off on the new Nam experience. . . ."

"Get that outta my face, Mex," JD laughed, cringing from the monstrous prize.

Mex shrugged, "Your loss, amigo. This is the nose of the officer in charge of that fire-fuck com center. We caught up to him 'bout ten days ago."

"Thanks, Mex, but no thanks. I need skills, not luck," JD said. "I just hope I'm not rusty and lose my shit out there."

"Fuck, Doc," Jake cut in, "I seen FNGs lose it, I seen second tour lose it—forget that shit! You lost it before and survived, killin' a shitload of gooks doin' it. You're the toughest goddam corpsman I ever saw. Hell, you're scarier than the enemy half the time. You'll kick ass just like we taught your skinny ass."

"Still wish you'd get your crazy ass on one of our teams," Mex said, "but if anybody can get a stupid bunch of FNGs through a hot patrol it's you, Doc."

"Oh, shit," JD exclaimed, reaching into his personal property locker, "almost forgot. Here's a little something from back home."

He pulled out a collection of tapes and a new tape player he had gotten at the PX to bring with him. Some of the tapes he'd paid the guy back at the Corner Disco in Springfield to record for him; somehow the business transaction helped him feel easier about the trouble that night with Willy. He had three copies of two of the tapes for backup and only one copy of the other four. He had carried all he could.

"Sorry, Jake," he said, grinning though genuinely apologetic, "first casualty I couldn't fix back in hell—" he held out a tape that had been shredded by a hot piece of metal during Charlie's usual greeting at the landing zone, "some new guy all the country boys love back home. At least one of the two made it."

Jake swallowed hard, then howled like a dog and left the hooch. He sprang in again quite suddenly a moment later. Though he'd obviously run a sixty yard roundtrip, JD hadn't heard his feet hit the ground at all outside the hooch.

"Here," Jake handed JD a worn commando belt and holster. It reeked of jungle. "Marine issue—only ever used by a grunt name of Hamsel—broke in for efficiency. . . ."

A powerful kinship, of *family*, filled JD full to overflowing. Was this the feeling called *home*? It didn't matter. He was in a place where someone would always have his back.

CHAPTER 29

"Johnson, I don't like this . . ."

JD met Cal Johnson the day before the patrol. He didn't ask JD to be involved with the planning or flight over the recon zone. No matter how much bush-time JD had, he was just another corpsman to Johnson. JD didn't like the way he kept everything to himself. Ham taught him that mistakes couldn't be recognized when only one mind is doing the thinking in the bush. Now he understood Mex's words about Johnson trying to make quick rank.

He borrowed a set of unwashed, stinking jungle utilities and a filthy bush hat from Jake. He didn't want to go to the bush smelling new. Since he had nothing to do with the planning of the patrol, he spent the day cleaning his rifle and repacked his pack several times. The utilities matched Ham's belt and holster almost perfectly for stench. He was glad to have it for the same reason Jake had given it to him, his new sidearm. He'd gotten a newly issued Colt .45 this time; they'd decided to stop him from taking his .32 Colt when they'd searched him stateside. He'd shrugged and written a letter to go back home with the pistol. The letter was to, "my son sixteen years from now," and sealed in an envelope with his initials along the seal and a note not to open the letter until 1985 or later.

JD's stomach acted up like it always did the night before patrol. *Good*, he thought as he ran to the shitter, *my normal reaction*. He met Johnson on his way back to the hooch.

"What's the matter, Doc?" he asked. "Been away too long from it? You nervous about going out tomorrow?"

"Not nervous," JD said. "Cleaning out my insides so I don't make any bowel sounds or have to take a shit in the bush." JD smiled. "You know about that, don't you?" he asked.

"Bowel sounds? Don't shit in the bush? I've never heard that before," Johnson said. "I heard you were a member of the Valley Dogs—some say the best team ever in recon. Old Valley Dog bush tricks, is that it?" Johnson asked.

"No tricks. Good habits."

"Habits? It's been awhile since you've been out in the bush. Your habits are gone. Maybe you are just scared," Johnson said.

"You're not scared?" JD asked.

"No. I know what I'm doing out there. Just keep your head down and follow my orders; you'll be okay."

"How'd you learn so much about the bush?" JD asked.

"I attended Recondo School and several jungle warfare programs before I came to Nam. I've never lost a man on patrol since I've been here."

"You attended stateside jungle warfare training programs, and you've been on, what, four or five patrols in the bush? You think you know what you're doing? Man, the Valley Dogs were the best, and the gooks got us. Don't confuse luck and skill. You've been lucky, that's great. When luck runs out, all you have is skill, and if the bad guys are lucky, your skills mean nothin'."

"I don't give a damn what you think. I'm patrol leader. I'm the head of this team. You do what I say, when I say. Other than that, you wait for me to tell you what to do. Understand?" Johnson said.

"Oh, I understand. I understand I've forgotten more than you will have the chance to learn. The only bush time you have is the time I've been gone. That's only a couple of months. I understand you don't know how to do your fucking job." JD walked away before either could say anything more.

Back in the hooch, JD smoked a joint. This patrol was not being put together right. He had a bad feeling. Team leaders don't bait team members the night before patrol. He tried to put all those thoughts aside and fix his mind in what-to-do gear instead of what-might-be or what-used-to-be gears. It was Nam. It changed. You dealt with it. You killed. You lived until your time was up. Simple truths in a land of simple truths.

The rush of the choppers taking off the next morning washed away JD's apprehension about the patrol. His mind cleared as he watched the green checkerboard landscape out the chopper's door. He didn't think about anything except which direction he would go when he jumped out of the chopper. He was ready to be back in the bush.

The team was dropped about a thousand yards from the DMZ. Their orders were to "check out Viet Cong activity in the area." JD considered it a milkrun. The only things you needed to watch out for dealing with the VC were booby traps and ambushes. They weren't like the NVA—the NVA would come after your ass.

The team moved for an hour through thick brush. The wait-a-minute vines hugged JD like they were glad he was back among them. He took his time removing them because he could only go as fast as they allowed. The other team members were fighting the vines, showing how inexperienced they were. They were burning up a lot of energy wrestling with the jungle.

The team came upon some flat terrain nestled between two small hills. Johnson made the team follow a well-worn path through the flat terrain between the hills. The movement was easier, too easy for JD, and following the path made him nervous. He knew it was trouble messing around trails in VC areas. Booby traps and ambushes always happened on trails.

JD saw footprints on the trail. The pointman followed them. JD moved up next to Johnson. "What-in-the-fuck is that dumb-ass pointman doing?" he whispered to Johnson.

"What're you talking about, Doc?"

"Why is he following the trail? There are footprints on it."

"I told him to. We know the enemy is somewhere around here. Those footprints should lead us to them."

JD's voice got loud. "No shit." He caught himself and started whispering again. "Following those footprints will lead us right into a fucking ambush. You'll find the gooks all right. They'll be all over our asses." JD's insides were bursting, but he forced his voice to stay low. "If you want to see where the footprints lead, get off this Goddam trail and walk parallel to it."

"The brush is too thick. It'll take too much time to fight through it," Johnson said. "We'll move down this trail 'til it thins out."

"Recon teams don't walk on roads in gook country. Tell you what—I'll walk point." JD walked off at a right angle to the path.

Johnson ran up to JD and grabbed his arm. "Wait a minute, Doc. I'll tell you when I need your help."

"Don't take it as helping *you*. It's *my* ass." JD pointed across the flat land to a ridgeline. "I'll protect your flank and meet you over there, if you make it. I'm sure the gooks know we're here," he said.

Johnson looked around anxiously. "Okay, Doc. We'll do it your way," he said sternly. "When we get back to base, your ass belongs to me."

"We get back, you can chew it all you want—sir, yes sir," JD said.

JD led the team away from the path about fifty yards before he started walking parallel to it. They had moved two-hundred yards when they came to one of the hills that rose on both sides of the path. JD went around to the opposite side of the hill and started up it.

Johnson halted the patrol. "Doc, why-in-the-fuck are you going up there? Keep moving parallel to the path," he said.

"You keep moving. I'm going up there to have a look."

"Goddamit, Doc, I'm tired of your shit. Keep moving or you're going to face a court martial when we get back."

"Your choice—*when we get back.*"

Johnson pointed his rifle at JD. "God damn it, I am giving you a direct order, corpsman. Keep moving or I'll shoot you right here."

JD's eyes narrowed as he stared into Johnson's eyes. "You're going to shoot me? Fuck you. Go ahead. The gooks will know for sure where you are. You'll wish I shot you when they get through with you. If you're going to shoot me, shoot me in the back." JD started up the hill. The rest of the team followed.

Halfway up the hill, they surprised two gooks watching the trail. The gooks opened fire on them. JD yelled for the team to throw grenades up the hill. They threw six grenades, but only five explosions went off. *Always a fucking dud in the bunch.* He dropped his pack and charged up the hill firing his rifle. Two other team members followed. The rest jumped for cover.

There were two dead gooks on top of the hill. Five more were running down the hill toward the path. "M-79. Bring up the fucking

M-79," JD yelled at one of the men who took cover. "Move your ass. They're gettin' away."

By the time the man with the M-79 reached JD, the gooks made it to the trail and found cover on the other side. The man fired wide of their position. JD grabbed the M-79 and pumped two rounds where the gooks were hiding. Two gooks jumped up and started running down the trail. JD fired an M-79 round, hitting one in the back. His body exploded. Nothing was left except two twitching legs. The other gook disappeared before JD could get off another round.

"God damn it, one got away," he snapped.

Johnson finally reached the top of the hill. "What happened?" he asked.

"Fucking gooks set an ambush for us. There's more around. You better give artillery our coordinates. We'll need fire support soon, I'm sure." JD started walking away from Johnson.

"Where you going now?" Johnson asked.

"To get my pack. I dropped it halfway up the hill," JD said.

"Why did you throw grenades instead of just working your way up the hill?" Johnson said.

"If we didn't throw grenades up, they would have started lobbing them down," JD said. "It's easier to throw them down than up, unless you do it first."

JD walked back to where he dropped his pack. The kid with the M-79 followed him. "I'm sorry I didn't move faster. This was the first time I needed to use this thing on real people. I was . . ."

"Yeah, the first time's always a bitch. You'll get over it. You'll be okay. Just remember, you're the only artillery we got," JD said.

An artillery shell exploded twenty-five yards down the hill. Someone yelled to warn of incoming. JD flattened to the ground. *What the fuck is going on?* The gooks wouldn't use artillery for a few VC. That didn't make sense. He ran to the top of the hill.

"Where's that shit coming from?" he asked Johnson.

Johnson's body was shaking. "It's ours. I gave them the wrong coordinates, and they started firing."

"They don't know the coordinates are wrong. Tell them to stop firing before they blow us to pieces." Another shell hit on the other side of the hill. "They're bracketing us for a barrage. Get on that fucking radio," JD yelled.

Johnson got through and canceled the firing mission. He looked bewildered and confused.

JD took over. "Let's get out of here. We've been here too long. The gooks have to have a fix on us." He kept the team moving. He wouldn't let them stop until they reached the top of the far ridgeline. The only delay he allowed was the time it took to give them a crash course in moving through the terrain, to move *with* instead of against the plant life.

JD was uneasy. There were a lot of signs that gooks were around them, yet they didn't see any other than the ones who had tried to ambush them. On the way to the ridge, they crossed eight or nine gook trails.

"Johnson, I don't like this. I know gooks are around us," JD said, "but we've only seen . . ."

"We'll sit tight here tonight. I'll call choppers to get us in the morning," he said.

One of the basic rules in recon was never sleep where you eat. It puts you in one place too long and gives the gooks time to get a fix on where you are.

"We've been here too long already. Let's move seventy-five yards deeper into the bush. This is too open," JD said.

Johnson was scared. It was dark. He didn't want to move. "No. We'll move in the morning when we can see. I told the men to set up a claymore defensive in case we get visitors tonight," he said.

Johnson was asserting his authority and leadership. He lost it back at the ambush, and all the team members knew it. He was trying to save face. JD backed off.

He didn't want to push Johnson too far. The team leader is in charge. There was enough to worry about without a struggle about who was running the patrol. JD didn't care if Johnson needed to feel like he was in charge, he cared about Johnson doing something so stupid it threatened their survival.

The morning arrived with two grenades tossed into the middle of the area where the team was sleeping. Two were killed instantly. Johnson blew up the claymore mines. The blasts exploded toward them. The only thing that saved the rest of the team was that they were on their bellies when the claymores went off.

After Johnson saw the effects of the claymores, he froze. He lay on his stomach and covered his head with his arms. Gooks fired from the brush. JD laid down a raking fire pattern into the brush. He yelled at Johnson to shoot.

The gooks didn't try to rush them. They must be VC. NVA soldiers would have rushed in right after the mines went off. They would have been wiped out.

"Shoot where? Where are they?" Johnson asked.

"Every-fucking-where. Just shoot into the brush!" JD yelled. Johnson couldn't see the bad guys. He couldn't see the shadows moving from one position to another. JD barked orders while spraying the surrounding brush. "Throw grenades . . . they're all around us . . . Get on the fucking radio . . . Get some choppers in here."

JD attacked the shadows moving around the team. He plunged into their ranks, shooting right and left. Only one man charging into their ranks surprised them. He was so close to them that they were shooting their own men while trying to shoot JD.

Choppers hovered overhead. They radioed to say they were low on fuel and could do only one pass. They were flying support for another mission and did not have time to refuel when they responded to the team's call for help.

One chopper swooped down. The hills buzzed with gunfire. JD and Johnson threw a wounded man in. Six gooks charged out of the brush at the chopper. JD flattened to the ground and mowed them down. Johnson jumped into the chopper yelling, "Go! Go!" The chopper took off.

CHAPTER 30

Images of home were leaving his mind. . .

JD watched the chopper zoom into the sky. The downwash of the chopper's blade stirred up a swirl of debris and flattened the tall elephant grass down to its roots. The roar of the motor drowned out all noise except the popping sound of gunfire and bullets ricocheting off the chopper.

A sharp pain ripped through his left shoulder. He screamed, but couldn't hear it over the "thump, thump" of the chopper blades. Another sharp stab of pain blasted through him as he dropped to his stomach.

The swirl of activity around JD seemed to move in slow motion. Time became confused. He was home with Jan at Bridgeview Beach. Her short afro radiated pulsating rainbow colors. He remembered the spot on the beach where they met and the feelings he had when he held her hand and looked into her eyes.

His son's face appeared in his mind. He remembered the way his chest swelled, ready to burst from the love he felt inside, when he saw his son for the first time. He remembered how his son's tiny hand held his finger when he was home. He brought life into the world and, like any other father, wanted to teach his son how to ride a bike, pee on trees, or write his name in snow.

JD was covered with blood, his body wracked with pain. Images of home were leaving his mind. Tears fell from the corner of his eye and tumbled slowly down his cheek. He was going to die alone in a strange country. He crawled to the edge of a deep tear in the earth and looked down into the darkness. A shell must have exploded and cracked through the ground to expose a cave below—or enemy tunnels. He dropped an empty M-16 magazine down the hole. It seemed forever until he heard it hit bottom, too long for it to be tunnels.

He turned around and saw a gook aiming at him. *You might kill me*, he thought, *but you ain't cuttin' me up.* He pulled a pin from a grenade, smiled at the little yellow man, then laid the egglike object beside himself. The gook dove for cover; JD rolled over the edge of the dark hole and fell in. His last thought, as he plunged into darkness, hidden from the enemy by the explosion of the grenade and the crumbling of the earth where he'd been, was the hope that maybe one day his bones would be found and returned home.

Twenty-three days after he returned to Vietnam, John Douglas was officially declared MIA.

*Only the dead
have seen the end of war*

PLATO

A NOTE FROM THE AUTHOR

I am a Vietnam War survivor.

I do not know why, or how, I survived.

War is the most profound event in a person's life. Brutal events are encapsulated into hard shells in your body, mind, and emotions. These areas become dead zones within you—dark places you hide from outsiders.

I was brought up to respect people—Vietnam changed that. At times, I knew my survival was an act of God. Other times, I felt God had forsaken me for doing what I had to do to survive. Vietnam was a living hell. Surviving meant giving up everything that defined me and going against my upbringing. I accepted killing as a natural act, and it was a burden that cut my soul.

I was born in Quincy, Illinois, but I considered Peoria, Illinois, home. Peoria is seventy-eight miles northwest of Springfield, the state capital and home of Abe Lincoln, and 180 miles southwest of Chicago. I lived with my grandmother, who owned a boarding house, while my parents worked in Chicago. Peoria used to be a small city with tree-lined streets and conclaves of ethnic cultures. Though there was racial tension and clear boundary lines existed between the white and black areas of town, it was home—and home was a sharp contrast to Vietnam. At least at home, I felt safe and knew I was loved.

When I was twelve years old, my family moved to the projects on the south side of Chicago. We lived on the seventh floor of a fifteen-story building at 3939 Lake Park. My mother moved me from Peoria after she found a job and place for us to live. I attended Oakenwald for my last two years of grammar school, went to high school at Tilden Tech, and spent one year at Southeastern Junior College. In 1965, I returned to Peoria and joined the United States Navy. After completing boot camp at the Great Lakes Naval Training Center in Illinois, I went to corpsman school in San Diego, California. Following combat training at Camp Lejeune in North Carolina and jungle warfare school in the Philippines, I was ordered to Vietnam.

I was only 23 years old when I went to Vietnam in 1967, but

that was an old man compared to the 18- and 19-year-old kids who served in the field. I served as a Senior Hospital Corpsman, known as "Doc," with the Third Marine Division, Deep Reconnaissance (Recon) Company until I was wounded and transferred to a—supposedly—non-combat support unit, the Third Shore Party Battalion. In Vietnam a non-combat unit was a paper designation in an office. But in war, all units are combat units. To the enemy, it's the uniform they attack. Non-combat means easy prey.

I had seen maps of Vietnam with black lines showing the country divided and the areas considered "enemy territory." But in the jungle, enemy lines were not as clear as those drawn on the maps. Every step I took in Vietnam felt like enemy territory. Recon teams operated behind enemy lines in six- to twelve-man units for seven to ten days at a time. Recon's motto was, "Swift, Silent, and Deadly." The enemy certainly believed in the motto because Recon fought the war the way they did—small units of men causing destruction, then melting back into the jungle. In fact, we were so feared that Hanoi Hanna, who had a radio program that played music from the United States, regularly told the country how much the reward was for killing or capturing Recon team members.

The patrols in Lost Survivor are based on my personal experiences. I know the strain, and pain, of humping through the jungle with more than a hundred extra pounds strapped to my body. The pack on my back, extra ammo, and medical supplies on my belt and in my pockets made every step a test of will. The strap of the overloaded pack would cut into my flesh like a sharp knife, with numbness eventually invading the pain. I have walked, eaten, and slept amid the musty, decaying smell of the jungle. It would leave a layer of grime on my skin. I have looked toward the sky during the day only to see darkness because of the high, thick jungle canopy. My ears have heard the sound of jungle animals in the night, the rolling thunder of exploding 1,000-pound bombs, and the agony of men screaming from pain and grief. I have felt the fear of walking through a mine field, my feet and mind anticipating the metal click of a mine armed to explode. I have fought through thick jungle bush with wait-a-minute vines clinging to my body as if protesting my mere presence in their jungle. As a corpsman, I have used my hands in an attempt to stop the draining of blood from men's bodies into the red dirt of the jungle floor. Fear of death was a common factor in every action, every day, and every thought. Death was visible everywhere in Vietnam, always reminding me of its possibility.

While in Vietnam, my memories of home were fragmented mental snapshots of places, events, and people. The longer I was there, the more my memories of home became vague images that I only thought of during rare moments of silence. Internal silence was next to nonexistent—I spent most of those quiet moments listening for danger, not thinking of home.

Music from home provided a sense of silence between the sounds of explosions and gun fire. Listening to familiar songs helped keep some home memories alive, and new music meant home still existed. The beats of home would have you snapping your fingers and dancing, mostly from your head to your ankles. Feeling the beat in your body made you feel like you were home.

Most men carried something physical from home on them. Touching something real from home was like a memory bookmark that allowed us to play a memory over and over. Simply getting a letter from home was more important than what was in the letter.

For thirteen months, I survived the brutal existence of combat in Vietnam, and then the day came for me to go home. I walked out of the jungle, got on a plane, and forty-eight hours later I was back in the United States. Although I was home, it took a long time for my mind to catch up with my body. My mind and emotions remained in Vietnam for—much too long. To this day, I still carry with me the vivid, emotional memories of Vietnam.

After my tour in Vietnam, I attended Radioisotope and Nuclear Medicine School at the National Naval Medical School in Bethesda, Maryland. Upon completion of the school, and until I left the Navy, I was placed in charge of the Radioisotope and Nuclear Medicine Laboratory at the Great Lakes Naval Hospital in Illinois. Ironically, I ended my military career where it began.

I had moments when I doubted whether I could make a life for myself back home. I would wake up some nights in a cold sweat, my body shaking, as my mind relived a Vietnam experience. I was always on the ready to react, to attack, to survive. I have even hidden in the dark, dead zones within me.

But helping others helped me. At Great Lakes Naval Hospital, I counseled returning wounded Vietnam veterans. I could talk with them because I was, like them, a combat Vietnam veteran. Then, from 1981 to 1986, I was appointed to the Governor's cabinet as Assistant Director of the Illinois Department of Veterans' Affairs. In that position, I counseled Vietnam veterans from all parts of the state. I also helped coordinate the state of Illinois' involvement in the building of the Vietnam War Memorial in Washington DC, and served as the fund-raising and government liaison for the building of the Illinois Vietnam Memorial.

Most returning Vietnam veterans fall, broadly speaking, into one of three types. Some came home and were so lost they returned to Vietnam; some came home and got lost in America; and some came home and joined life again. I was fortunate, after being home awhile, to be one that came home and found a life. Yet, just as the lingering memories of Vietnam always surface, the personal pain I suffer for my brothers who got "lost" comes back. I can't answer the perpetual question of why so many veterans were lost when they came home. I only hope *Lost Survivor* will help families and friends of war veterans understand the metamorphosis of man into soldier and soldier back into man. My fellow veterans can relate to this courageous, yet troubling, story for many of them have lived parts of it.

Thomas R. Jones Sr. served in the Vietnam War in 1967 as a Senior Hospital Corpsman with the 3rd Recon Battalion, 3rd Marine Division. He was awarded the Purple Heart, Presidential Unit Citation, Combat Action Ribbon, Vietnam Campaign Medal, and the Vietnam Services Medal. Although he survived the war, he – like so many war veterans – came back a different person.

After the war, Jones struggled with his memories of Vietnam – the killing, the brutality, the conflicts. Jones turned to his computer as an outlet for the feelings that stirred inside of him and wrote Lost Survivor, a tale of a young Vietnam soldier who reluctantly adapts to the jungles of Vietnam, but not to the home to which he must return. Although Lost Survivor is a work of fiction, the book is a blend of Jones' personal experiences combined with stories about people he knew.

When he returned from the war, Jones was placed in charge of the radioisotope and nuclear medicine laboratory at the Great Lakes Naval Hospital. During that time, he worked with returning Vietnam veterans to help them reintegrate into society. From 1981 to 1986, Jones served as Assistant Director of the Illinois Department of Veterans' Affairs. In that position, he counseled Vietnam veterans across the state. He also coordinated the state of Illinois' contingency activities during the building of the Vietnam War Memorial in Washington D.C., and served as a fund-raising and government liaison for the building of the Illinois Vietnam Memorial.

Today, Jones is Chief Deputy Director of Budget and Fiscal Management for the Illinois Secretary of State. He and his wife, Carol, live in Springfield, Illinois.

TO SURVIVE IN YOUR WORLD

Color drains from dreams, disappears, grey scale
shadows mix, remind me of life before
this place when the tick-tock click of momma's
clock soothed me to sleep between whispers sweet
from my lover's lips, and the world was real.

Violent scars on the edge of fantasy
askew from your memories of me, and you
cannot enter the world I've lived—would not
want the me I became—I cannot be
the one you loved, that's *once upon a time*

when I wasn't lost, before life became
kill or be killed—a place I could not see
color outside yellow fear—jungle green.

I lost myself to survive in your world.

Siobhan
10/25/05